BIRD SHADOWS

We gratefully acknowledge the support of the Canada Council for the Arts and the Ontario Arts Council for our publishing program. We also acknowledge the financial support of the Government of Canada.

Bird Shadows is a work of fiction. All the characters portrayed in this book are fictitious and any resemblance to persons living or dead is purely coincidental.

Cover design: Val Fullard
Cover art: Jennie Morrow

Library and Archives Canada Cataloguing in Publication

Title: Bird shadows : a novel / Jennie Morrow.
Names: Morrow, Jennie, author.
Series: Inanna poetry & fiction series.
Description: Series statement: Inanna poetry & fiction series
Identifiers: Canadiana (print) 20210185791 | Canadiana (ebook) 2021018583X | ISBN 9781771338011
(softcover) | ISBN 9781771338035 (PDF) | ISBN 9781771338028 (EPUB)
Classification: LCC PS8626.O772 B57 2021 | DDC C813/.6—dc23

Printed and Bound in Canada.

Published in Canada by
Inanna Publications and Education Inc.
210 Founders College, York University
4700 Keele Street, Toronto, Ontario M3J 1P3
Telephone: (416) 736-5356 Fax: (416) 736-5765
Email: inanna.publications@inanna.ca Website: www.inanna.ca

BIRD SHADOWS

A NOVEL

Jennie Morrow

INANNA PUBLICATIONS AND EDUCATION INC.
TORONTO, CANADA

Bird shadows, disconnected, abandoned on the ground;
millions of shadows from thousands of species, their shape
changed by each tip of the wing, each flutter, each swoop.
Made large and small by each rise and fall. Black manna
from the sky.

Collect them up, shuffle, and the game begins.

Would you say this smudge resembles, in any way, a dove or
perhaps a vulture? Could this be the shadow of a sparrow or an
eagle soaring at a hundred feet? Can we ever know for sure?

Spirit shadows. Cast in human flesh. Spirits of all species,
as dissimilar as a hawk from a chicken, but so alike to the eye.
And so, the game begins.

Would you say this body is that of a kind and giving person
or a con artist flying very high?

Let's pretend we are so good it doesn't matter. Let's put
the hawk in the chicken coop and teach the chickens that:
if they are nice they will pretend not to notice,
if they are fair they will make room for it on their perch,
if they are righteous they will believe that God has changed the hawk
into a chicken
...if they are smart they will fly the coop!

—Jennie Morrow

Mother's Day, 1995

In a field at the edge of the ocean, fourteen white wooden crosses cast lengthy shadows in the early morning light. Two women, dressed in jeans and loose-fitting shirts, unload large square paintings from the back of a silver Dodge Caravan. Two men quickly screw an extra eyelet into the back of each stretcher so the canvases can be secured to the crosses at their bottoms as well as their tops. From time to time, a slight breeze from the direction of the water infects the large areas of canvas with a kite's dream of flying. By ten o'clock the four workers have created a spectacle. The fourteen paintings on fourteen crosses have been spaced ten feet apart. Paths have been mown through the long grass from one site to the next, creating stations. Stations of the Cross.

This is an account of one year in Brood Bay, of how it is remembered in the conscious minds of a few people—memories, fallible memories. Ahhh, but the dreams of those few people construct fantasies that are closer to the truth. Like when I dreamed of my brother-in-law, Warren. He was wearing his dark suit and was hanging from an angle beam on the wharf, caught by a gaff hook in his shirt collar. On his face was a look of bewildered horror—as if he had just realized that he'd gambled on something huge and lost.

Who am I? I'm an artist. Some would say a bit of a misfit. I'm guided by my own scheme of logic. It doesn't happen to coincide with the prevailing current of thought in the place where I live. That doesn't mean that I'm crazy, just displaced. There are many spots in the world where I could live and be thought normal—or so I tell myself. It might be true.

I'm motivated by beauty. I live here in Brood Bay because it has lots of that—beauty, that is. The people around me don't care so much about the beauty. I'd say they're motivated by something else, but I'm not sure what. If I start to guess I will come off seeming unkind, and it's a little early in my story for me to give you a bad impression. I'm too stubborn to fake it to fit in. I have tried. A little bit. For the sake of my sister, Helen. She tells me I make things worse.

I'm an observer. Gotta observe to be an artist. I try to not to be judgmental, but sometimes my observations solidify into opinions based on what I've seen. Is that a bad thing? I suppose that's what happens to all of us, and then we get caught thinking we know things that we don't. And that, in a nutshell, is what my story is about.

Helen's people are churchgoers. I know that they're basically good people, but, as I've said, they're ill-equipped to understand me. They try to be nice, but I can't shake the feeling that they're tolerating me, even though I'm all wrong in my beliefs, on the off chance that the Lord might decide to work through one of them and fix me up. Make me right. Make me worthy. In their presence I feel a strong urge to explain myself. Perhaps defend would be a better word. It's like needing to pee so bad that you have to cross your legs and clench your teeth. I'm sure it makes me act funny.

I go to church with Helen's family now and then when one of her kids is doing something that requires a familial audience. I try to be a good aunt. But the artist in me comes first, aunt second. It makes sense alphabetically.

After attending church with Helen's family at Christmas, I wrote in my journal: *Went to church with Hel—had hoped it would make her happy, but it didn't seem to. I looked for Jesus there. I really did, but I didn't find him.*

It may sound like I was looking to be saved. To "find the lord." But keep in mind that I'm an observer. I was referring to my search for features appropriate for Jesus: a refined nose, without the pudginess of self-indulgence, without the tip of snobbery; warm eyes, eyes capable of seeing souls—understanding, twinkling eyes. I was looking for ears tuned to the sound of other people's voices. And a gentle mouth. A mouth closed as often as open. A mouth used for kind smiles. A mouth that spoke truth. And temples. I wanted my Jesus to have temples fit for God.

I studied a group of children as they sang, making a game of trying to match child to parent. Some were easy. One red-haired child, one red-haired adult. Others were a challenge. I craned my neck around in search of a pair of enlarged nostrils. Helen frowned viciously and shook her head.

I turned back to the front and refocused my attention on the children, fascinated by the eyelids of a particular child. She noticed me staring. I think I frightened her, what with the intensity of my expression. My reputation didn't help, I'm sure. But I couldn't help myself. Her eyelids appeared to be stretched over balls; she had a Lucas Cranach, Botticelli kind of look, like Edith Piaf. I decided that I might give my Jesus eyes like those. That settled, I moved on to mouths. I definitely wouldn't give him a sharp jaw or wide mouth. I had no use for the big-toothed, predatory mouths that are so popular among movie stars and preachers.

Preachers. I turned my attention to Pastor Wallace. He was not a bad-looking man. For some reason God seldom "calls" homely men to become pastors. Have you ever noticed that? God usually "calls" men with a nice hairline and good teeth. God says, *Slick back thy hair and polish thy face, and if thou should choose to have a moustache, keep it well trimmed.*

Pastor Wallace possesses a well-trimmed mustache. He has a habit of keeping his upper lip pushed up slightly on one side while talking so that at least some of his lovely white teeth are on display. I also noticed that Pastor Wallace gestures a great deal while preaching. It's as if his hands are confirming what his mouth is saying, giving a second opinion. His movements distract me, like a magician's. I often catch myself following his eyes as he raises them heavenward, his hands as they take turns sweeping outwards or coming together, his knees dipping, and his head tipping, and then I suddenly realize I've been so distracted that I haven't heard anything he's said for quite some time. As I think I mentioned, I'm a visual person. That's my problem. Or one of them, anyway.

I have to admit though, that Pastor Wallace is a master of his craft. He's careful not to cause discomfort in the congregation by making eye contact. People are able to enjoy staring at him without the fear of being challenged by his eyes. He seems to be looking at the upturned faces he's addressing, but his gaze actually stops at the spaces between heads. Everyone assumes it is the person behind who's receiving his attention. In this way, he can maintain perfect concentration throughout his performance, completely unaffected by the expressions on the faces of his flock. He's a piece of work, that Pastor Wallace. He sparkles with the brilliance of cubic zirconia.

My name is Rube Smith. A pitiful name for an artist—the Smith part, that is. I would give just about anything: an ear, an eyebrow, or several toes off either foot for a last name like Boissonnault or Rodenhizer—that last one would go well with Rube—but I'm stuck with Smith. It sounds like a generic brand of human being. My married name was better—Finch. It was more memorable; however, I had worried when saying it to someone for the first time that it sounded a bit too much like "rude pinch." It doesn't matter now. I gave the name back to my husband when we divorced along with a few other names that I threw in for nothing.

I'm thirty-seven, and I'm childless. As I said, I had a husband, but, as he so often pointed out to me, I didn't measure up. We used to live in Halifax, and he stayed there when I moved back home to Brood Bay. Most women my age have at least one husband in their past. It's like riding a bicycle: most people try it at some point. Some wobble uncontrollably and wind up in a tangle in the ditch, and some ride off to glory. It's largely about setting out with confidence and a willingness to make minute adjustments along the way. Of course, it also depends on the bicycle.

Enough about me. Let me tell you about Brood Bay. It's a lovely looking little fishing village on the Nova Scotia side of the Bay of Fundy. Notice that I said *lovely looking*. That's important. Every small village has its invisible peculiarities. Brood Bay is no exception. However, within a fifteen-minute walk from my house there are fish shanties that have been salt cured, sand blasted, and wind blown until they look more like a product of nature than man. There are fishing boats of every colour tarted up with hot pink balloon buoys and viridian green ropes. There's an impressive stretch of beach, so heavily influenced by the sky and tides that it displays a hundred variations of gorgeous within the span of one day. Saleable subjects for an artist, just there for the taking.

So, the village of Brood Bay.... It consists of an elementary school, a corner store, a post office, a church, a library, a seniors' home, a garage, a fire hall, a wharf, a lighthouse, and a four-kilometre-long sandy beach. Not much gossip is ever swapped at the lighthouse. That leaves, however, a complex system of contacts, spread throughout the rest of the village, as intricately woven as a new fishing net. In Brood Bay stories that begin as innocent exchanges are soon transformed into titillating tidbits. A generous person could claim that the inaccuracies result from interruptions: the recess buzzer at school, a boat engine starting up at the wharf, a church bell ringing, or the fog horn groaning. "She apparently told him to get out of her way or he'd be wearing his supper" could be transformed into "She 'pparently told him to get out the other day and he was only wearing his uppers." An exchange of the same piece of gossip might, on the first telling, be preceded by "I don't know whether this is true or not," on the second telling by "I heard something from so and so, and she should know," and finally by "I need to add someone to our prayer list because...."

Misunderstandings happen all the time for a lot of different reasons. To keep peace, most people avoid addressing injustices, but we pay a price for our polite silence. I'm reaching out, through my story, to anyone who has been damaged by anger and frustration inspired by a self-described righteous person. I may or may not be a generous person. You can be the judge of that. I'm setting down in words what seems to me to be a reasonable explanation of the events that led up to Mother's Day, 1995. That's all I can do.

The Gospel According to Pastor Wallace
Mother's Day Eve, 1995

Pastor Wallace averted his eyes from the spectacle of Pastor Obie settling into his chair like a cat wiggling its behind into a litter box. "Appreciate you coming, Obe."

"Don't mention it," grunted Pastor Obie. "It's an interesting idea, holding a special service for orphans in Africa on Mother's Day."

"Thank you." Pastor Wallace dipped his head briefly in humble acknowledgement. "Having it in the evening lets the mothers have a much deserved lie-in with breakfast in bed and without worrying about getting everyone out the door to church. The mothers deserve it, God knows." He raised his hands in playful submission. "Where would we be without mothers?"

"We wouldn't be alive for starters," chuckled Pastor Obie.

"Too right. There would be no 'we' without mothers."

The muffled clatter and clink of a table being set suggested a short wait for dinner. Pastor Obie allowed his eyes to wander around the office, taking in the mustard walls, the weary filing cabinet, the long-suffering desk. He scanned the titles in a bookcase, finding nothing of particular interest, and turned back to Pastor Wallace.

"I worry that I'll be intruding tomorrow. Even though your children are away, I'm sure you had Mother's Day plans for Rebecca."

"Well, actually, to tell you the truth, I had a reason for inviting you to come early. There's something else going on tomorrow, and I'd hoped you'd attend with me. Then we can take Rebecca out. I've made reservations."

Pastor Obie raised his eyebrows in interest.

"There's going to be an art show that could prove to be somewhat," Pastor Wallace paused and worked his lips for a few seconds, as if crafting a word designed specifically for this occasion, "controversial. Out in a field if you can believe it. Just for one day. Just for the afternoon."

"You're interested in art?"

"Not particularly. But this art is something I'd really like to see. I've heard about it, and I expect some of the people in the church might check it out, so I thought I should see it for myself."

"What kind of art?"

"Well," Pastor Wallace nodded as if Pastor Obie had just hit the nail on the head, "that's the thing. I've heard it's about religion and churches, and that it might be offensive to some." The word offensive was coupled with a direct gaze; clearly it was meant to be the selling point. "I'm also interested because of a connection between the artist and some members of my church. The artist, Rube, is the sister-in-law of Warren Pritchard, one of our deacons. You'll meet Warren tomorrow.

His wife, Helen, left him last year, and I attribute a lot of the blame for that to Rube. She's a bad influence, that one." He frowned at the pen in his hand and turned it absently over and over as he spoke. "He's having a hard time right now, Warren is. If your church would say some prayers for him, I'm sure he'd appreciate it. You couldn't ask for a finer man, but that's often the way."

"Amen to that."

Pastor Wallace smoothed his dark hair and straightened his tie. "His wife left him last September, just out of the blue. They were a good Christian couple with two lovely children. I feel for those children. I also feel for Warren, but it's the children that you hate to see hurt. And there's no need for it." Pastor Wallace swung his head up and tossed the pen on his desk. "Absolutely no need!"

"Well, maybe she'll go back to him," said Pastor Obie consolingly. "It might be she was just going through something. It happens. Good people suddenly act like idiots. You shake your head and watch them make fools of themselves, but all you can do is pray and let the Lord take care of it. Pray and wait. And hope."

Pastor Obie crossed his bulky legs and tried to shift in the chair. It gave little room for maneuvering. The irritation seemed to catch in his throat, and a few coughs were required to clear it. "Is there another man involved?"

"Well, not out in the open," admitted Pastor Wallace grudgingly. "They say there is, but no one knows yet who it is. Helen, Warren's wife, has gotten herself an apartment, but Warren says he knew there was somebody else before she left. She started acting different, you know, not like herself."

Pastor Obie shook his head. "Well, we'll pray for the both of them. And for the kids."

"And for the kids," echoed Pastor Wallace. His lips curled. "Helen's sister, Rube—now there's a piece a work. A real wingnut. She lives in a shack out beyond the bridge, in the woods. Moved back here about four years ago. Warren and Helen tried to interest her in church, but it wasn't long before it was clear that it wasn't going to take. Do you know what she said to me the first time we were introduced? This'll give you an idea of what kind of woman I'm talking about." He chewed on the edge of his lip then slid his gaze in Obie's direction and sniffed in disgust. "It was at one of our church suppers. Well, I went over to where Helen and her sister were standing, and I smiled and said hello and leaned over to read her name tag." Pastor Wallace levelled his eyes on Pastor Obie and paused. "And she said 'Rube—rhymes with boob.'"

Pastor Obie made a sucking sound in the roof of his mouth. He shook his head, and after a few minutes of sober contemplation he asked, "What time did you say this show was?"

"The ad in the paper said ten o'clock. It said everyone was welcome."

This story really begins about a year after I moved into my house, when my niece, Harriet, who was nine at the time, showed up at my door with her friend, Melissa. I was glad of the unexpected company, so I quickly set out a snack of cucumber slices, cookies, and tropical juice. As we ate, Harriet pointed out to Melissa the "special" circumstances of my lifestyle. She explained my propane fridge, my solar panels, and my wood stove and outdoor toilet without so much as a hint in her tone of anything other than pride. I was touched. I thought she deserved a little more to work with, so I led the girls upstairs to my studio so that Harriet could show Melissa my recent work. Harriet visited often, but this was a new experience for Melissa. She had never been in a "real" artist's studio before. Harriet proudly adopted the persona of tour guide, and Melissa followed her around, touching, with shy reverence, the edges of paintings and the tubes of paint lying on my work counter. Melissa left that day dreaming of art lessons. After that I agreed, with her parents' permission, to devote one evening a week to teaching both girls. However, as I learned later, her parents would only agree to allow art lessons if they were taught by a Christian teacher. I guess they were afraid I would permit the use of impure colours. Maybe even black.

This flavour of thinking was not new to me. I shrugged the whole thing off as if it wasn't important. As if it didn't hurt. I said to myself, *Ah, well, you're either in or you're out, and I'm out.* But for days the unvoiced anger nipped at the edges of my sense of peace like a dog barking when you're trying to take a nap. It's not surprising that, as I slept, my subconscious processed the incident and generated a dream that not only captured the emotion but also inspired the first of what would become my *Stations of the Cross* paintings.

In the dream, I stepped through a doorway to the outside in response to the sound of a prayer gong. Many people milled about, choosing places in which to pray, their left hands raised in the air. I raised my left hand, but after noticing all the heads turned toward me, faces staring, rigid with outrage, I lowered it back down. It was clear from their hostility that my place was not with them. I noticed a tree in the distance beside a stream and went to it, hoping for a place to pray. The ground beneath the tree was muddy, so I sat, then laid in the mud, thinking, *If the only place for me is in the mud, I will wallow in it.* I turned my head back and forth, feeling sludge squish in my hair.

I awoke unsettled. After breakfast, I walked along the beach with my head down and my hands shoved deep into my jacket pockets. As I processed the symbols, gradually grinding the dream into small pieces, masticating the emotions with the bile of my anger, an image began to take shape, presenting both a challenge and an opportunity. I embraced it, glad of the chance to shift my energy from the negative brooding of the hard done by to the positive current of the creative. The result was a painting: four feet high, three and a half feet wide. It was unwieldy, impractical, but large enough to accommodate life-size figures so that the faces, particularly the eyes, engaged the viewer. Many subtleties were needed to refine the expressions: eyelids lowered ever so slightly; nostrils made visible by the tilt of the head; chins protruding; lips pursed or curled; eyes flat, cold, dark. I painted them with their left hands raised. They seemed to be saying, *How dare you assume to have the right to pray if you are not one of us?* I stood in front of them, in front of the painting, and stared them down.

Long, curving, snakelike strands of hair wrapped around the figures in the foreground before leading back to the head of a figure lying at the base of a tree beside a stream. Lines from a poem by William Blake came to mind:

Earth raised up her head,
From the darkness dread and drear.
Her light fled: Stony dread!
And her locks covered with grey despair.

The painting was unlike any of my other work. I was stunned and a little humbled. I showed it to my friends, Janet and Gordon. They both agreed it was *real* art. They hurried on to assure me that my other paintings were also art but of a different category. I knew what they meant. They were right. After they left I hauled out my dream books in search of more material to work from. I unearthed another thirteen dreams. They all circled the topic of religion; several took place in a church. They also had, in common, a strength of emotion—either sadness, joy, peace, anger, or love. Hardly saleable. My only hope was to paint feverishly in an attempt to purge my psyche and return to my "paying work."

The Yellow-Bellied Sap-Sucking Power Tripper gravitates towards an environment in which it will be surrounded by smaller, weaker birds. Their habitat of choice is one that ensures any reports of their salacious or hostile behaviour will be met with denial.

Helen lived with a familiar low-grade sadness that she suspected was depression, plus a muddle of sympathy for people on the street who looked less fortunate or lonely. She told herself that, by comparison, she had every reason to be happy and she should be thankful. Her fear was that, due to some shortcoming of her own, she was letting down all the less fortunate people who would trade places with her in a heartbeat.

This sadness existed within her like an extra organ. Occasionally it became inflamed and sent out pains that upset the functioning of her other organs. Mostly it lay dormant, providing an extra weight to counteract any unexpected impulse towards joy. It was not the fact that she missed, needed, or desired joy that bothered her the most. She missed peace. She had, on so many occasions, just gotten snuggled down into peace when Warren upset the whole business. She was plagued by the question of why he would not allow her to just quietly be. One of the saddest things about her melancholic state was that she felt elbowed out of her relationship with God, like a third party on a date. She suffered guilt over the sadness and sadness over the guilt, unable to rally her spirits for so much as a sincere hallelujah. Warren had come between her and God, and she lived in his shadow.

The rules of their relationship were not the ones recommended by marriage counsellors. Helen was well aware of those rules. In recent years Warren had become a counsellor himself. The rules of Warren's house went like this:

Rule number one: nothing Warren did was ever discussed at the time it was happening. This resulted in things being left unresolved, and it enabled Warren to avoid facing the unfairness of situations.

Rule number two: nothing Warren did was ever discussed after it had happened—a week later, a month later, a year later. According to Warren, the past is past, and only a small-minded person digs up things from the past. If Helen persisted in trying to force a discussion, Warren resorted to lines like, *Oh yes, and you think you're so perfect. It must be nice. Perfect Helen, the saint.* He was prepared to keep up this undermining of her argument until she broke down and burst into tears of outrage and frustration. Then he would move on to the next stage, implying that she was mentally unstable: *I worry about you. I'm afraid that someday you're going to go right over the edge.* He would then show tenderness, comforting her and treating her like a sick relative. His real affection seemed to have been misplaced, like a pencil put behind his ear and forgotten.

Helen also worried that someday she would go "over the edge." She indulged herself in a secret fantasy life as an attempt to stabilize her sanity, reassuring herself that no one would be harmed by it. It was better than any alternative that she could think of. It allowed her to maintain her image in church and keep her home intact for the children. It fed off her anger, diminishing it, re-directing it, providing an interlude until Warren provoked another episode.

Her fantasy was of having her own apartment. She would begin working with the daydream the day after an argument, and she'd keep it alive for hours or days, depending on how long Warren's sulking or her anger lasted. It was like a salve.

Sometimes she sat with a pen and paper and calculated the cost of providing a home for herself. She walked the back streets of town on her lunch hours checking out *For Rent* signs, imagining what was behind the window containing the sign, and then incorporating the space into her fantasy. She furnished many imaginary apartments in her mind, always with a stuffed chair in a south window with potted geraniums on the sill, always with books piled on the floor beside the chair. She stocked the imaginary refrigerator with food that she liked but seldom bought—food that Warren objected to. In this fantasy, the children treated her with respect and they were happy. This part of the fantasy, the part about the children, was the most difficult to create and maintain. It was the part that made the whole thing seem impossible.

She knew she was being childish and unrealistic, self-indulgent and disloyal. The secrecy of it both shamed and excited her. It excited and soothed her when she first drifted into the fantasy. It was like saying, *So there! Do you think I care? Do you think you can hurt me? I could do just fine without you! In fact, I would be happier on my own!* But eventually the fantasy would wear out and lose its flavour. It would begin dimly, vaguely, taking shape as she worked on it, but if she began to seriously consider the possibility of turning the fantasy into reality, it was as if the sun was suddenly glaring on something previously lit by the soft glow of candlelight, suddenly emphasizing all of its flaws. At that point, it became more painful to sustain the fantasy than to give it up.

To be fair, there were occasional periods lasting from
to four months when Warren was actually relatively easy
live with and she was content. All she wanted, after all, was a happy, peaceful home. And Warren could be sweet. It just didn't happen often. When it did, the family welcomed it like a warm day in May, like a place by the fire, like the sighting of a rare bird. Being nice was not his natural state—it required effort. He seemed conscious of a scarcity of goodwill, of a need to ration his kindness; he took pains to spend it wisely, where it would be most noticed and earn a high interest. He also seemed conscious of record keeping. Perhaps that was the accountant in him. If an act of kindness is recorded in the books of thirty people observing it, isn't it, therefore, worth more than if only two or three people record it? Warren was like a miser, fearing shortage. He was afraid that his lack of compassion would be discovered, so he cultivated witnesses who would testify to his goodness. He surrounded himself with people who thought he was wonderful, and Helen was painfully conscious that these people would stand by him in the event of a dispute. This knowledge spawned two variations of her fantasy: one in which Warren goes too far and is seen by the world as being the man she knows him to be, and another in which he dies and she is spared.

My mother was a practising Catholic. My father had explored many religions (he read a lot), but he stayed unaffiliated until his death. Brood Bay is mostly Protestant. Even as a child, as an outsider, I was aware that religion had flaws, like a once-valuable vase with its crack turned to the wall. Helen converted to Protestantism when she married Warren, but I became fixed in the role of observer, much as my father had been. You see, I have both an eye and an ear for detail. I am offended by the inflated value given to words, especially

I think of churches as meeting places for worst, where liars flourish thanks to the *good* people to admit to their suspicions lies.

view—and I apologize, but I'm going to wax philosophical here for a minute or two—Original Sin was committed the first time a human being *thought* in words. Before that, they grunted or used gestures to communicate needs, warnings, and general news, but eventually they began to construct ideas out of words. Abstract thinking was born. The subsequent accumulation of words resulted in an eloquence that allowed deceit. Lies were born. An omniscient God was created in a hurry, but the concept backfired: only the honest people, the true believers, were deterred—like a lock that's easy to pick. The hazard of hell that morphed out of the concept of a judgmental God traumatized the good people and enabled the bad. God became a tool that the liars used to bully the innocent into believing them. Power fell into the hands of the people who could collect the most words. The right-brained attribute, memory, ruled. No... religion is not a good fit for me. Religion seems to complicate something I intuit to be very simple, and I have difficulty with any concept that requires subservience. Rules grow out of religion like morning glory in a flower garden, wrapping themselves around the spirit and strangling the natural impulse toward good. I prefer to dowse for truth with my paintbrush. The option of acquiescence does not exist for me in important matters such as belief in God. I need to search for authentic feeling, authentic thought. When I attend church with Helen, I feel alienated from the congregation by the emphasis given to memorization as opposed to original thought. I can understand that, for someone who is not creative but who has a good memory, memorizing the Bible and finding opportunities to quote the memorized passages would make them feel creative. The passages do, indeed, sound very poetic, but my dreams give me access to an undercurrent of awareness that is my subconscious. They communicate to me through words and images simultaneously, giving equal value to thought and emotion.

As I said, church has never been a good fit for me. Apparently, I was born without the necessary buttons. People grope about me from time to time, attempting to trigger guilt and shame but without success. It always leaves me feeling molested.

I discussed this with my father toward the end of his life. Helen's anxiety over his approaching death had become all mixed up with horrid imaginings of hell and damnation. She had an urgent need to save him and was wrought with disappointment when in the end he died a sinfully peaceful man. She'd said, "What kind of funeral will he have now? Where will we bury him?" I listened to Helen's lamentations, and then I rented a boat and spread my father's ashes on the sea.

It seems a shame that such things as death and dying have to be twisted up in words that tug and sting like snarls of hair at the nape of the neck. In the end my father's farewell contained the swish and slap of waves against the side of the boat, the clang of the bell buoy, the call of the gulls, and the whisper of *Peace be with you* as the ashes were given flight.

Now I go to church to hear the music. Once, shortly after my father's death, while adjusting to the lack of demands upon my time, I'd wandered into the cemetery during Sunday service. The singing voices of the congregation had followed my progression from marker to marker, and in my loneliness, the incoherent words of the hymns were replaced with an imaginary communication from my dad. I allowed myself to hear, "I am with you in every sense. I am the touch and the taste. The sight, sound, smell. I am everything. I am the shrine, the shrive, the shroud, and even the shrubbery." I freely admit that my father would never have talked to me in those words. Somehow between here and there a poet must have intercepted his message. Perhaps I'm to blame. Or maybe William Blake.

I settled myself in the bushes at the edge of the cemetery and I listened. I like hearing the church sounds from the outside, the shuffling and the hollow coughing. The pastor's words are reduced (or elevated) to mere tones, and the muffled responses come in waves like the sound of a car passing an open window—suddenly there, suddenly gone. I like not being able to make out the words. It's better that way; it allows me to flow with the general hum of things, pretending the words are whatever I want them to be: *Thank you God for the amazing grace of the shadows of leaves wavering on the church wall, for the patches of warm sunlight on the white shingles, for the smell of the spruce trees, for the texture of the tombstones, for their lichen and moss. Amen.*

I was in good company. There was Mary, wife of Wayne, who lived from December 12, 1841 to September 19, 1901; her baby daughter, Miranda, who lived from January 16, 1868 to May 3, 1868; and the Nickersons: Donald, Louise, and Louise's brother Harold.

After my first trip to the cemetery, I began taking a snack and a thermos of tea to eat and drink while the offering is being taken. And then, after the service ends and the last car has driven away, I stride back through the woods toward the shore, gathering mushrooms. Then I walk home by the beach feeling placid and reflective, like a tide pool—close to a large, thundering body of water, but quiet and contained.

Trippers can usually be found in an environment that has a moderate climate and a placid, if somewhat stagnant water supply. Their survival rate decreases in direct relation to their proximity to strong tides or fast currents.

It takes a smart person to recognize their weaknesses and contrive ways of functioning effectively in spite of them. My weakness is my lack of willpower. I admit it. I'm stubborn. I'm determined, and I've even been described as formidable (I secretly took pride in that last adjective) when possessed by the urge to complete a particular project, such as the construction of my house—just ask my carpenter. But a lack of willpower surfaces in me when restraint is called for, when the best action would be inaction, when an urge needs to be ignored. Generally speaking, most of my urges are associated with creative projects. I seldom cross paths with attractive men, and I'm not so good looking that they seek me out. My social life, since my divorce, consists mainly of dinners and movies with Gordon; sometimes these take place at a restaurant and the theatre, but more often we spend time in one of our houses, enjoying a home-cooked meal followed by a movie rental. Gordon is an amusing but unsatisfying date. He's gay. On the plus side Gordon makes me feel good about myself, better than I have felt in years.

I met my husband, Robert, at the hospital bedside of a mutual friend back during my art school years. He scrutinized me with what I considered—I wasn't totally stupid—to be unjustified interest. I appreciated the attention and privately vowed to at least *become* interesting; I would read better books and educate myself in the complexities of wine and classical music. Alas, for all my efforts, I became less and less interesting to Robert with every passing day. He married me, but I was mostly a blank page that he could write himself on. He always knew more than I did, was always one step ahead of me, but I kept chasing after his approval like a hound chasing a rabbit. It is with chagrin that I look back on those years.

I developed an unflattering impression of myself. Like a homeowner confronted with an appraisal that is contrary to the long and sentimental relationship they have had with their house, I objected to the evaluation while, simultaneously, compiling a to-do list. It was embarrassing to realize that I had blundered along for decades unaware that I wasn't very bright. It would have been too depressing if not for my art. Art gave me at least one area in which I could excel. It was not an important area—in fact it was a rather frivolous area from Robert's point of view—but at least it was one that did not showcase my stupidity.

Robert and I built a house together. I remember that part of the marriage fondly—the smell of new wood, the thrill of discovering that I could participate in a form of creation that was not insignificant. I left the building site each day exhausted and dirty but satisfied I had accomplished something real with my time. I deserved to live after all.

Robert and I worked well together. It had been clearly established that he was the job foreman; he read the "how to" books and designed the house. I made several creative contributions to the plans that secretly pleased me, but Robert deserved the credit for figuring out the important details, like how to construct a wall on the floor and then raise it up and put it in place. He was good at following written instructions; I was not. He assigned me simple, repetitive tasks—planking over the floor, shingling an outside wall (I even helped shingle the roof)—and I did him proud, except for the fact that he never seemed proud.

After the divorce I didn't actively seek a replacement for Robert. Painful memories can prove to be an effective antidote to the temptations of loneliness. I didn't actively seek a replacement for Robert, but in the spring of '94, at a farmhouse potluck, I found myself gazing up into the tanned, clean-shaven face of a handsome, attractively dressed man. I knew instantly that I was in big trouble. I was in the middle of my *Stations of the Cross* paintings and didn't have time for a man. And yet, I wondered, if this man proved to be interested in me, how would I be able to resist?

Gordon and I had gone to the potluck together. Gordon is handsome and witty and gay on a good day. On a bad day he is cranky and rude and gay. On a day when he's had a few glasses of wine, he fluctuates between the two, making little sense to anyone but me. We were balancing our plates on our laps while leaning against the outside wall of a veranda when we caught a fragment of conversation from above: "I'm going to try to grow parsley this year. I've never grown it before, but each year I like to try something new."

Gordon, gazing thoughtfully towards the hen pen, declared, "If I come back as a plant I'd like to come back as parsley."

"You can't come back as parsley," I said.

"Why can't I?"

"You just can't."

"Why not?"

"You wouldn't make good parsley."

"What do you mean I wouldn't make good parsley? How can you not make good parsley?"

"You probably wouldn't stay in your row for one thing."

"So? Who's to say I have to stay in my row?"

"The gardener. If you're going to be parsley you have to have a gardener. If you want to do your own thing, come back as a cranberry." I sat, nodding thoughtfully, pulling tufts of bread from a roll and poking them into my mouth. "I just don't see you as a vegetable. Sorry." I tasted the pickled carrots. My tongue quivered from the vinegar. I shoved them to one side of my plate with my fork. "You're not practical enough." I paused for a moment, considering. "Helen!" I poked the air with my fork for emphasis. "Now Helen would make a good vegetable. You and I, we're destined to be fruit."

"Thanks," said Gordon indignantly.

"Me, I don't want to have to depend on being planted. I want to be able to incarnate whenever and wherever I want to."

"You might be right." Gordon sighed. He frowned at his socks. "I wasn't sure whether I should wear the navy pair or the green pair, and now I fear the green ones were not the right choice. It's the first time this year that I've worn sandals." He sighed again and returned to the topic at hand. "I just never thought of it that way. I'd hate to be dependent on someone to weed me." He looked off into the distance. "It would get so boring having to stay with your own kind all the time, having some old farmer come around worrying about cross-pollination."

"Helen would make a good potato."

"No, I'm not so sure."

"Why not?"

"She's not that bad." Gordon grimaced. "I've always been suspicious of potatoes. They're so beige. It's unhealthy the way they all huddle there together underground in their little piles; there's something so secretive about it. I suspect incest. Just look at their eyes. Do they look inbred or what? You're right, Rube. I think I'll be something red and juicy. Something irresponsible." He fingered the gold chain around his neck. "Something that can get ripe and just fall on the ground." He sipped his wine. "How about you?"

I held up my glass and, with a slightly demented expression, said, "Something that wine can be made out of... a blackberry." I pause. "Vegetables get ripped off. They live their whole lives just to please the farmer, then what does he do?" I turned and looked at Gordon, feigning indignation. "He devours them. I'd just as soon feed the birds."

"Oh well, it all comes out the same in the end." Gordon got up, wiggled his behind, walked over to the wire pen, and threw his crusts to the chickens. He stood watching them scramble, then walked back past me looking for a garbage can. "Chickens are so honest in their greed."

I set my plate on the ground and, still holding my empty wine glass, closed my eyes and tipped my face toward the sun. The commotion of sound made me smile—voices and laughter and music. And then a voice from above, a man's voice, startled me.

"You're going to catch a cold sitting on the ground this early in the year. Or at least that's what my mother always told me."

I suddenly became conscious of my purple tights that were peeking out, like eggplants, between the tops of my little leather boots and the bottom of my brown corduroy skirt. I opened my eyes for a second and saw a man looking down at me. Another quick look told me that he had a great hairline and lovely temples. I'm a sucker for good temples. Have I mentioned that? I tried to appear relaxed and indifferent, with my head back and my eyes closed. I wasn't completely sure whether I looked demure, as I hoped, or ridiculous, as I feared. I waited behind my orange eyelids, then opened my eyes again. He was gazing off toward the hen pen, rocking back and forth a bit on his heels, his left hand in his pocket and his right one holding his wine glass. I watched the ever so slight tip of his pelvis as he rose on the balls of his feet. I could smell the strong erotic odor of the hen manure.

He suddenly turned toward me, and I realized he'd asked a

question. *Shit.* I blushed. As I struggled to remember his last words, Gordon returned and rescued me.

"I'm thinking of getting a refill." Gordon held up his empty wine glass. "Anyone else?"

I struggled to my feet. "I'll go." I raised my eyebrows in the man's direction.

He smiled and handed me his glass. "Any red will do."

I returned in time to overhear his plans to spend four days in New York later in the month. He had tickets to see *Hamlet* at the Belasco Theater. I'm not crazy about Shakespeare, but I could fake it given the chance. I imagined myself sitting next to the man—whose name, I discovered, was John—and became so lost in my fantasy that I didn't realize the conversation had swung around to me. "Tell John what you're working on now, Rube," said Gordon. John looked at me with interest. I frowned and took a sip of wine, suddenly remembering how much work I had ahead of me if I wanted to finish the fourteen paintings for *Stations of the Cross.*

Too much alcohol can complement the ego and encourage its stupid ideas; alcohol is like an insecure friend sucking up, looking for your approval. It told me I was sexy and brilliant, that John was bound to ask me out. Indulging my ego now and then is not a bad thing, but as the fog of intoxication began to clear, out of the mist came the details of my life—the importance of working on my fourteen paintings. As much as I would have liked to humour my heart, I couldn't afford to take time out for a relationship. And yet, as I mentioned, I've never been known for having strong willpower. After the party, and while still under the influence, I reached for the pair of barber scissors that dangled from a cup hook on the side of my medicine cabinet and hacked away at my dark shoulder-length hair, lifting it in clumps away from my head and forcing the slender blades through its obstinate thickness. When my scalp looked like the stubble of a mown field, I switched from scissors to razor and finished the job.

"There," I sighed, "that'll do it." My regret was immediate, the effect of my new image sobering. I was a drunk driver who had heard the unmistakable thud of a bumper hitting a body. I was a husband waking up to a hangover and a wife with a black eye. I was an idiot who had done the only thing she could think of to do... while inebriated. The logic of my madness went like this: if I looked ugly I would turn down any and all invitations from handsome men and I'd stay at home to paint. I needed money. I needed to paint. I'd given my sense of vanity the work of my inadequate willpower. It made perfect sense if I didn't take into consideration the other areas of my life that were affected by it, like the fact that some of my income came from babysitting. How would I explain my bald head to the neighbours? And, perhaps more importantly, how would I explain it to Helen?

The Gospel According to Pastor Wallace
Mother's Day Eve, 1995

Pastor Wallace frowned and nodded, his eyes moving from object to object around his office, then spoke as if addressing a small gathering: "If Helen gets in with the crowd that her sister hangs out with...." His voice faded temporarily. "They're a party crowd. Drinkers. And Helen has free time now when she doesn't have to answer to anyone, when the kids are with Warren. My sister lives just down the road from one of their crowd. She says there's times, at least once a year, when the cars are lined up on both sides of the road clear down as far as her driveway." His voice had become a sour whine. "Didn't take Rube long to hook up with that bunch after she moved back here."

"But maybe Helen won't feel comfortable in that environment. Did she party when she was young?"

"Not to my knowledge. She and Warren married almost right out of school. That makes her pretty innocent." Pastor Wallace glanced at his watch.

Obie continued in a tone that exposed his lack of real interest in the subject. "Sounds like the two girls are almost opposites. Odd how that happens—children brought up in the same house going in such different directions. It's amazing, the differences you see in families. When they leave the nest they either fly or they fall. I'd say from the sounds of things Rube fell pretty hard."

"I like that. Fly or fall. Have you ever preached on that theme?" asked Pastor Wallace.

"No, I don't believe I have."

"I think you could make a powerful sermon on that. Mind if I use it?"

Pastor Obie raised his hands in acquiescence. "Go ahead."

Pastor Wallace silently considered the possibilities. *Just because you've fallen, it doesn't mean your wings are broken.* He liked that. People could make the connection to angels if they were so inclined without him saying anything directly. He was tempted to start jotting down notes, but he thought that might be a little rude. *We all have to leave the nest sometime, and we will either fly or fall. We all have to have faith to fly. Birds need faith to fly. Just imagine looking out from that little nest....* Hadn't he read somewhere that bumblebees shouldn't be able to fly because of the size of their bodies relative to the size of their wings? He wondered if he could work that in. *Those that don't believe fall to the ground; those that believe fly.* He leaned back in his chair.

"What about Warren?" Pastor Obie asked.

Pastor Wallace turned toward Obie, still distracted by the thoughts of birds that were flitting around in his imagination.

"What about Warren?" Pastor Obie repeated.

"Oh yes, he came from a good nest—I mean, a good home."

Pastor Obie shifted in his seat.

"Is your back still bothering you?" asked Pastor Wallace. "That chair's not worth much. We could move out into the living room if you'd like."

"Oh no, no. This is fine. I just needed to change position."

They showed their teeth to one another to prove that they were agreeable fellows.

So after I shaved my head, I realized I'd solved one problem but created several more. On Sunday I gazed into the mirror at a scalp that looked as attractive as a pig's backside. *Hmmm, I may need to avoid the village for a while.* I winced at the thought of the babysitting jobs I'd need to turn down, the loss of income that I couldn't afford. I sat with pen and paper, calculating my upcoming expenses. *How long can I delay ordering propane? When is the phone bill due?* I scrutinized my cupboards, estimating how far my food supplies could be stretched. Money-making schemes were hatched and rejected in the time it takes to drink a cup of tea. One possibility was left, like fortune-telling dregs in the bottom of my teacup. Gordon worked at the Avis Car Rental agency. I had, in the past, driven for them when they needed a vehicle returned to Halifax. I could do that without hair. Who would notice if I wore a hat? Who would care?

I called Gordon at his office on Monday. "I have a little problem that's going to make it difficult for me to do my odd jobs."

"Oh yeah? What's wrong?"

I hesitated, drawing a long breath. "I've done something you might consider kind of stupid."

"Yes, go on. Why do I feel like I should be in a confessional wearing a white collar?"

"Bless me father for I have sinned. I've shaved off all my hair."

"You've what?"

"Yeah, you heard me." I began to count in my head to fill the silence. I got as far as six before Gordon responded.

"I don't believe it."

"Believe me. Really."

"Why would you do that?"

"Well, do you remember John?"

Gordon's voice softened. "I sure do."

Gordon called back fifteen minutes later. "Hey, you're not doing anything tonight. I'll pick you up and take you to supper. At Janet's. We've been invited."

"Right. You couldn't wait to call and tell her about my hair, could you?"

Janet lives in an apartment over the top of her bookstore in a hundred-and-fifty-year-old building she purchased after her divorce. It's located on Potter Street in Yarmouth, the town nearest to Brood Bay. Its clapboards are painted dark green with turquoise trim. Over the sidewalk is a sign that reads *Words of a Feather* above a picture of a hand writing in a book with a feather quill.

I allowed Gordon to deliver me to Janet's door like a lamb being led to the slaughter. Thinking of nothing other than the promised plate of chili, I rang the bell. We waited, Gordon in his brown leather jacket and cords and me in my grey baggy pants, white t-shirt, and black braces. A black felt hat was pulled down over my ears.

"Now don't you look cute?" said Gordon. "Where in hell did you get that hat?"

"Frenchys. Where else?"

Frenchys is a chain of used clothing stores that Nova Scotia is famous for. The clothes, imported from the US, are of better quality than many of the new ones available in the Yarmouth stores. The bulk of my wardrobe comes from

Frenchys. There's no shame in shopping there. Rich and poor alike boast of their brand-name finds. Gordon, however, is an exception.

"It looks it."

"Thanks."

"It wasn't meant as a compliment."

"Well I chose to take it as one."

As we waited, we listened to the sound of Janet thumping down the stairs inside; turning the locks; and cooing to her cat, Blanche, as she scooped her up before opening the door.

I removed my hat, and Gordon broke into a laughter that began as a squeal and then sank into mad, guttural rhythms that resembled an exotic birdcall. Janet took my chin and turned my head this way and that, muttering, "Black and white... I'll use black and white." I should have run away, but the smell of chili had assaulted my senses before we'd even climbed the stairs to Janet's apartment, and I couldn't bring myself to leave.

Janet is breathing down the neck of forty. She wears her grey hair short and spiked on top. She lives with a pair of glasses hanging on a chain around her neck and large metallic earrings dangling at each side of her head. We'd met in her store shortly after I moved home. We were both recently separated, so we started recommending self-help books to one another. That led to comparing stories of our exes. The friendship was cemented when I helped Janet make a papier maché coffee table to celebrate her divorce. The base was a life-sized figure of a man on his hands and knees as if he were ready to play horsy with a child. The top was glass.

I respect Janet's work ethic. We share a determination to be independent. Janet earns extra income as a photographer, and sometimes, especially in June, she calls upon me to tend to the shop while she shoots a wedding. I also respect Janet's intelligence. My memory for trivial facts is short. Incoming data is sorted into two categories: *may possibly be of use someday* and *this has nothing to do with me*. The later is swiftly deposited into a chute; it usually takes between five minutes and two days for me to forget it completely. Important information—such as how to mix that particular shade of blue (the one that's slightly warm but also a little greyish) by mixing alizaron crimson, viridian green, and titanium white so that the small amounts of blue in each of the colours adds up and, if the proportions are exactly right, the red pigments and the green cancel one another out—is not something that can be worked into casual conversation. Robert, my ex, read voraciously and accumulated useless facts with the dull doggedness of a spoon collector in a tourist trap. I was so impressed by the scope of Robert's intelligence—because at that time I was still thinking of information as intelligence—that I let him do most of the talking. Now, with friends like Gordon and Janet, I've discovered the joy of taking part in a conversation. And I don't feel so stupid after all.

Janet's living room spans the front of the building and is cluttered with overflowing boxes of books and a peculiar collection of furniture. It has the air of a lived-in stock room, complete with the odor of aging paper. She has a bulky old red couch on the far wall holding a gaudy collection of souvenir pillows with gold fringe and images of Niagara Falls, the parliament buildings, mounties, and the coronation. The open bedroom door reveals patches of a wide-board floor painted a gleaming bright turquoise.

In the kitchen, Janet has placed an antique dining room table in front of a large, three-sectioned window. Two spaces are reserved on the sill, in the middle of plant pots, for Blanche and Janet's other cat, Bernie. Renovating the window was Janet's one indulgence when she bought the building. It gives her a view, as she eats her supper, of the sun setting beyond the rooftops that slope down to the harbour.

After we were settled inside, Gordon looked at me with an evil, amused glimmer. Janet narrowed her eyes and stared while working her brows as if ciphering. I tried to return my hat to my head, but Gordon snatched it away from me and tossed it into a chair on the far side of the room. "You look so different," he said, examining the back of my head. "All these funny little bumps and things. It makes me wonder what my scalp would look like."

"There's one way to find out," said Janet as she served up the chili. "Rube, put some music on." She nodded in the direction of a CD player on an old bureau in the corner. I chose Art Tatum, and soon a piano version of "Tea for Two" filled the air. Gordon settled at the table, waited until Janet and I were seated, and then asked me, "What did you do with your hair? Did you save it? I'd like to have some of it."

"For what?"

"Oh, I don't know. I could make something from it perhaps."

"Like what? A voodoo doll?"

"No, I don't know. I'd have to think about it, wouldn't I? It just seems a waste to throw it away."

Janet snorted. "I can see it now. Him working it into his pottery. Moustache cups with a moustache."

"Or a soup bowl with a hair embedded in the bottom of it," Gordon suggested.

I cringed. "That's disgusting! But I could see it appealing to you."

"I could mail it to Warren with a note saying, 'I'm holding your sister-in-law hostage. Pay up or her fingernails go next.'"

"I hope to hell if I'm ever kidnapped, they don't send the ransom note to Warren."

"Ah, dear, dear Warren," said Gordon in a reminiscing tone. "What's he going to say about your new hairstyle?"

"I don't want to think about it." I grimaced.

"He's a strange bird."

"How's the series coming?" asked Janet.

"Oh, slower than I'd like, but it's coming."

"Which one are you working on now?"

"The dream about pulling down the blinds in the church."

"I loved that dream," said Gordon. "How are you doing it?"

I sighed. "I don't know. No offence, Gordon, but I'd rather not talk about it. You know, if you talk about something too much while it's in the works it loses energy and fizzles out. It's like a pinhole in a balloon—the tension gets lost and the energy is directed toward the little pinhole, and it gets all soft and sad looking."

"There's nothing sadder than a deflated balloon," said Gordon. He thought for a minute. "Well, maybe one thing."

Gordon uncorked his bottle of wine and proposed a toast. "Here's to the hairless, the bald, and the brave. May they never have trouble with stubble or mind the shine."

Janet laid down her fork and turned to me. "Rube, I was thinking—I could get some really great shots of your head while the hair's gone." Janet and Gordon's eyes met, and they almost winked at one another before turning back to me. "It seems too good an opportunity to miss. I mean, you may never in your life be bald again. What d'you say? Just a few."

"Are you nuts? Helen would kill me."

"She wouldn't know."

"Yeah, right."

"No really. Why would she have to know?"

"Someone will see them."

"No, they won't. I promise."

"Where would you get them developed?"

"I'd develop them myself. I'll use black and white." Janet waved toward the door to her darkroom.

Gordon said wickedly, "I dare you, Rube."

"Knock it off, Gordon. I don't take dares."

"Oh, come on. It'll be fun."

"For you, maybe."

"Don't you owe me one?" asked Janet.

"From when?"

"I don't know. I must have done something for you at some point that you haven't repaid me for."

"If you did, I didn't know about it."

"Well then, I'll be indebted to you. You do this and I'll owe you one."

"Come on, you guys. You planned this, didn't you? You invite me here for dinner and I think, 'Oh, isn't that nice. I have such good friends,' and all along you have an ulterior motive."

"Pay her," said Gordon. "She'll take money. She needs it. I know because she called me asking if there were any driving jobs she could do out of town. She can't do her regular part-time jobs now that she's bald. Pay her."

"How much?" Janet was all business.

"Okay. Thirty bucks an hour."

"Are you nuts? I'm not rich. Or crazy."

"Hell, that's not much." I was indignant. "Think of what you're asking for. There's the risk factor."

"What risk factor?"

"The risk I'd be taking that Helen would see the pictures."

"How could she? I promise you she won't see them. I give you my word."

"Right. I'd rather have your money. Thirty bucks an hour. You can take a lot of pictures in an hour."

"Fifteen."

"Twenty-five."

"Twenty and I'll give you dessert."

"But you were already going to give me dessert."

"Not necessarily. Did I mention dessert when I called you?"

"Dessert goes with supper. When you invite someone to supper, you give them dessert. No strings attached."

"It's cheesecake," said Gordon slyly.

"Mind your own business, Gordon. What kind of cheesecake?" I looked toward the kitchen counter.

"Blueberry. Last year's. Frozen."

I groaned and settled back in my seat. "You bitch." Then, reluctantly, I agreed to Janet's terms. "It's a deal."

Janet began examining my head like a taxidermist would a dead animal. My long face appeared longer than ever. My big eyes appeared bigger and my eyebrows hairier. Janet reached over and ran her hand across my scalp. "There's a bit of fuzz. We'll have to shave it again, but first I'd like to get a few shots with back lighting. Go ahead and have your bath. Gordon and I will get set up."

I carry a bath bag with me when I visit friends. Bathing is difficult at home. The absence of electricity means water for a bath has to be carried from the well or pumped at the kitchen sink by hand. It is then poured into large pots on my wood stove and heated. Most of the day is required to heat enough water to fill the cast-iron tub that sits to one side of my airtight stove in the living room. I usually make do with three inches of water in the tub or a sponge bath in the kitchen.

I closed Janet's bathroom door, started running the water, and sat on the toilet to wait. Staring at me from the opposite wall was a large photograph of Janet, straight on, almost life-size, sitting on a toilet. It was rather disconcerting, like a mirror with someone else's face. I could hear Janet and Gordon laughing and talking as they gathered up the dirty dishes. I thought of Helen and chuckled.

I emerged from the bathroom half an hour later to find Janet waiting with two red Christmas balls. She hung one on each of my ears and then ushered me to a space in front of the big kitchen window where the evening sun provides strong back lighting. Janet directed me to turn my head for a three-quarter angle from the back with one ball showing completely and the other partly visible. She took another shot dead on from the back, then a couple in profile without the balls. Then Janet straightened up and announced that it was time to shave the stubble. Gordon had, by then, come up with a few ideas of his own.

Bernie, the cat, was reclining demurely along the back of

the couch. Gordon suggested mischievously that I sit in front of Bernie and wrap his tail across my neck. *Fine. Not a big deal.* I went along with it. The tail twitched during our first few attempts, spoiling several shots.

Janet said, "I want your shoulders bare. Wait here and I'll see what I can find." She went into her room and looked around, returning with a wide-elastic haltertop.

In the first pose I stared, level, straight ahead with robotic eyelids half lowered. In the second, my head was turned toward Bernie so that the artery behind my ear and down my neck was prominent. Bernie began to sniff and lick my face but lost interest before Janet could catch it on film. Gordon fetched a can of tuna from the fridge. He dabbed water from it on my neck and cheek, sniffed his fingers, and then hurried off to wash his hands. If this were being done in other company I would have been mortified but, despite my weak protests, my creative core was plugged into the possibilities my baldness presented. How could I blame Janet for her enthusiasm when her eyes were sparking with inspiration? I told myself that I was not a pathetic moron. I was a business woman who had negotiated a lucrative modelling session. I was making lemonade from lemons. I never could understand what was so wrong with life handing you lemons in the first place. I love lemons.

Once she was satisfied with this pose, Janet began wandering around the apartment mumbling, "Texture... I need texture. I need a background that will contrast with your smoothness." She stopped in front of her wood stove and stared at the window. A large black piece of wood was laying in a bed of smouldering orange chunks. Flames curled and peaked in wisps and flares, gauzy grey tipped with bright yellow centres.

"Perfect!"

"Right," I said. "I'll just remove my head and sit it on the stool in front of the window. No problem. I'd do that for you. Anything for a good picture."

"Get down." Janet began pressing on my shoulders and didn't stop until she had brought me to my knees. Then she pushed the stool in front of me before just as quickly snatching it away. She got down on the floor herself, sprawling on her stomach with her arms across the stool; her back arched; and her head, chin out, straining for an upright position.

"Get like this," she said. Then she scrambled up and dashed to the living room for her camera.

Gordon sat at the table and poured himself another glass of wine. He said dryly, "We can call it 'Profile from Hell.'"

Janet began to set up, but she paused when she noticed two black streaks on the window of the stove. "You can relax for a minute. I've got to clean the glass." She pulled a bottle of ammonia from under the sink and snatched a few paper towels.

"Is that a good idea?" asked Gordon. "Maybe you shoudn't do that while the window's hot?"

"No, but it's okay." The ammonia sizzled as it touched the glass, and the paper towel steamed. Janet rewet it after each swipe.

"It stinks. It smells like piss," spat Gordon in disgust. "This just keeps getting better and better. Now Rube, Janet has set the mood for you. Time to reposition yourself before the flames of hell, breathe in the stink of urine, and smile for the camera. Come along like a good girl and prostrate yourself for art."

I dropped once again to the stool and managed to get my head upright in front of the window without breaking my neck, all while Janet was making suggestions.

"Look cold, disdainful, remote, smouldering."

Disdainful was the easiest—I rolled my eyes to one side and looked directly at Janet for that one. Still not satisfied, Janet roamed the apartment looking into the corners like a cat trying to find a place to do its business. I stood up and stretched, twisting my neck back and forth, and accepted my glass of wine from Gordon, who continued to smirk. Janet returned to the kitchen and declared, "We've gotta go to a cemetery. I need texture. Just imagine a lichen-covered tombstone for the background."

I screwed my eyebrows into a twist. "It's dark out. Piss off!"

Janet dropped onto a chair at the table and tapped her lower lip as she stared into her imagination. Gordon and I knew better than to interrupt. We used the time productively: we consumed more wine. Finally she said, "What would really be great—I can't get this image out of my mind—would be your head in the sand, surrounded by round beach stones."

Gordon hooted, spitting his wine halfway across the table.

I groaned. "Oh, come on."

"We could dig a hole and bury her," suggested Gordon. He howled.

I tugged at the top of the damned stretchy halter in an effort to regain enough dignity to support my protests. "Not on your life." I pointed a finger at Janet. "You're getting carried away." I shifted the beam of my glare to Gordon, who was wiping tears from his eyes. "And you're not helping matters any."

"We could do it Saturday, weather permitting. Somewhere remote. Barrett's Beach. There can't be much traffic there. Come on, Rube. Be a sport. You know I'd do the same for you."

"I know I would never ask you."

"I'll give you a hundred dollars."

My eyebrows shot up involuntarily and quivered. "One fifty."

"No. One hundred."

"Can you imagine what it is going to feel like to be buried up to my neck, depending on the two of you to dig me out?"

"Oh, all right, I'll give you an extra twenty-five for the entertainment factor," said Gordon. "I might even bring my own camera and take a few pics."

"No. I'll do it and I'll take your money too, Gordon, but you can't bring your camera. I don't trust you."

The Gospel According to Pastor Wallace
Mother's Day Eve, 1995

Pastor Wallace fiddled with a paperclip chain. "Rube built this house.... I haven't been in it but, well, why'd she build this house with no electricity and no toilet? Her father had a perfectly good little house that the girls inherited after he died, but she sells that and buys a piece of land and builds this house off by itself with nothing but wood for heat and an outdoor toilet." The increasing tempo of his speech belied the intensity of his anger. He was going downhill fast, like a freight train loaded with coal. "And when I say she built it I mean that she worked on it right alongside her carpenter as if she were a man."

The two men held one another's gaze as if reluctant to go on. Obie had to ask, "Is she a...?"

"No, I don't think so." Pastor Wallace sounded as if he'd never heard a more absurd idea. "She likes men just fine."

"You mean... she's promiscuous?" A light of interest sparked in Obie's eyes.

"You could say that."

"It's not surprising, I suppose. Artists often are. I wonder why that is." His voice trailed off.

"I couldn't honestly say, with any authority, what she lives off of," said Pastor Wallace suggestively.

"How old is she?"

"Oh, I'd guess late thirties, older than Helen. She's a good-looking woman. Quite pretty when she fixes herself up."

Fog wiped my face like a damp cloth as I struggled to make my way up the beach over rocks made slippery by the receding tide. Not a hint of a breeze, but the air seemed to hold excitement like it was dancing on the spot, shaking off its salty smell. The handle of the bucket almost cut through my leather work gloves. I stopped and rested on a driftwood log before hauling the bucket of gravel up the rough path to my driveway. I adjusted my toque for the fifth time and cursed both my slippery baldness and the spring potholes that made hauling gravel necessary.

Approached from the driveway, my house is not very attractive. Two small windows face in that direction, one on each level. A small deck squares off the L shape formed by the main section of the house and the porch. It faces southeast and is protected from the wind off the water, making it a perfect place to sit in the early spring. The shed roof of the house slants from south to north with three skylights and a solar panel. The higher side of the shed roof is on the north, providing an upstairs studio space. When I built it, I tried to keep things simple; I wanted my house to be a shelter from the weather, not a piece of real estate. I skimped on the luxuries of plumbing and electricity, but I made sure of enough windows to afford good light and an appreciation of the spectacular view on the ocean side. There is open water straight ahead, and to the northwest there is the Brood Bay wharf with its breakwater and fishing boats.

I have two identical outbuildings. One is a toilet, the other a tool shed. I could have built one larger building and divided it to serve both purposes, but I like outbuildings, so I have two. I like the way they relate to one another, the spaces that are created between them, the way their shadows reach out and touch each other's walls at different times of the day. They're like the children of the main house, a boy and a girl, distinguishable from each other only by the symbols on their doors. The tool shed has a female symbol painted on it, the toilet a male. There is only one other small difference: the "male" building attracts flies on warm days.

Occasionally I am questioned about the need for two toilets, usually by a man who is attending one of my rare parties and is unfamiliar with my property. When asked why I bothered having two toilets, I smile slyly and say that I'm a Gemini. I tell him I find it "balancing."

When I'm alone in my house, I feel as if the walls and floors, windows and doors are hugging me with their familiarity. I know my home with the intimacy of both a mother and a lover. I created it, watched it grow, nailed floor boards to floor joists, measured off rooms, raised skeletal walls, and fleshed them over with the zeal of an evangelist. And I live, a mother within her child, constant in my sense of wonder, reassured by the reliability of my surrounding surfaces, measured distances, predictable odors, and patches of sunlight.

My house is bordered on three sides by trees; the fourth faces the ocean. Privacy is important to me even though my neighbours are only a short walk away. The road at the end of my driveway is paved and well populated with houses that are, for the most part, at least fifty years old. The area has grown up over many years as a result of the fishing activity around the wharf, and the architecture has the charm of practicality rather than the ambiance of a resort village. A few homes have been purchased in recent years by summer people who were attracted by the extraordinary five-mile beach, but the majority of the fifty or sixty families have lived here for most of their lives.

I kicked off my boots in the back porch, and then, with my toque still on, I went into the kitchen and poured myself a glass of sherry. I carried this, along with an old quilt, through the living room and out to the deck on the ocean side. Three wooden lawn chairs sit in a half circle, one painted periwinkle blue, one fuchsia, and one chartreuse. Wrapped in the quilt, I snuggled into the blue chair and put my feet up on a mustard-coloured foot bench. The damp air made me feel acutely aware of all my senses. I took a sip of sherry, closed my eyes, and set my senses adrift. They lifted to the top of a distant tree for the caw, caw of a crow, then came back to hover over the smells of salt and spruce and sweet wet grass. I let them glide down over the bank to where the water was roaring and whispering, and I pictured the gulls drifting on the surface of the waves, gracefully adjusting to the movement beneath them like motorcycle riders. I watched the shore from the gulls' eyes, seeing tufts of grass bursting from the sides of the bank and spruce trees on the very edge of the bluff bending flirtatiously toward the sea then twisting back, suddenly shy. This image shifted gently as the water beneath me rose and fell. The gull blinked, losing interest, and I was back on my deck, relaxed and ready for another sip. A soft feeling of peace had formed about me.

I believe that this feeling is God. I believe that God should settle nicely around you, like a gentle fog, damp and sweet and natural, softening the edges, lifting at times to reveal things that you suspect are there but can't quite see, now and then allowing a beam of light to break through, to touch and clarify areas which are normally not given attention. And, like the fog, God should be allowed to remain mysterious.

I heard a car door slam. I called out, "I'm back here."

Helen barely rounded the corner of the house before she asked, "Isn't it kind of damp to be sitting out?" Then she looked at me in my toque and blanket and said, "I guess you're dressed for it, but I think it's a little early for me." She was wearing a pale rose dress and tan pumps. She stood with her back hunched, rubbing her arms.

"You're dressed up. Church today?"

"No, I just came from Winnie's funeral."

"Oh. That's right."

"Can we go inside? Really it's my hair I'm worried about. I don't want it to get damp from the fog."

"Right. Hair." I took a deep breath. "We can go inside." I shuffled to the door, still wrapped in my quilt. I crossed through the living room to the kitchen, Helen close on my heels, then shrugged the quilt onto the cot in the corner. With the finesse of a seasoned stripper, I pulled the toque off my head and hung it on a peg. Never had a stripper felt more naked than I felt as I turned to face my sister. Helen was frozen, half lowered onto a chair. Puzzlement gradually gave way to horror, horror to disgust.

"Merciful God, Rube!"

I laughed awkwardly. "You don't like it?" I crossed in front of Helen to the stove.

"What are you trying to prove now?"

I lifted the stove lid and poked a few small sticks in, then leaned down and opened the side draft.

"What happened to your hair?"

"I shaved it off." I slid the kettle over to the hot spot on the stove.

"What would ever possess you?" Helen paused. "Did you have lice or something?"

"Thanks."

Helen threw up her hands in exasperation. "Well, what do you expect me to think?"

"I got tired of my hair." I turned toward Helen and suddenly saw myself through her eyes. I hate it when that happens. Ideas that seem good when I'm alone end up distorted, all bent out of shape as soon as Helen looks at them. I asked, "Do you want a coffee?"

Helen neglected to answer. She had her hard-pressed look of forbearance on her face as she searched the upper wall opposite, as if God had promised to post an inspirational message there—something about patience. All she found was cobwebs.

I opened a cupboard door and took out two red mugs.

"I don't understand, Rube." Irritation hardened her voice. "Surely you don't think it looks good. You want to shock people? Is that it?"

"No. You know me better than that. I don't give a damn what people think of it." I shrugged. "Hair can be a nuisance. Who needs it?" I scooped grains of instant Maxwell House into our cups, added a teaspoon of sugar and a slop of milk into each, then handed one to Helen and placed my own on the table.

"You can't blame people for thinking you're strange if you do things like this. I'm tired of trying to defend you, especially to Warren." We stared at the steam rising from our coffees.

"You've gone too far, even for an artist. People are going to say you're crazy."

"They're *going* to say I'm crazy? Is this something new that I should try to avoid?" I snorted in a feeble attempt to imply victimhood.

Helen sighed. She held her mug with both hands, wrists draped elegantly, elbows placed firmly on the table. She looked at my head and then, blinking quickly, turned her gaze toward the stove.

"What? Do you think my naked scalp is indecent?" I asked.

"Quit being childish."

"There's something," I waved a hand, "pure about not having any hair."

"Pure! Good Lord! There are other ways to make yourself feel pure." The fire snapped in the wood stove and the kettle began to rock, like someone hopping from foot to foot on hot asphalt.

Helen toyed with a permed curl, tugging it straight and feeling it spring back into place. I eyed her from across the table.

"Why are you wearing earrings?" Helen was suddenly offended by the silver seagulls that were dangling from my earlobes. "They look ridiculous."

I could feel a rebellious look begin its slow crawl across my face.

"Rube, why have you done this?"

"Okay," I said, "I'll be honest with you. There was this potluck supper last weekend—"

"You haven't been going around like this for a week," Helen interrupted.

"Yes, I have." I grinned.

She ran her hand over her face and hair, leaving it to rest, as if forgotten, on the back of her neck. "Who's seen you?"

I tipped my head from side to side as if compiling a list, then said slowly, "No one. Except for Gordon. And Janet." I smiled at Helen. "And they don't count."

"Thank God."

I began to slowly fill Helen in on the story of the sexy man, John, from the party. I neglected to tell her about my new series of paintings; instead I generalized with, "I need all my time to work." I rubbed the little bristles on my scalp as I talked.

When I finished, Helen asked, "What are you going to do about your hair?"

"Mail it to John in a ziplock baggie."

"Oh, for God's sake. Be serious. If you stop shaving it, how long will it take to grow out?"

"I have no idea."

"Well, please stop. If Warren sees this..."

"What if he does? What I do with my hair is none of Warren's business."

"You don't make it easy for me. I try to defend you, but you don't help when you do stuff like this."

"Defend me?"

"Yes, defend. I either have to listen to him rant and make fun of you or I have to try to explain things away. And the kids... what kind of impression do you want to make on the kids?"

She had me there. I might not care about Warren, but I didn't want to have the kids thinking of me as mental. I winced and with a long sigh I apologized. "I'm sorry. It wasn't a good idea. I realized that right away, but it's the kind of thing that can't be undone."

She closed her eyes and shook her head. "While it's growing out you'll have to stay away from him. And the kids. And everyone. I'll bring you what you need. I'll tell Warren that you're not feeling well."

"Ah yes. We must never ruffle Warren's feathers." I smiled, remembering Gordon's favourite name for men like Warren: Yellow-Bellied Sap-Sucking Power Trippers. "You don't have to lie. No one will see me. I'll wear a hat if I go out."

Helen looked at the toque on the peg and snorted softly. "I think I'd better. But the deal is: if I do these things for you, you have to promise that you won't go out."

I hesitated, remembering the upcoming photoshoot. "Can I go to the beach?"

"Yes, you can go to the beach."

I smiled. "Okay. But I don't really think all this is necessary."

"Never mind what you think. Is it a deal?"

"Sure, all right. I'm easy to get along with."

Mates of the Yellow-Bellied Sap-Sucking Power Tripper are encouraged by the Tripper to use their beaks almost exclusively for carrying food to the young. They are seldom heard chirping.

Pastor Wallace preached on passivity at Winnie's funeral. He said, with the woeful sincerity of a politician, "Winnie never had a bad word to say about anyone," and then, two minutes later, he said it again. And again. Helen counted five times. He said it as if it were the highest praise that a woman could be given. Helen realized, with some shame, that it would never be said about her. She left the funeral feeling anxious and slightly depressed. Warren returned to the church after the cemetery committal for a deacon's meeting. He would catch a ride home later. She pulled out of the parking lot in their 1985 Accord intending to drive home, but then she decided to visit Rube instead. She knew exactly what Rube would say about Pastor Wallace's eulogy, but she needed to hear her say it.

Rube would say, *Some virtue. With a husband like that maybe Winnie should have said something bad. Perhaps then her kids wouldn't have had to put up with all the crap.*

Helen hadn't known Winnie very well. She'd visited her in the hospital the week before she died, but mostly out of a sense of duty. Helen had looked at the situation the way you look at a can of tuna that you've found in the fridge—one part of you knows that you would be irresponsible if you didn't acknowledge the potential for food poisoning in the dried-up bits stuck to the sides of the can, while another part of you doesn't want to throw away the remaining moist and edible chunks.

She knew Winnie's face—she'd seen it every Sunday. She knew her clothes and her posture, and she could recognize her singing voice, but she'd never really talked to her for any length of time. She hadn't felt comfortable sitting in a hospital room trying to find something to say, putting Winnie in the position of hostess. Hostess without a teapot, without a crumb of conversation. Winnie's life had been reduced to the rings left behind by an empty cup, and Helen had still required something of her. Why? Because she knew she would be asked at the funeral if she had visited Winnie and she had wanted to be able to answer yes. Yes was the right answer. Secretly she thought that Winnie should have been left alone to die in peace without a steady stream of do-gooders parading in. But that was the wrong answer. So Helen had gone and visited Winnie and prayed with her and held her hand, wondering all the while what Winnie really thought and believed. Death was much discussed at their church, but it wasn't the same as holding its hand or looking into its eyes. Take what you dare from the tuna can, watch out for the rust, and be careful not to cut yourself on the edges. It's borderline expiry time.

The Gospel According to Pastor Wallace
Mother's Day Eve, 1995

Pastor Wallace sat thinking about the Mother's Day message he had prepared. He said, "There are so many kinds of women. Do you ever look at some of the young girls in your church and wonder what kind of women they'll turn out to be? I mean, sometimes you can pretty well tell; sometimes they're as disagreeable and," he paused, trying to find a polite replacement for the word *mouthy*, "outspoken as they can be, and I say to myself, 'Oh Lord, here comes another Beulah Burns.'"

The two men laughed.

"Then other times they're sweet and kind. You think they must be the daughters of Winnie Earle."

"Who's Winnie Earle?"

"Ah, Winnie Earle passed away a year ago, I'm sorry to say. Wonderful woman. Never said a bad word about anyone. Didn't have an easy life either, but she bore it with a smile. Bore five children too. Her husband was kind of a hard man, stern, but a Christian." Pastor Wallace had picked a paperclip up off the desk and was cleaning his nails with the end of it. He frowned in concentration. "I expect it wasn't always easy for Winnie, but she didn't complain. Fine woman. We miss her. She set a fine example."

"The church needs women like this Winnie of yours," said Pastor Obie. "Needs the other kind too—though they sometimes try your patience, they usually get the work done."

"True," admitted Pastor Wallace. "That's so true."

Saturday was sunny and calm. I wasn't. Gordon picked me up at eleven. Unsure of what to wear I settled on jeans, a grey sweatshirt, and a yellow rain jacket. Gordon sang along with Patsy Cline as he tapped his steering wheel. I said, "God will get you for enjoying this so much."

He laughed. "You could enjoy it too if you put your mind to it."

"God will make your hair fall out prematurely, from all

over your body." Then I looked at his receeding hairline. "What am I saying? He's already making it fall out."

He chuckled. "Don't be a poor sport now. You're getting paid well for this."

"I know. I calmed myself all morning by thinking about the groceries I'll buy. I can even put a little propane in my tank."

We pulled into the back lane behind Janet's building. She appeared almost immediately carrying two shovels, a broom, and a foil survival blanket. Then, after setting them down beside the car, she disappeared back inside and returned with a canvas bag bulging with odd shapes. She was wearing sweat pants and an oversized windbreaker.

"What's with the broom?" asked Gordon.

"For smoothing the sand after she's buried," answered Janet matter of factly. She turned to me. "So how're you doing, kid?"

"I'm fine."

"It's your first time being buried, I suppose."

"No. Harriet and Sean buried me when they were little. Their dog came and licked my face. I couldn't push him away. It was awful. They thought it was funny, but I hated it."

"Well, we don't have any dogs today, so you're all right."

"How long do you think this is going to take?"

"I don't know. It depends on how fast Gordon can dig."

"Excuse me," said Gordon. "I'm not going to be the only one digging here. I don't see why Rube can't help dig the hole." He looked at Janet. "And you'll be helping of course."

"I was only kidding."

It was a half-hour drive to Barrett's Beach. I was fairly confident I wouldn't see anyone I knew. It was too early in the year for sunbathers, and Barrett's Beach was not as popular for walking on as some.

We had the hole dug in ten minutes. The idea was for me to sit in the hole while Janet and Gordon refilled it with sand until it looked as though my head was lying on the sand among the beach stones. I suggested that perhaps Janet should choose the stones she wanted to place around my head before they buried me—I anticipated that this part would take a while. Finally, it was time for me to wrap myself in the survival blanket and climb in.

As Gordon shovelled sand into the hole, bits hit me in the face, causing me to spit and squeeze my eyes shut. It smelled of salt and seaweed, and my mouth became gritty. I said, "Hey, watch out for the eyes."

Janet pulled a pair of sunglasses from her pocket and positioned them on my nose. A small pile of sand was left over, and the jackets and shovels were thrown onto it. Janet took up the broom and smoothed the sand. She was being fussier than I thought necessary. I rolled my eyes to the right so that I could see the waves. Their closeness alarmed me. The tide was coming in, and the beach was level. It wouldn't take long for the first lick of water to reach my mouth. Janet was about to set up her camera when we heard a car engine come closer and stop.

I asked, "What is it?"

No one answered. Someone had parked on an old road farther up the beach. We listened. One door slammed, then another. We heard voices. Facing in the opposite direction, I was dependent on Janet and Gordon to keep me informed.

"Are they coming this way?"

"I don't know yet. They've got a dog with them."

I said, with a touch of hysteria, "Don't let that dog come near me."

"Yes, they're coming this way. What should we do? Should we dig her out? I don't relish the idea of trying to explain this one."

"We can't dig her out now. I haven't taken any pictures yet. Let's just sit tight and see what happens."

"I'm sitting tight. I'm sitting tight. What else can I do?" I closed my eyes and tried to meditate on trust and vulnerability.

"What if they come over to see what we're doing?" asked Gordon.

"Please don't let that dog come near me."

"We won't."

"I know," said Gordon, "I'll go tell them that Janet's terribly allergic to dogs or afraid of them. I'll ask if they can put it back on the leash until they're well past us." Gordon got up, threw his jacket over my head, and went off in the direction of the intruders.

"Don't you go anywhere," I hissed at Janet.

"They're snapping the leash on. Good idea. Leave it to Gordon."

We waited until the dog was well past before returning to our work. I struggled to overcome a growing sense of panic. The tide was rising. Janet placed the stones one way, then another and another, constantly checking the view through her camera. She swept the sand, blew on it, and complained of her inability to get it smooth enough for the effect she wanted.

Gordon lit a cigarette and smiled wickedly at me. He had marked the high-water line within my view with a stick so that I could monitor the tide's progress. Every time Janet appeared to be wrapping things up, he kept coming up with new ideas that made it necessary for me to remain buried longer.

"What if I were to lie down beside Rube so that my head is facing upwards and in profile and hers is facing the other way?"

This done, he suggested that we wait until the first shallow waves had passed by my head and receded. He said, "The water will make the sand far smoother than you've been able to get it with that bloody broom."

"No. No way," I protested.

"Gordon's got a point, Rube. I think it's worth a try."

"Get me out of here."

"It would give the sand a nice sheen."

"Dig me out now."

"Don't panic. It will only take a few minutes. We'll have you out in no time."

Gordon chuckled with delight; satisfied that Janet had taken his bait. "You'll only need to have two or three waves go past your head. Five tops. Don't worry."

I was powerless to do anything more than make faces. A tongue of water was already licking the sand inches from my head.

Janet said, "Gordon, go fetch me that piece of wood up there. See the one that's square, like a piece of beam?"

Gordon didn't move. He looked at Janet soberly.

"The short piece, Gordon. It won't be heavy. Hurry."

"Excuse me. Did you say fetch?"

"Oh, for heaven's sake. We don't have time for this. Gordon, would you be so kind as to *deliver* that piece of wood to me? There—is that better?"

Gordon moved off in the direction of the wood.

Janet said, "I can set my camera on it. It should be just the right level."

I noticed the couple making their way back up the beach. "We've got to finish up now," I said, "before they get any closer. Come on."

"No way. Gordon was right. These will be the best shots." A wide sweep of water passed my head, then receded. "Great. It won't be long now."

"But how are you going to cover my head this time? You can't use a jacket. They'll know you wouldn't throw your jacket over a pile of sand that's in the water."

"Gordon will think of something. Here he comes. Great, Gordon. That's perfect."

Janet was careful to wait until the next wave receded before setting her camera on the piece of wood. She knelt in the wet sand so that she could look through the viewfinder.

"See Rube," said Gordon, pointing to Janet's wet pant legs, "you're not the only one who's making sacrifices."

"Gordon, the people are close. The water is close. This isn't fun anymore."

"Almost done. Almost done," he reassured me.

"They're going to see me."

"No, they won't. Janet and I will block you."

Janet stood up. "Done."

"Great. Now keep your legs together and let's stand close as if we're lovers."

Gordon had positioned himself so that his legs blocked my head from the approaching couple's view. Janet's legs, next to his, widened the screen. They embraced, seemingly oblivious to the water swirling around their feet.

I spat out, "God! You look more ridiculous than I do!"

Gordon winked down at me seconds before I gagged on a mouthful of salt water.

"Rube's been sick. I'm gonna help her a bit 'til she feels better." Helen's back was to Warren; she was at the sink washing dishes, and he was lingering at the kitchen table, reading his copy of the *Vanguard*, the local newspaper. She turned when he didn't respond, crossed over to the table, and picked up his empty coffee cup.

"Did you hear me?"

Still no answer.

"I'm talking to you. Hel–lo!"

Warren lowered his paper an inch. "Huh?"

"I said, Rube's been sick and I told her I'd help her out 'til she's feeling better."

"Yeah."

"Like you care." Helen slapped the dishcloth over the faucet and yelled, "Harriet! Dishes!"

Harriet emerged from the living room and snatched up the dishtowel from the bar at the end of the counter. Her dark ponytail swung back and forth as she wiped the dishes and stretched to deposit them on the second shelf.

Helen called into the living room: "Sean, could you bring those jeans in off the clothesline for me, please?"

When he failed to answer, she called out again. "Sean?"

That's not my job," Sean grunted from his place on the floor in front of the TV.

"Sean!"

Sean appeared, scowl and all, to stand behind Warren.

"Just bring them in," said Helen firmly.

"Dad?"

"Sean's jobs are putting out the garbage, shovelling snow, and washing the car," said Warren through his paper.

"Sean." Helen levelled her eyes at Sean.

"Oh, just do it, Sean. To keep the peace," Warren said, snapping his paper as he folded and turned it. He ran his tongue across his bottom teeth, ending with a sucking sound in the corner of his mouth. Sean stopped next to the door and rammed his feet into his trainers.

Harriet asked her mother, "What's wrong with Aunt Rube? I heard you say she's sick. Maybe I'll go visit her this afternoon."

"I don't think that's a good idea. You might catch it."

"What's she got? AIDS?" asked Sean. Warren snorted, and Sean laughed at his own joke.

The Gospel According to Pastor Wallace
Mother's Day Eve, 1995

Pastor Wallace straightened up in his chair. He said, "Warren mowed the cemetery all last summer. He charged us nothing for his labour, just for the gas—saved us a tidy sum. He's like that. Good guy. A good man, Warren. A good man. He had no idea at the time that he'd be in financial difficulties now. It doesn't hurt to shore up a little extra good work for insurance, and Warren's done that, praise the Lord."

Pastor Obie nodded and turned his nose in the direction of the study door. He thought he detected a whiff of dinner cooking.

Pastor Wallace pulled out the right bottom drawer of his desk, reached beneath some papers, and produced a package of Fig Newtons. "It may be a while before dinner," he said as he offered them to Pastor Obie. "Take a couple. Here, they're only little."

It is characteristic of this species that, though they often display a lack of interest in contributing toward their own nests, they cannot seem to do to enough to aid other birds in their colony.

Warren didn't buy the ride-on lawnmower for himself. He was not a selfish man. He needed the ride-on lawnmower to mow the cemetery. Theirs was not a large church and, as one of the deacons, Warren was painfully aware of rising costs and diminishing revenue. New members were hard to come by. Young people were marrying and moving away, and old ones were dying. Oil prices and taxes were steadily going up. The cemetery had been mowed for twenty-one years by a retiree for little more than the price of gas until the onset of arthritis forced him to quit and it became necessary to divide the work between five of the younger men. The whole business became a nuisance, but they couldn't afford to hire someone to take care of it.

The idea to buy the new bright-red ride-on mower felt like an inspiration. Almost like a request from God. Once he thought of it, he felt committed, as though not buying it would be to deny God, to disappoint Him. Warren prayed as he ran his hand over the gleaming engine cover. It was beautiful. His first new bicycle had been shiny red. A voice said, "Climb on. Give her a try." He was in the seat, his legs spread out on each side of the engine before he realized that the voice did not belong to God, but to a salesman.

"This model here has a nineteen-horsepower Briggs & Stratton twin-cylinder platinum engine."

Warren gripped the steering wheel and then ran his hand gently over the vinyl. He thought of how grateful everyone at church would be when he announced that the mowing problem was over.

"You've got your Turbo-Cool feature. It will either mulch or discharge the clippings." The salesman tapped the mower with the forefinger of his chubby white hand. "And it has your automatic, hydrostatic drive transaxle." His jowls wagged as he nodded his head knowingly. "You don't need to brake or use your clutch to change speeds. She's a beauty."

The washer and dryer huddled forlornly in a dingy corner of the basement. The light from the cobweb-covered window was supplemented by a bare bulb hanging above the dryer, but it did little to brighten Helen's work area. The space had a damp-lint, grey-water feel and smell, like it was a by-product of the house, not a part of it. For the first six or seven years after they built the house, Helen had wiped off the top of the dryer carefully and folded the clothes on it as she looked around and dreamed of what it would be like when the space was finished into a proper laundry room. Back then she enjoyed handling the clothes of her family, checking for wear and loose buttons. She loved the feel and fragrance of laundry from the dryer, the comfort of a family of clothes, united in their fresh smell, mingling together in their warmth and softness. But in time, Helen began carrying the basket of clothes upstairs and dumping it on the bed for folding.

The last time she reminded Warren of the laundry room project he snapped at her. The house was now ten years old, and she'd become more realistic. The laundry room would never happen. Laundry had become just another chore. But on fine days, it still gave her pleasure to hang out a nice line of washing, especially in the early days of spring when the breeze held the fresh tingle of melted icicles.

Helen was unloading the wet clothes out of the washer into her basket when she heard two vehicles pull into the driveway. She paused. She recognized their own car through the basement window above the washer, and she moved to another window in time to see a brown truck with the tailgate lowered. She watched as two planks were leaned into the back. She glimpsed familiar pant legs and sneakers moving about in front of the window: Warren's and Sean's. After listening for a few minutes, she recognized the voice of a man from their church. His name was Arthur. She picked up her basket of wet clothes and then went up and out to the deck in time to see a sparkling new ride-on mower being unloaded down the ramp into the driveway. With the basket balanced on her hip, she approached the men and inquired, "What's this?"

"What's it look like?" asked Sean.

"Whose is it?" She looked at Warren. He examined his hands and indicated to Arthur that they were dirty.

"Be right back," he said and headed for the house.

Helen followed him and stood in the middle of the kitchen floor, still holding the basket, as he worked soap into his hands and rinsed them under the tap.

"What's going on? You didn't buy that, did you?"

"Well they didn't give it to me." He tipped his head slightly as he looked at her over his shoulder.

"What did you buy it with? We don't have any money!"

"Hey, don't worry about it." Warren wiped his hands on a dishtowel and started for the door.

"Warren, we need to discuss this!"

"What's to discuss?" he said, his hand on the knob. "The old mower broke down, so I bought a new one."

"Couldn't the old mower be fixed?"

"No."

"Couldn't you have gotten a push mower like the old one? Why did you have to get one of those things? It must have cost a fortune!"

"Look," snarled Warren, pointing a finger at Helen, "you don't mow the lawn. Maybe I have better things to do on Saturdays than spend the whole day pushing a lawnmower!"

"Well Sean's old enough to help with that now. It would do him good."

"Sean will help." Warren redirected his pointed finger toward the driveway. "With the new mower." Warren left the kitchen, slamming the door behind him.

Helen stood looking at the closed door for a full minute before going to the basement and throwing the clothes in the dryer.

Helen found me lying on the squeaky metal cot in my kitchen, covered with a green wool blanket, reading *The Passions of the Mind* by Irving Stone. I kept reading, sneezing, blowing my nose, and dozing off. All on repeat. I had read almost every page at least twice, once before napping and once after. Predictably, sleeping with Freud was affecting my dreams.

Helen asked, "How on earth did you catch a cold?"

I coughed and smiled sheepishly, remembering the chill of the wet sand. "Ahhh. On the beach." Then, to change the subject, I asked, "So what did Warren say when you told him I was sick?"

"He wanted to send you flowers."

"Right."

"You're responsible for me telling a lie." Helen pulled a

chair out from the kitchen table and sat down.

"So I'll go to hell. I'm halfway there anyway. Besides, I didn't tell you to lie. It was your idea."

"Yes, but..." Helen stopped.

I sat up and swung my legs over the side of the cot. "Maybe God is punishing me by making me really sick. Maybe you are such a good person that God turned your lie into truth for you."

"And maybe you have a fever and you're hallucinating."

"I hope so."

"How long have you had it?"

"Since yesterday."

"Got anything to take for it?"

"Garlic. Can't you smell it?"

"Got lots of Kleenex?"

"This is my last box." My voice was muffled by mucus. I honked with gusto into a tissue and tossed it into the wicker wastebasket on the floor by the cot.

"I'll bring in mine from the car before I leave."

Helen settled back into her chair and began looking around my kitchen. The windowsill was full of clay pots filled with rosemary, thyme, and basil. Dishtowels were hanging on hooks behind the stove. Mounted on the wall beside them was a wooden rack with six arms that could be braced up to hold clothes. Two of the arms were propped out, and three pairs of underpants, a bra, and a pair of grey wool socks were draped over them. Down below, the oven door was hanging open. A rusty metal object was lying on it.

"What's that?" asked Helen, pointing.

"Isn't it great? I found it on the beach. I don't know where to put it. I thought of above that doorway, but it's too high. It should be more eye level so it can be appreciated better."

"What's to appreciate? It's a rusty old hunk of junk."

I shook my head and sniffed. "You haven't looked at it. It's quite lovely when you really look at it." I held it against the backdrop of the white enamel stove. "Its strength is in its form."

Two pieces of metal, rusted uniformly and pitted like sandpaper, formed the upper section, suggesting graceful wings. A small latch-like slab of metal, which measured one inch by five inches, was attached to the left wing and crossed over to the right, passing through a small bar. Obviously moveable at one time, these pieces had atrophied beyond function but had nevertheless maintained the dignity of their design. There was something pleasing in the symmetry and the clear, perfect roundness of the holes in the metal, cast at one time for a purpose but now tricked into being decorative.

Helen said, "It wouldn't go in my house."

I looked at her. "Then I won't give it to you. It'll go in mine. I just have to find the right spot."

The room became quiet except for the crackling of the fire. I rose, opened the fridge door, took out the milk, crossed over to the cookie jar, and began placing raisin cookies on an antique china plate with gilded edges.

"Oh. You're using it," said Helen, eyeing the plate.

"Yes." I smiled at her as I set the plate on the table. "I've been really enjoying it—thank you."

"I thought... when I bought it... you might want to put it up on your wall or something."

"Well, I s'pose I could, but my walls are quite full."

Helen's eyes wandered around the room. She nodded. The walls were cluttered with an odd collection of paintings; dried flowers; macramé hangings; bits of debris from the beach; and little shelves, some made from driftwood, with rocks and shells placed on them. She looked back at the china plate and sighed.

I asked, "So is anybody sick at your house?"

"No. Not yet."

"Anything exciting going on?"

Helen stood up, opened the stove lid, and peered into

the hole. "Well, Warren bought a new ride-on mower last Saturday. I guess *he* would call that exciting." She chose a piece of firewood from the oven and poked it into place before sitting back down.

"Brand new? As in straight from the store?"

"Brand spankin' new. Bright shiny red."

I whistled. "Must be nice."

"It would be nice if we had the money."

I quietly fingered the satin edge on my blanket as if I wasn't particularly interested, silently willing Helen to go on. Helen seldom complained about Warren.

"He wants me to take the money I've been saving for a camcorder and use it to pay the visa bill. He charged the mower."

"Don't you dare."

"I told him I wouldn't."

"I bet that went over well."

"He's still mad."

"Let him be."

"It's taken me two years to save that money."

"Is it in a joint account?"

"No."

"Then do you want me to tell you what Warren can do?"

I used up Helen's box of tissues over the next few days—plus a roll of toilet paper—but, in spite of my runny nose, I was content. I enjoy colds. I like feeling waterlogged, mellow, tired, hazy, and drugged. Heavy and soft like a watercolour sky. It always feels as if the fever and the drip excuses me from any past or present indiscretions. All is well in my world when I have a cold, except for my nose, and nothing else matters. I use the downtime for romantic fantasies. This time, the fantasies involved the handsome man, John, from the potluck. He hadn't called me, so it seemed I had shaved my head for nothing. Oh well. I lay awake at night snuffling and strangely aware of the distance between myself and other people. I avoided remembering times when I had convalesced in houses where the sounds of family moving about kept me company. Such memories made me lonely and homesick for homes long gone. I told myself that being cared for is often an illusion anyway, stimulated by the sounds of someone else stirring about as if they're taking care of you when, really, they're probably just making themselves a cup of tea. It wasn't like that when I was little, though. When I was little, I would wake up with a cold and hear the sounds of my mother in the kitchen below, the clank and grate of the stove lid as the fire was being lit, the creak of the kettle swinging by its handle as my mother carried it to the sink, the urgent gush of the water rushing to fill the very void it was echoing in, and the groan of the pipes in the wall. These sounds played on the cold air with a clarity peculiar to chilly mornings. The entire house—the stove, the kettle, and the pipes—knew that not only was my mother up and about in the cold, but that I, Rube, was still snug beneath the covers. There was no reproach in the sounds. They were a chorus singing, "You are cared for." They were the sounds of love.

Now, if I want my stove lit I have to get out of bed and light it. I left my bed with my shirttail dragging, knowing that neither me nor the bed would be as warm when I returned. Then I snuggled down, shivering, while I waited for the house to heat up. There was no one to listen to the sounds I made. My two woodstoves are the closest thing I have to dependents, and the dependency is mutual. If I take care of them, they'll take care of me.

The living room was chilled after a rainy night without a fire in the airtight stove. I pulled my bathrobe around me. I had managed to keep the kitchen stove going overnight, and I dressed quickly beside it. The wood box in my porch was as empty as a beggar's belly and, sick or not, I needed to go outside and fetch wood to fill it. I put on my raincoat, slipped my feet into black gumboots, grabbed a pair of heavy work gloves, and tramped out the door.

It took five armloads to fill the box. The effort caused me to break out in a sweat. I lowered the oven door and made two more trips to the woodpile. The wood was wet and messy, but an hour or more in the oven would dry it out enough to burn. I brought in another armload and laid the sticks on the floor beneath the stove. After putting my boots back by the door, my work gloves on the warming shelf, and my jacket on the back of a chair near the stove, I swept up. Then I sat down for a cup of tea, exhausted.

My basic needs are simple. Meeting my needs gives me a satisfying sense of accomplishment. Successfully bringing in the day's firewood was reason enough to pause and congratulate myself. One of my needs had been met.

I thought of my mother as I drank my tea. I inherited from her the idea that it's important to distinguish between a need and merely a want. My mother was also conscious of the difference between investing and spending. It was not that she thought spending was bad, more simply that people shouldn't fool themselves, when they spent, into thinking they were making an investment. It's quite simple: a house or any physical property is an investment; money spent to buy and maintain it can be regained at the time of sale, and it will probably appreciate in value. A car, on the other hand, will depreciate, so money spent on it is spending. Money used for gas to travel to work is invested; money used for gas to joy ride is spent. Money for books is spent unless they are textbooks, in which case it's invested, and so on.

My father had loved reading, and he had defied the system by buying books at a rate that rankled my mother. She tried to persuade him to trade the books in after reading them, but he usually refused. Now and then, he even went so far as to commit a particularly unforgivable sin by stopping for coffee when he was less than ten miles from his own kitchen.

Senseless waste.

I am aware that I appear poor. Most people live by a different set of values. However, I don't feel poor. Well, I do some days, but I'm talking generally now. I feel fortunate. My needs are met, and things just seem to come my way, partly because I am able to see value in things that other people overlook and partly because I am open to receiving.

I've invested in a few very nice antiques, and alongside them are things from the dump or things that had been put at the side of the road on pick-up day. Life for me is like sitting on a riverbank watching things float by. If something particularly nice drifts past, I reach out and grab it. The rest I let go.

The Gospel According to Pastor Wallace
Mother's Day Eve, 1995

"Rube pulled a bit of a fast one on us," said Pastor Wallace. "She had us all praying for her good health. She probably never felt better in her life with all those extra prayers being said for her. And she wasn't even sick, just pretending. Had us all thinking she was desperately ill. We thought she had cancer—and why wouldn't we? Here's Helen saying Rube's sick and she has to go over there all the time to help her, and Rube's as bald as an eagle, so naturally we thought she'd been through chemotherapy. We should've known better though, considering what she's like."

"Bald?" asked Pastor Obie incredulously.

"Yup, bald. Freddie, who drives the propane truck, goes to my church. Well, he got a look at her when he was delivering her propane. He said she seemed to be trying to hide the fact that her hair was gone, that she wouldn't come out from behind the line of clothes she was hanging when he drove into the yard. Vanity was all it was, vanity. But he saw her." Pastor Wallace sighed. "But it was all a scam. That's what she's like. The Lord showed us what she's all about." He paused, nodded, and shot Pastor Obie a sideways look. "Billy Wood, from our church, is a tax assessor, and he was appraising a building owned by a friend of hers. He said he never saw anything so evil looking in his life—pictures and negatives. Scared the daylights out of him. They were hanging in a darkroom with just a red light on. He took a peek at a half dozen of them. Said they were 'red light' stuff all right. You can imagine."

Pastor Obie grimaced as he tried to imagine.

The Irving propane truck pulled into my driveway, catching me at my clothesline, bareheaded. I ducked behind a blanket, waved to the driver as he jumped down from his truck, and then busied myself with the clothes, trying to stay behind the line of laundry so that he wouldn't catch a glimpse of my head.

He said, "Great day to be alive."

"Sure is." I pinned up a pair of jeans, then stepped back behind a sheet.

He looked around slowly as he waited for the tank to fill.

"Did you mind the winter out here?"

"No, not at all. The house is well insulated. I had dry wood this year. Bought it from Leo Burton."

"Makes all the difference. Gotta be dry."

"Sure does."

"Selling many pictures?"

"The odd one."

My clothes basket was empty. *Now what?* Thirty feet of exposed ground lay between me and the back door. I glanced in the direction of the tool shed. To get there, I would need to come out from behind the clothesline at the end. I would be visible while I opened the tool-shed door, but once inside I could pretend to be busy until the he left. I walked down the line of clothes. Just as I reached the end, I said, "I saw some tracks over around my back door the other day, in the mud. You wouldn't know what they are, would you?"

He turned toward the house and bent over. I came out from behind my cover, unlatched the tool-shed door, and was in before he straightened up. "Don't see anything. What'd they look like? A big animal?"

I called from inside the shed, "Not real big. They just didn't look like a dog or a cat, and I wondered. I don't want rats."

"Must've rained since then cause I can't see anything."

"Maybe so."

"You shouldn't have a problem with rats this time of year, not if you didn't have them over the winter."

"Well, I won't worry about it then." I shifted the shovel for sound effects and clattered a few plant pots. I noticed that he was finishing up, so I shouted, "You can leave the bill in the screen door there. Thanks."

He called out, "You have a nice day now," as he climbed into his truck.

The phone was ringing when I entered the house. I picked it up and, hearing Janet's voice, settled into a chair.

"I'm calling for two reasons. One, a book was brought in this morning that I think you might like—*William Blake: His Art and Times*. Loads of illustrations in it. I'm looking at one right now. You probably know it. Looks like God is picking nits out of a woman's hair. What does it say here—*Ahania*. Anyway, it's ten dollars. Are you good for it?"

"Save it for me. What's the other thing?"

"The pictures. I've developed them."

"Good?"

"Some are. Some are, well, ridiculous. But a couple are great."

"Can you bring them here? I promised Helen I wouldn't go out." Then I added abruptly, "Oh, hell—you can't leave the shop. I'll be right over."

I grabbed a hat and locked up the house. The bookstore was empty. I helped Janet blow out the half dozen prayer candles that were placed around the shop, then Janet turned on the baby monitor and beckoned me to follow her upstairs. She pointed toward the glass-topped coffee table before disappearing into the blackness of the darkroom. "Clean that off so I can spread them out."

I stacked the books on the floor beside the sofa, swiped the sleeve of my sweatshirt across the glass, and pushed the ashtray to the side where Janet would be sitting. She plunked down next to me and rifled through a pile of eight by tens, deciding which to show first. She pulled one out—it was of me, back lit, in front of the window. My face was faded into dim shadows, but the light from behind created a thin, bristly, halo effect in the stubble on my scalp.

"I look almost angelic." I stared in wonder for a full minute at the magic of lighting, before sighing and saying, "Wow."

Janet lit a cigarette, took a drag on it, and placed it in the ashtray. She laid another photo next to the first. I hooted, "I look positively evil!"

Janet giggled. Staring back at us, out of a backdrop of flames, was a wicked unearthly skull with a depraved gleam in its eye. She said, "The negatives of these are as interesting as the positives." She passed two negatives to me. I turned to the light of the window and held them, one at a time, by their corners.

"God, they're wild, absolutely wild."

"The one I think you'll really like is here." Janet gently placed a photograph in the middle of the table. It was of me on the beach; my eyes and mouth were closed. I looked like a marble statue after time had removed the eye colouring. My head was reflected in a film of water, a film so thin that my head also cast a shadow to the left, onto the sand, through the water. I picked it up and settled back onto the couch. Both a reflection and a shadow.

"God, how I wish I hadn't promised Helen. This is wonderful! I could use it on a brochure the next time I have a show." I looked at Janet. "What are you going to do with it?"

"I think I'll start by entering it in a competition, if that's all right with you. It's the best thing in my portfolio."

"Like I could stop you. It's fabulous. You've got to. It's… there's something about it. The other two, they capture the two extremes, but this one…" I pause. "It seems to capture both sides at once."

Janet picked up the first photo, the one with the halo. She studied it, narrowed her eyes, and looked off into nowhere, her cigarette poised inches away from her mouth. Then, before drawing on it, she said, "I have an idea."

William Blake was inducted into my league of kindred spirits many years ago when I received a volume of his poetry from my father. I kept this book next to my chair, referencing his words the way some people reference their bibles. Lines from his poems began to cross my mind like weather systems. I recognized in Blake an independent dedication to own his vision of the world, whether it coincided with those of his contemporaries or not. Among his engravings, especially the early ones, were images that were awkward in their proportions and composition. These endeared him to me and made me appreciate his later work all the more. He was a bit of a misfit—a Christian who disliked any form of institutionalized religion, an artist whose engraved copies of famous paintings caused him to be looked down upon by other artists as being unoriginal and therefore unprofessional. He was a visionary who was not understood by his contemporaries.

I set *William Blake: His Art and Times* on the kitchen table to peruse with my meals.

I was standing in the middle of my studio, hands on my hips, chin thrust outward, face twisted into a sneer. When

I paint faces, I take on the expression I'm painting. A smile on my face makes it easier for my hand to paint a smile; a frown makes it easier to paint a frown. The downside of this is that my emotions reflect my expressions, and vice versa. Therefore, to paint cold, hateful faces it's necessary for me to feel cold and hateful. So I was in a foul mood.

The "dream" image I was struggling with consisted of the laughing, jeering, life-size image of a man with his mouth wide open and his eyes glimmering with cruelty, repeated again and again over the canvas. He stood, in a suit and tie, before the doors of a church. He was positioned high above the viewer, looking down on them.

Once again, William Blake's words seemed appropriate.

Love seeketh only self to please,
To bind another to its delight,
Joys in another's loss of ease,
And builds a Hell in Heaven's despite.

The work was in its seventh day. Seven days of scowling and jeering. An unidentifiable anger was crippling me. I left the studio, cleaned my brushes in the kitchen sink, carried firewood for the stoves, pumped water for the water pots, and then slumped in my chair and stared at the slush I had tracked in from the back door. My world had settled into the grey sludge of a cesspool. I'd been driving myself too hard, depleting my hoard of confidence and enthusiasm. I'd been left destitute. I had been in that place before. The familiarity should have helped, but it didn't. *If only my work was better…. But then, what difference would it make? Who cares? I should be doing something useful in the world—helping people. Instead I'm indulging myself in the fantasy that I'm doing something important.* I told myself that I was the worst kind of person with no talent. I was a person with no talent who was too dumb to realize it. I was making a fool of myself.

Eventually, out of desperation, I turned to my homemade cards of inspiration and chose one about negative space. It read: *Negative space is important. You need your negative space as much as a painting needs its negative space. Be still. Don't dismiss the stillness of "empty time" as time wasted. If you cut the negative space away from the subject in a painting, the painting will not fit in its frame. Without reflective time, you cannot align yourself with your four-dimensional framework (the fourth dimension being your absolute centre). Always be aware of the force created by your negative space, relax, and be at peace with it. You are in no condition to evaluate anything at this time; you can only let time pass.*

I returned the card to the file; put on my boots, toque, and jacket; and went outside, wanting to walk until I was exhausted. I crossed the bridge—breathing deeply, sucking the salty air into my lungs—and then paused at the wharf. I stood staring dully at a group of barrels huddled by a shed, comforting one another with their rounded shadows. Rusty anchors, faded buoys, plastic bait boxes.

As peculiar as it sounds, I have my preferences as far as debris goes. Wood and rusty metal are honourable, almost alive in their decay. You could say they were involved, at least, in a process. However, I regard plastic with contempt. It is lifelessness.

It was low tide, and the beach sprawled for miles. Matted humps of rockweed, snarled with bits of green and orange rope, were pushed in a ridge along the upper edge. The hard density of the sand made it easy to walk on. I saw other footprints scrunched out, the treads heavy. There were two kinds, plus dog tracks. But other than myself and the crying gulls, the beach was empty of life.

I walked for an hour on the fine line between opposites. On one side of me, the frenzied energy of the waves matched the chaos of my emotions; on the other side, the absolute stillness of the stones and the bright reflective clarity of tide pools promised relief. When I turned to make my way back, I felt a shift. It was as if the chaos had been transferred to the other side to be absorbed by the dullness of the sand. The worst was over. My tide had turned.

Helen's car was parked in my driveway. "Oh no," I muttered under my breath when I remembered that I'd left the door unlocked. Even so, I went in expecting to find Helen sitting at the table. The kitchen was empty. I passed through to the living room, calling out to her. No answer. I backtracked toward the stairs to my studio. *Oh God, please don't let her be there!*

Helen was perched on a stool with her shoulders slumped and her feet tucked behind the rungs. Her hands were fingering the bottom edge of her blue cardigan. Her eyes were riveted on the painting of people with their hands raised. I waited for my presence to be acknowledged. Helen seemed unwilling to do so, so eventually I said, "It's from a dream I had. They all are."

Helen remained as motionless as the figures in the painting and just as silent. I kicked off my boots, creating a pile of sand on the plywood floor. I threw my jacket on a cardboard box full of small canvases and asked, "Do you want to hear the dream?" Helen turned toward me with an ambivalent expression, dropped her gaze for a second and then looked back at the painting.

"Why not?" she said.

When I finished, she asked, "Is that what we look like to you?"

"The dream illustrates a feeling, Helen. That's how the people looked in the dream." I walked over to my table, removed a brush from the bottle of turpentine, and began to wipe it on a white cotton rag. It was an attempt to relieve the awkwardness. It failed.

"I've never seen people in my church or any other look like that! They're," Helen paused and then spat out, "hostile."

She was right. But she didn't understand. I had only painted what my subconscious had presented to me. Did that make me responsible? I turned to Helen, took a deep breath, and tried to explain. "It's exaggerated. That's art. That's the way dreams work. It's about beliefs not being considered valid because they're not the same as the beliefs of other people. It's about being treated with disdain, being excluded."

"Why should you be included in something if you're not part of it?"

"I only wanted to pray in the dream." I threw up my hands.

"But you wanted to pray with them. Why should you expect to pray with them if you don't belong?" Helen rose from her stool and began to survey the other paintings leaning against the wall with the adversarial attitude of a health inspector in a greasy spoon restaurant.

I tried again. "I only wanted to pray. It didn't seem like it was a matter of belonging or not. It seemed to be a matter between God and me. I didn't understand the whole belonging business. What was it to them?"

"Don't you think you exaggerated their expressions a bit?" Her voice was sharp.

"That's how they looked in the dream. Sometimes dreams exaggerate things."

"If it's part of their beliefs that they're supposed to stay apart, then..." She didn't finish. She had lifted her hands briefly and dropped them again.

"Staying apart I can respect. But being small-minded and vicious has no place in anyone's beliefs. Trying to hurt people who are on their own path just because they're not on your path is not right." I stopped. "I'm sorry, Helen. I didn't mean to say those things. I'm sorry."

"Isn't that what you're doing? Trying to hurt people?"

"No. I'm not trying to hurt anyone. How do you feel when

you look at that painting?" I indicated the faces with my paintbrush.

Helen paused. "Angry. Upset, I guess."

"Is that God's work? Is anyone that goes around with that attitude," I gestured toward the painting again, "doing God's work? What if they looked at Jesus that way, not knowing it was him they were looking at? A lot of good people don't go to church because they don't want to be part of that."

"But that's just how they looked to you in your dream. It's not how they are. It's not how they look to me."

"You're on the inside. Most things don't look the same from the inside. The feeling of the dream is real. That's the important thing." I began mixing yellow ochre and cadmium yellow together with my brush.

"That's your problem," snapped Helen.

"Aren't they responsible for treating people in a way that doesn't encourage a feeling of brotherhood?" I shrug. "That encourages separateness?" I dabbed the painting and then returned to my palette to add a little white.

"What would you have them do?"

"I'd have them respect other people's beliefs. They don't have to accept them as being their own, but respect them as being the other person's. That's all I'd ask. Not treat me as if I'm unfit or contaminated or something."

"Nobody treats you that way. We welcome you into our home, share our Sunday dinners with you, and let you bathe and do your laundry. You ungrateful—"

"Yes, but...?"

"But what? Maybe you should practise what you preach."

"You sound like Warren."

"Well, you're free to go to church or not. It's a free country. Nobody has said anything about your beliefs or lack thereof."

"There. You see what you just said? 'Lack thereof.' You treat people like me as if, because our beliefs aren't all lined up in a row and affiliated with a church, they don't exist. You think it's fair game to make remarks like that." I crossed my arms. "You think it's fair for ministers to stand in pulpits and preach that people like me are going to hell. You think it's fair to teach children that people like me are to be avoided like pedophiles, and that it's fair to tell people like me that we don't have a right to our own voice. If we speak out, we're evil and in the grips of the devil." I stopped and stared hard at Helen. "I'm not evil, and these," I sweep my arm out toward my paintings, "are my voice. Your church may be good for you, but it's not good for me. I don't have to be wrong for you to be right."

After a long silence, Helen asked, "What's that one?" She pointed to the profile of a bald woman wearing a bathrobe and sitting in a church pew staring straight ahead, vacant. A stained-glass window was visible in the upper left-hand corner, and irregular lines of paint ran in a grid-like fashion across the painting, even crossing her face.

I said, "I've chosen lines of William Blake's poetry to go with each of them. For this one, it's 'They clothed me in the clothes of death and taught me to sing the notes of woe.' In the dream, it was Pastor Wallace's wife, Rebecca, that I saw sitting in a pew like that. I'd say the bald head represents a lack of identity, strength, sexuality, words, voice. Beneath it all, she's naked; beneath her skin, she's hollow. I've seen a lot of women like that. They think you can't tell. They're like blown-out Easter eggs. Brittle. Fragile. Trimmed up on the outside but empty."

Helen asked slowly, "Do you see me like that?"

"You're getting there."

Helen stood up and moved about the room. "What are you going to do with these?"

"I don't know yet. They're not exactly saleable."

Helen breathed a tired sigh, turned, and walked toward the top of the stairs. She said, "I never know what to expect from you next."

I followed her down the stairs to the kitchen. When she was about to open the back door, I said, "They're my dreams, Helen. When people look at them, they'll interpret them according to what their beliefs are, according to what's going on in their lives. I have no control over what other people see. They could learn a lot about themselves by how they react if they ask themselves questions."

Helen left quietly. I was even more upset and depressed than before my walk on the beach. Self-doubt began to creep back in through the cracks that I had temporarily sealed. *What's wrong with me that I would have such dreams in the first place?* Perhaps I felt lacking because I couldn't sum up my spiritual beliefs efficiently by saying, "I am a... whatever." I tried to remember a single sentence that had been said to me by someone from Helen's church that would justify my feelings of being looked down upon. My memory failed me. Again.

I finally finished the painting of the laughing faces on Wednesday. I allowed myself a holiday before beginning the next one. The jeering faces piece was still wet on Friday morning. I made a place for it against the far wall, then leaned a large blank canvas against my table and settled back into my stuffed chair with a cup of anise tea. At first I was easily distracted, looking up each time a gull flew over my skylights, sweeping my studio with its fleeting shadow. I found myself, several minutes later, still staring at the clouds moving in and out of the skylight frames. Then I pulled my attention back to the blank canvas. Too many eyes were watching me; too many mouths from the other wet canvas were stretched open in derision.

I looked over at the painting of the laughing faces and wished I could cover it without smearing the wet section. Finally I rose and carefully turned it face to the wall, with only the top edge touching. That part, at least, was dry.

I sat down again, pushed my head back so I could feel the top edge of the chair against my neck, and closed my eyes. The dream played out in my memory. It had begun with me standing at the end of a church pew. The half dozen people in the pew slid over, making room. I sat in the empty space their movement had created. The people slid over once again. Thinking they were making room for others, I followed suit. They moved away from me again, and again, until they were up against the far end of the pew. Only then did I realize they hadn't been making room for me. They'd been trying to distance themselves from me. The congregation behind us, having witnessed it, laughed.

I thought of the thousand people reputed to have been in William Blake's last painting. He had worked on it for twenty years, but it had since been lost. All that effort gone, time wasted.

I circled the imaginary setting of the church interior in my mind. A wide gap between the other people in the pew and myself would be illustrated most effectively from behind. Best not to see the faces. I could express the feeling through the postures. I saw the back of my own neck, my head bent forward and my shoulders slumped. The most vulnerable part of the body is the back of the neck, or so it seemed. The other people would be upright, heads tilted so that even from behind one could imagine the chins raised and noses just a bit too high. The shoulders would be stiff and uncomfortably close. *Yes, exaggerate it a bit. Make it look ridiculous.* The viewer's first reaction should be laughter at the bunched-up people. The viewers would be in the position of the rest of the congregation who had laughed in the dream, so let the viewers laugh. Then their next response would be to the other figure at the far end of the pew. Let their next emotion be sadness. If they laughed first, they'd travel more emotional distance to arrive at sadness. The viewer's eye needed to be led into the painting toward the group of people first. *How can I do this?* Lighting was the obvious way.

I sat considering. I stared at the white canvas, but I no longer saw white. I saw forms and colour. I would make the viewer enter the painting from the upper right-hand corner; I would add a stained-glass window there, using the brightest colours in the painting. The angle of light would filter across the top half of the painting and touch the silly people. I had begun to think of them as silly people. *Should they have brightly coloured clothes that would set up a relationship with the stained-glass window? Or would dark clothes be better?* I chewed on my lower lip as I considered this. I didn't think of them as people who would wear colours. I decided to dress them in greys, greys with splotches of colour from the windows. I could have some fun with that. I began to imagine patches of colour that looked like paint splatters. I checked myself, realizing I was getting carried away. Besides, the light from the windows would be hitting them from the opposite direction, on their fronts, away from the viewer.

I stood and began to walk around my studio. I could forget the beam of light. I could draw the viewer's eye to them by contrast if I dressed them in blacks and whites, and if the rest of the painting was in middle tones. The solitary figure could be in grey—bluish grey to indicate loneliness.

Like Blake, I believe that the viewer experiences a higher satisfaction by having to work to achieve understanding.

I began to foresee difficulty in getting the perspective right. The repetition of the rows of pews could be tricky. The altar would be raised. *Should there be people between the solitary figure and the altar?* There would have to be. *So if the viewer looked at the painting from the point of view of a person sitting behind, how would all the heads line up?*

I sighed. I needed a photo of a church, any church, from the eye level of a person sitting in one of the pews. A good photo to start with. I checked my camera and found that I had three shots left on the black-and-white film. All I had to do was get into a church and steal a few images.

The Gospel According to Pastor Wallace
Mother's Day Eve, 1995

Pastor Obie shook his head and reached for another Fig Newton. "A curious thing happened one day." Pastor Wallace paused and looked at his nails. "It sent chills down my spine." He checked Pastor Obie's face quickly, then continued. "She snuck into the church one Sunday, Rube, before the service. No one was there. She didn't hear me come in. She was acting... I've never seen anyone act like that before. She was acting strange."

"How so?" Pastor Obie leaned forward like a dog on a scent.

"It's hard to describe. She was moving in peculiar ways. Like she was seeing something I wasn't, but in a creepy way. Sort of crouching, like this." Pastor Wallace scrunched his neck down into his shoulders. "She was going from pew to pew, moving around. She had a sack with her. I don't know what was in it. I interrupted her before she was through."

"Lord help us!" exclaimed Pastor Obie.

"Yeah, really!"

"Sounds like she might be into something like the occult. So what happened?"

"She snuck out. I was in the back, and when I came out she was gone." Pastor Wallace shifted in his seat. "I said a prayer right then and there to cleanse the place of any evil influence, and later, after I'd told a few of the others about it, we said another prayer together. We didn't mention it to Helen and Warren. Didn't want to make them feel responsible. But it was disturbing." Pastor Wallace shook his head and sighed wearily.

"You hear about these things, but you don't expect them in your own community."

"No. You certainly don't. You most certainly don't."

My familiarity with Pastor Wallace's routine, acquired during my cemetery picnics, gave me confidence that I could easily have ten minutes alone in the church before the first parishioners began to arrive. I just had to creep in after Pastor Wallace unlocked the doors and returned to his house. Carrying my camera in a canvas bag, I made my way purposefully to a pew halfway up the aisle and slid along toward the middle, pushing my camera bag in front of me. I stopped to consider the view and, deciding it wasn't quite right, advanced a few more rows. I moved back and forth along the pew, sliding my corduroy-covered bum on the varnished seat, and tried to visualize the shot as it would be when populated with shoulders of various sizes. My attention was totally focused on the visual, as if the plugs for sound and smell and touch had been disconnected. I didn't hear the soft-soled shoes on the front steps or the sound of the floorboard creaking just inside the threshold.

I stroked the side of my face thoughtfully, lost in my imagination. I was absorbed in the shot framed with my hands. I widened the frame out, stretched my arms a little ahead of me, and then folded them over my chest and settled back to think some more. I definitely had some problem solving to do before my camera could come out of the bag.

I didn't hear Pastor Wallace suck in his breath.

I slouched a bit in my seat in the hope that the perspective would be improved. *No. That doesn't help. What if I stretched myself up a few inches? Yes. That's better.*

How can I get a little higher? Not possible while sitting. I rose from the seat and stood hunched over with my knees bent. *Yes.* I was getting closer to what I wanted.

I didn't hear Pastor Wallace gasp.

I swung one leg behind me and half kneeled on the pew to steady myself. "Yes," I hissed with a celebratory raised fist.

This would be it if I moved one or two rows back. I scooted out into the middle aisle and swung around hastily toward the door, toward Pastor Wallace. Suddenly, the imaginative cocoon in which I'd been working was cracked open; I was paralyzed, becoming *Statue of Woman in Flight.*

"You!" he spat. I could tell that, until this moment, it had not occurred to him that the figure could be that of someone he knew.

We faced off, our mouths hanging open impotently. A long silence followed. Racing through my mind was a frenzy of images of myself. I wondered if it would help if I showed him I had a camera in my bag. I said, "Ah, hello."

Silence.

"I didn't hear you come in."

Pastor Wallace murmured, "Obviously." We stared at one other. I offered a nervous little laugh, hoping to lighten the atmosphere.

"It's quite nice, empty like this."

Pastor Wallace had collected himself enough to manage indignation. "It's God's house. It's never empty." He emphasized both *never* and *empty.*

I blinked, then understood. "No. No. Of course. I meant no people."

Pastor Wallace moved up a few pews toward me. He was making a visible effort to compose himself. "So. You've decided to join us today? How nice."

I didn't know quite what to say. "I, ah, don't know. I was just," I shrugged and gestured with my hand, "checking out the vibes."

"And how are the," Pastor Wallace paused before adding evenly, "vibes?" He stood in the centre of the aisle, between me and the door. I looked toward the pew I had been moving to.

"Pretty good. I thought I'd give this pew a try."

"Be my guest," said Pastor Wallace with a sour smile.

I settled in place and, conscious that he was still looking

at me, painted a meditative expression on my face. When he neglected to move I said, "The vibes are very good here. Yes, very good."

Pastor Wallace frowned and then moved hesitantly down the aisle to the front of the church, giving me barely enough time to snap two shots before he turned to look at me. Still frowning, he passed through a little side door. I made a hasty escape.

The Gospel According to Pastor Wallace
Mother's Day Eve, 1995

Pastor Obie examined his fingers, stretching and flexing them. He drummed the arm of his chair, then said, "You say there was no warning that Helen and Warren had problems?"

"Not a bit," said Pastor Wallace. "I remember them at our church picnic in the spring. She was taking pictures of everybody. Not pictures, but with a movie camera. What do you call them?"

"Camcorders?"

"Yeah. She was having a good time. Who would have guessed?"

Though a loud honking and a conversational gabble are characteristic of Trippers gathered together, a sullen sulkiness is often evident when they are alone with their mates.

The way Warren told it, his marital problems began in June when Helen purchased the camcorder. He painted a picture of a defiant wife recklessly spending the family's savings on a frivolous plaything instead of paying bills. He painted with a finicky detail, hiding his brushstrokes and exaggerating certain shadows. He had no respect for the use of white, no understanding that too much of it can bleach out a painting. He was blind to the multitude of soft greys at his disposal. He left out a few necessary details—he didn't mention that he and the mower were responsible for the size of the visa bill or that Helen was responsible for earning the money in the savings account. That's the thing about super realism. Items can be added or taken away without affecting the viewer's ability to believe.

Helen used a different style when she described that day in June, the day when she first dared to challenge Warren's authority. She used a few strong, angry, and impulsive strokes because that was the way it happened. Warren pressured her to withdraw her savings to pay the visa bill. He forced her hand. There's no erasing India ink.

Warren demanded that she return the camcorder. Helen refused. Warren simmered dangerously, and then he brooded. Harriet and Sean couldn't miss the connection between their father's foul mood and the new camcorder. They were careful not to show enthusiasm for the camcorder and thereby divert the anger toward themselves.

Helen recorded snippets of her family, like news bites. And one evening, when she was alone in the house, she put the tape in the VCR and watched it. She saw her family in a detached way, as if they were characters in a sitcom, characters that behaved in a way she didn't like. She watched the tape over and over again. Harriet scowling and saying, "Oh, Mom. Please. Not now," as she pushed the camera away or covered the lens. Sean saying, "Get that thing out of my face, woman. Get a life." Warren turning to look at her with cold contempt.

Helen remembered the hope she had felt while saving for the camcorder. She decided there was nothing more depressing than *remembered* hope after the thing you had been hopeful about has gone sour. The camcorder afforded her the luxury of watching people with her full attention, unconcerned about them looking back at her. Knowing that she wouldn't be called upon to respond gave her great freedom. She could observe people in a new way when she watched her tape in the privacy of her own living room.

Helen took the camcorder to the July 1st church picnic. She recorded everyone. They were flattered by the attention. Even Warren smiled good-naturedly into the camera, the corners of his eyes crinkling in an attractive way. He shook his head as if accustomed to indulging her. They all indulged her. They giggled and teased. The things they laughed about weren't really funny, but it seemed important that they laugh. They were nice people, and nice people laugh. The conversations struck Helen as being a bit prefabricated. Almost fill in the blank. I say *A* and you say *B*. Then I say *C* and you say *D*. Odd that she had never noticed that before. There was a lot of *Hi, how are you? Are you still working in the same place?* Helen noticed that sometimes the person asking the question didn't even wait for the answer. There was a lot of *Praise be* and *If the Lord's willing*. Lots of words.

As she examined the faces, Helen felt the warmth of familiarity. Yes, these were her people. She and Warren had been going to the same church for the entire fifteen years that they had been married. Church had always been an important part of Helen's life, a staple in her spiritual diet. She didn't agree with some of the things Pastor Wallace said but, over all, the experience of sitting in her regular place was soothing. She belonged there, watching Pastor Wallace as the words grew from his mouth, styled and smoothed like strands combed from the Good Book and braided together with his own wisps of belief. Helen didn't go to church for the words. She went because when she was there, she felt like her family was intact, sitting together; she felt they were a unit, clean and in their best clothes. They were doing the right thing, and it made her proud. It put things in perspective. And there were times when she heard exactly what she needed to hear and went away feeling better for it. She went to church because it was her holy place, her holy time. The church smelled of God. God filtered in with the dusty light and filled the silence.

It didn't matter what they said to one another at the church picnics, whether it was profound or banal, as long as they were being kind to one another. She watched the children playing. She could remember when most of them were born. She chuckled when she saw an old dame, renowned for her gossiping, lean over to one of her friends, her mouth moving excitedly.

Helen rewound the tape several times and rewatched the part that included a woman named Christine. By the third viewing she decided that she didn't really like her. It seemed like a sin, but she couldn't help it. It was like a sin, and yet it felt honest. Christine was just a little too perfect for words.

Rube had commented once that she didn't like people or colours that were too pure. She had said that a painting done with pure colours, straight out of the tube, was pretty hard to take. Each pure colour might be okay on its own, but they're a bit much when you put them together. She said that you had to neutralize them by mixing them with a little bit of their opposite. She said that perfectly pure people affected her in the same way. Helen had never forgotten it, and now, when applied to Christine, it seemed true.

Helen allowed herself total, sinful honesty as she watched the tape. She watched Christine shifting some of the salad bowls on the table, glancing up at the camera and smiling, trying to appear casual. "Oh, Helen. What are you up to now? How are you? Set that thing down so we can talk." Helen had set the camera down but left it running. Christine asked, in her squeaky-clean voice, "How are things at work? Still like your job?" Before Helen could even begin to answer, she went on to say she felt she'd made the right choice by staying at home with her children. She spoke as if every woman had that choice to make, but that some, like Helen, were more selfish and chose to put their careers ahead of their children. Helen couldn't remember ever having a conversation with Christine in which Christine didn't mention her choice to be a stay-at-home mom.

Every so often Christine would laugh her little, short laugh when there was nothing funny. Sometimes she would compliment Helen, but in a way that didn't feel right, as if she were saying, *I know that this isn't true, but I will pretend for your sake because I'm a nice person and you probably don't get many compliments.*

Helen had tried to be friendly toward Christine when they first met; she had even called her one Saturday to ask if she'd like to go to Frenchys, but Christine had said, "Oh, no. Thank you very much for asking, Helen. That's very nice of you, but I can never find anything at Frenchys. I guess it's just me. Perhaps deep down I just can't get used to the idea of wearing used clothing."

By the fifth viewing Helen felt almost good about her dislike of Christine, as if a place in her stomach was satisfied by it. The honesty felt like protein, easier to digest than sugar.

And then, quite by chance, Helen stumbled upon another revelation. On the day of the picnic, she'd left the camera on the picnic table, with Warren, when she went to the toilet. Though it was still in the same place when she returned, it was obvious that Warren had been fiddling with it, inadvertently creating clumsy footage of children playing by the water followed by a long stretch of nothing but bushes. Watching the tape, Helen's first reaction when she arrived at this part was to wonder if the day might come when Warren would relent and enjoy the camcorder. Clearly, he was curious about it but didn't want to admit it. He hadn't pressed the off button hard enough, a mistake that Helen had made several times herself, and it had continued to record after he'd set it back down. On the fifth viewing Helen didn't rewind when she came to this part; her kettle had begun to boil in the kitchen so she jumped up to make her tea, leaving the tape running. Upon returning she was surprised to hear the voices of Warren and Kenny Duncan deep in conversation; the patch of bushes was still on the television.

"Five hundred. I'm going to lose money on the job now. I'd been counting on that tax money when I did the estimate. But what can I do? Even if she doesn't call Revenue Canada, it will be bad for business if word gets out. It'll make me look dishonest. I don't figure it's stealing to keep the government out of my pockets."

"No, but the people you charged taxes to won't think much of it if they find out you didn't turn the money in."

"Well, Warren, don't say it like that. It's not like you didn't know about it. Come on. You said to think of it as a little extra money for myself."

The talk stopped abruptly. Helen picked the camera up soon after.

Helen rewound the tape back a little further so that she could pick up the beginning of the conversation, the part she had missed while making her tea. Her mind was racing. Kenny Duncan, a contractor and electrician, was a friend of Warren's whom she'd never liked. He'd always given her about as much respect as he'd given the children, and everyone knew that Kenny Duncan didn't like children. But he was one of Warren's clients, so she had tolerated him.

"Have you talked to her?" asked Warren.

"Yeah, I just can't believe my luck!"

"Well, what did she say? Do you think she would dare to do anything about it?"

"I don't know. I came down pretty heavy on her. I told her it was none of her business."

"Gee, I don't know if you should've done that."

"What else could I do? Had to make her worry a bit so she would think better of making any phone calls. I told her I'd change her bill and beyond that it isn't any of her business."

"How'd she figure it out?"

"Darned if I know. I've been doing it for years, and no one else has figured it out yet. The bitch. If she calls Revenue Canada... I could go to jail for this."

"Well they won't be able to prove anything from your books. Just sit tight. That's all you can do."

"The bastards! They get you coming and going!"

"How much were the taxes on her bill?"

"Five hundred. I'm going to lose money on the job now."

And so on. Helen sat back in her chair, stunned. She felt guilty for what she'd heard, like she should jump up and hide the tape before she was caught listening to it. So Kenny was in some kind of trouble over taxes and Warren knew about it, was involved in it. It sounded like Kenny wasn't turning in the tax money he was collecting on some of his jobs. He was treating them as under-the-table work but still charging his customers tax as if they were legitimate.

Helen recalled a recent incident on Sunday after church. The family had been walking toward their car and Helen, realizing that Warren was no longer with them, had turned and scanned the suits until she'd caught sight of him beside the church steps talking to Kenny. They'd moved around the corner of the church until they were halfway between the parking area and the entrance to the cemetery. Helen, trying not to stare, had wondered why they needed that much privacy. She and the children had continued on to the car. Once inside the incubator atmosphere of the car, the warmth of the trapped air had lulled her. She'd always liked being inside a car on a cool spring day with the smell of the sun on the upholstery and a variety of surfaces reflecting or absorbing the brightness. It had made her sleepy, and, still waiting for Warren, she'd closed her eyes and luxuriated in the heat, thinking of the roast she had put in the oven and the wonderful smell that would greet them when they walked into the house. The door opened on the driver's side, and a cold draft, rushing in with Warren, jolted her. He looked anxious and she asked quickly, "What was that about?"

"Nothing."

"It must have been about something."

"It doesn't concern you."

Warren's tone had been brutal, shattering her dozy mood and snapping her back to reality. She had turned her head towards the side window and watched the bare trees and beaten-down grass on the edge of the road as they drove home.

I sat, rocking silently, next to my wood stove. I was in my slippers and robe, waiting for the day to find its shape, watching my kitchen slowly wake up in the grey early-morning light. The only sound was a low animal-like murmur from the fire in the wood stove. A candle burned on the table beside me. I leaned over to blow it out, sniffing its waxy odor. Meditation could not begin until I had established a sense of where I was at mentally and emotionally; it was a bit like going back and forth on a radio dial in search of an interesting station. I was tuning myself. I began with a prayer of protection, then drew a deep breath in and exhaled slowly. Deep inhale, slow exhale. Repeat. On my inner eyelid, I saw an irregular turquoise shape surrounded by a pale green band, so I focused on it. I tried to hold onto it, but it faded into muddied brown. I balanced on the brink of thoughtlessness. Time passed. Then a feeling, like a small droplet, trickled in on my left side, followed my inner curve, and came to rest in a pool at my centre. I breathed the peace in and out, working it, kneading it like bread, encouraging it to expand and multiply until it became an astringent, cleansing my spirit, sensitizing it, opening its pores. A draft of exhilaration swept up my spine. I was ready for the day.

The dream I had been having just before waking was troubling me. It had felt like a warning dream, but there hadn't been anything especially unsettling about it—just the feeling. I recorded it, as I did all my dreams, and made a mental note to tell Helen about it, just in case.

I waited for the water to boil for tea—a slow process on the wood stove. This gave me time to think. After a breakfast of toast and tea, I dressed, went upstairs, and opened the interior window in the upper wall of my kitchen so the heat could rise into my studio. Wrapped in a ragged quilt, I settled into a stuffed chair in the corner to consider my work.

I wondered how to begin illustrating another dream, one in which a huge mound of white had almost covered the pulpit of a church. I had known, in the strange way one knows in dreams, that the white substance had been put in the church to represent snow, but that it was fake. It was nothing but salt or sugar. As I watched, three beautiful women had glided down the white mound as if on skis. That part of the dream was not unpleasant, but then a young man had threatened me. I'd run and jumped into a hole in the floor, sliding down a tunnel like Alice in Wonderland. The young man had continued his pursuit underground.

It was not going to be easy to work with so much white and still convey the feeling of distrust and danger. Even though the painting had not yet taken form in my mind, I had already chosen lines of William Blake's poetry to accompany it:

And standing on the altar high,
'Lo! What a fiend is here,' said he:
'One who sets reason up for judge
Of our most holy mystery.'

Finally I rose and cut four large pieces of newsprint from a roll. I taped the first one onto a large birch panel, set it on my easel, and began to draw with a black felt marker in large sweeping motions. Then I tore that paper off and taped a fresh one in its place. I drew, tore the paper off, replaced it, and drew some more. When I'd used up the four sheets of paper, I cut four more. By the end of an hour, I'd begun to sense the division of space that I thought would work. This one was going to be a bit wild. It needed to be.

Too tired to begin painting, I considered the next dream in my collection. I was certain this one summed up my spiritual path. Just remembering it brought back the extraordinary feeling of peace and joy that I'd felt upon waking. In the dream I'd been riding in an open vehicle with a driver. We approached a church. People stood on the steps of the church watching us. The people seemed to think that I was coming to their church, and they looked surprised when I drove on by. Farther along we came to another church with more people waiting, and once more, we passed by. Eventually we arrived at a house. A woman invited me inside and offered me a seat. As I looked into the eyes of the woman, I realized that I was looking at myself. There's something powerful about looking into your own eyes—not their mirror reflection, but your actual eyes.

The room, in the dream, had been semi-dark. The woman apologized, at first, for the darkness, and then she admitted that she preferred it that way. I agreed, saying it reminded me of when I was little and would be sent to bed before the other, older children. I would lie in the semi-darkness thinking, while the other children were still playing. I had looked up and noticed that the woman's curtains—my curtains—had a beautiful fluorescent design of the eye of a peacock feather.

It wasn't difficult to decide which of Blake's lines should go with this painting: *The pride of the peacock is the glory of God.*

No one knew about Helen's fantasies about having her own apartment. They were between her and God. Helen didn't discuss her feelings with me. There was an invisible line that we never crossed.

"So, your camcorder isn't as much fun as you thought it would be."

"You know Warren."

"Yes, I know Warren."

"Maybe by Christmas. He'll have cooled down by then, I hope. I'll take it out again then."

It was early July, and Helen was sitting at my table watching me put the groceries away. The basket of clean laundry was on the floor in front of her. These visits had replaced the high-tension Sunday dinners that we used to have, when Helen always had to handle Warren and me like booster cables. Now we could talk about things that Warren would have sneered at.

I said, "I had a strange dream the other night about you and Warren."

"Strange in what way?"

"Strange because I can't figure it out."

I stuffed the empty grocery bags under the skirt of my cot and settled on the floor with my back leaning against it. "In the dream there was a window in the side of your house that had been covered over from the inside. You were removing the inside wall, exposing the window, but Warren wanted it left hidden. The window that you uncovered was double the size of what could be seen from the outside of the house. I wondered how that could be. Also, and this was the really strange part, sunlight was coming through both the covered side of the window and the exposed side."

I looked at Helen, studying her face, trying to read her thoughts. Windows usually represent eyes—both how you see and how you are seen. But this hadn't felt like a dream in which my subconscious had chosen Helen and Warren to represent aspects of my own personality. It had felt like a dream I should pay attention to. I liked the part about the sunlight coming in, in spite of the outside wall covering half the window. But I still felt that I was missing something. I waited for Helen's response. She laughed and raised her hands, saying, "Beats me." Then she changed the subject. "Remember the old lawnmower, the one that had to be replaced because it was beyond repair?"

"Yeah."

"Well, Warren sold it the other day."

"For parts?"

"No. For seventy-five dollars. I saw it sitting at the end of the driveway with *For Sale* on it. I asked Warren how much he wanted for it, in case anyone stopped when he wasn't home. He said 'Seventy-five dollars,' and I said, 'Isn't that high? It's only good for parts.' But Warren insisted, and before the day was over I saw him selling it to Cecil. And it seemed to be working. Cecil was pushing it up and down the lawn."

"Cecil?"

"Yes, Gladys's husband, Cecil. You know Gladys and Cecil. They live up along the stretch, north of the park. A little green house with lots of clutter around. They say he drinks."

"Oh, yeah. I know who you mean." It made sense that, if there was something wrong with the mower, Warren would feel justified in selling it to someone like Cecil. Better than selling it to someone from his church. "Did you say anything to Warren about it?"

"No, what would be the point? Things are peaceful now. I don't have the energy to stir it all up again."

"I don't know how you do it."

"Ah well. It could be worse. A lot of women have it worse than I do." Helen looked out the window, thinking of Cecil's wife, Gladys. "I should be thankful."

"Or so they tell you."

Helen missed my last remark. A memory of Gladys and Cecil was replaying in her mind. She had glimpsed them through their living room window one evening while on a walk after supper. Finding herself too far down the beach when darkness started to close in, she'd taken a shortcut to the road. The trail had led her past Gladys's house. She remembered the apricot light from the front window. Helen had stood in the darkness and watched, spellbound, as Cecil turned from the teapot on the kitchen counter with two steaming mugs and walked slowly through the archway to the living room. He was talking all the while in soundless words to Gladys, who received the tea with a casual smile and turn of the head. It had made Helen wonder. This did not look like a home in which violence ever occurred. There was not a speck of tension or exaggerated gratitude. This was a small routine act. This was domestic harmony.

I curled up in my living room easy chair after Helen left. I intended to bring my journal up to date, but my mind was caught by the sight of the sun squeezing through the narrow blinds of a south window, on an angle, bouncing off the shiny gold metal on the side of my airtight woodstove. It reflected on the brickwork next to the stove in a crisp, thin line of yellow—orangey on the edges, curving irregularly, delightfully sharp on one side, softened on the other. I sat enthralled. The sun moved a tiny bit and, from its new position behind the leaves of the trees, presented a new show: a soft ballet of shifting, flickering leaf images, irreverent shadows that toyed with the lights and darks of the stove like children playfully teasing a castle guard. The stove sat, firm, solid, purposeful, with its cold empty window staring straight ahead.

It's natural for me to tap into the little bits of beauty around me—the delicacy of soft, crisscrossed shadows and the celestial blue of the shadow on the white-painted window sash where the crack of light squeezes in at the edge of a blind. Bits of beauty are everywhere, like electrical outlets. I run on them. They charge me; give me energy. My God is there, in those elements of beauty, just as any artist is present in their creation.

I thought about my series. I'd decided upon *Stations* as a title for the show. There would be fourteen paintings, and there are fourteen Stations of the Cross. I had sold a painting in the local gallery the preceding week. Feeling flush, I had splurged on enough stamps to send off proposals for my show to two university galleries. The package cost three dollars and seventy-five cents to mail, and the self-addressed stamped envelope required that much again in postage. I knew the exact amount because I had already mailed it off once and received it back, rejected.

Finally, I rose and went to the kitchen to do something useful. I decided to make cookies. As I opened my carton of eggs, I noticed that Helen had brought white ones. I always bought brown eggs. I took one out of the carton, set it on the counter, and looked at it. It was beautiful. I went back to the fridge for the rest of the eggs, removed them from their carton, and placed them gently in a large mixing bowl. I stood enraptured by the way they rounded into grey. It was a dove grey with no highlights or dark shadows, just a gentle soft-toned roundness. I put the bowl of eggs on the kitchen table and sat in front of it so that I could give it my full attention. I noticed the way the shadows cast from one egg onto another were more uniform in tone and had clearer edges. I noticed that the dark depths of the bowl could be seen like black shapes between the eggs. Some of the eggs near the side were reflecting back the colour of the bowl in a dull, almost luminous way. I hated to crack one, but when I finally allowed myself to, I was newly excited by the colour of the yolk as it lay in the purity of the sugar....

Trippers delight in soaring to astonishing heights on updraughts of hot air. They will frequently plunge from these heights onto their unsuspecting prey.

Eventually even Warren grew tired of his sulkiness. He awoke one Saturday in an exceptionally good mood. After his second cup of coffee, he rose from the breakfast table, stretched, and, like an omnipotent provider of all good things, asked the children what they would like to do, as if anything was possible. It was decided that Sean and Harriet could each invite a friend for a trip to the mall.

And so it was that Helen ended up alone at home on a sunny spring Saturday, alone to clean in peace. She wondered, as she puttered, if maybe the winter could be blamed for their collective crankiness. Perhaps the warm weather would change things. She went about her work feeling content, like there was no other place on earth she'd rather be. First, the living room drapes came down for dry cleaning. The sun was on the opposite side of the house, so the light from the large window was subdued, discreet. The open space of the bare window made the room feel lighter. The change was refreshing. She decided to leave the drapes down and, instead of having them dry-cleaned, use the money to buy material for valances. The sheers would be enough. Why had it never occurred to her to do that before? Drapes were out of style. Especially her ten-year-old, faded, rubber-backed ones. The thought of new valances made the furniture lighter and the job more enjoyable. Starting out, she hadn't intended to re-arrange the furniture. It just happened and, as it happened, her emotions became rearranged. The tiredness that had been weighing her down like a wet wool coat was shoved into a dim corner; the nitpicky aggravation accumulating inside her like dust balls was swept clean.

Helen wasn't consciously aware that the new position she chose for Warren's chair wasn't immediately visible upon first walking into the room or that it was in front of the big window, where he would be backlit (and therefore in shadow) during the day. She wasn't consciously aware that the lamp on the side table, next to his chair, was set low enough for him to be able read at night without illuminating his face. Helen didn't consciously choose the new spot for her chair, to the left of his but two or three feet back, giving her some degree of privacy. And, in all fairness, she hadn't placed the high potted plant beside the left arm of Warren's chair so that it would screen his profile from her peripheral vision as they watched television together. Helen made all of these changes without questioning her instincts. When she was finished, the living room smelled fresh and Helen sparkled. She sat at the kitchen table, smiled into her teacup, and waited for her family to come home.

Sean charged through the door into the kitchen and was about to head through the living room to his bedroom when he stopped. She heard him say, "Cool."

Harriet, curious, followed Sean and said, "This is different. I like it. I think."

And then came Warren. Warren surveyed the living room from the archway like a relief worker assessing damage. "What did you do this for?" he asked.

Helen felt the sun go behind a very dark cloud. "For a change," she said.

"I liked how it was before." Warren's voice was flat.

"I'll put it back that way after a while," offered Helen as if she actually believed he would settle for that.

"I don't want my chair way over here. And where are the drapes?"

"I took them down for cleaning, but I was thinking," she hesitated, "it would be nice to leave them down, to just have the sheers and a valance to take the bareness away from the window."

"Put them back. Everyone can see in at night. I don't want to sit there in the middle of a bare window. I don't want to sit *there* at all. I wish you'd ask me before you go frigging around with my chair!"

Helen rose and dumped the rest of her tea into the sink. Sean and Harriet stood holding their plastic shopping bags. They waited until Warren had gone down the hall to the bathroom, not moving until he'd closed the door. Then they walked softly past the bathroom to their bedrooms.

Poor Warren. He was so good to his family, and this was the thanks he got. He couldn't leave his wife home alone for five minutes without her making a disaster of the place. It was no wonder he was upset.

Harriet closed her bedroom door quietly. She flinched at the crash of the toilet seat lid being thrown back against the tank and tried not to listen to the sound of her father urinating. The toilet seat lid slammed down. She sat in the middle of her bed, hugging her knees and rocking back and forth. Something in the bathroom cracked, something glass on the arborite countertop. She looked across at her tape player. No, she'd better not. The linen closet door in the bathroom was wrenched open and off its track, making a racket. The shopping bag at the foot of her bed caught her eye. She'd save enjoying her purchases for later, when things were better.

The vanity doors beneath the sink were opened, one after the other, then slammed. God-fearing men are allowed to behave like this in bathrooms. God does not see into bathrooms, so they need not fear eternal repercussions. It has something to do with plumbing or God's appreciation of a man's need for at least some privacy.

Harriet jerked slightly with each bang and wondered what Sean was doing. His room was quiet. She could imagine him lying on his bed staring at the ceiling. Perhaps he would go for a walk with her later. She removed her socks and fingered her bare toes. It would be fun to put nail polish on them. Water was running in the bathroom sink. Muffled sounds came from the living room; her mother was shifting furniture. The water glass crashed into the sink. Harriet looked at the top of her bureau. She would tidy it up later. The bathroom door opened. She shot a nervous glance toward her bedroom door and listened intently, wishing her mother wasn't in the living room. She waited, holding her breath. The back door banged shut. She exhaled.

Sounds of movement continued in the living room. Harriet wanted to go help her mother, but she thought better of it. Her mother didn't like to be seen crying. Harriet quickly swung off the side of her bed, knelt on the floor, lifted the edge of her bedspread, and pulled out a drawing tablet. She climbed back into place. The tablet already contained drawings of most of the objects in her room. She drew a tired breath and looked around. She'd draw Elizabeth, the doll, again, this time from the side. She liked the wide-eyed clarity of Elizabeth's face and was proud of the perfect state of her original blue lacy dress. Harriet leaned back against the headboard and began to draw.

Someday she would show her drawings to Aunt Rube. But not to her father.

Helen drove, hardly seeing the road before her, across the bridge and into the parking area by the beach. She felt flat, as if she had fallen from a considerable height. No wonder. She'd let down her guard and had been foolishly happy while cleaning her house. She should have known better.

Drawing a deep breath, she made her way to the water's edge. Her throat was raw, as if she'd swallowed a glass of seawater. How many people, she wondered, who walked on the beach, did so in a desperate search for peace? When would life become easy? She walked for fifteen minutes before sitting on a driftwood timber beyond the high-water mark, next to an ash pit of blackened stones. The ground was littered with pop cans, a whisky bottle, and a piece of birch bark that had been shed by a log on its way to the fire.

She stood, stretched, and resumed her walk. A rough path led steeply from the beach to the woods above. She climbed to the top, feeling some satisfaction from the exertion. The air smelled of spruce and sea, of sunlight, of childhood.

The path meandered along the bank until it came to an old shack, barely hidden from the shore by scraggly brush. It had been built from salvaged goods, a mishmash of materials optimistically painted barn red. An assortment of debris lay scattered about: a rusty stovepipe, an old chair, and a propane barbecue.

The door of the shack hung open, attached by only one hinge. Just inside the door and facing out, as if for the purpose of surveillance, sat a platform rocker covered in a badly picked red fabric. Another chair, in even worse condition, sat behind it. A couch slouched and sagged in the far corner. It held a dirty ashtray and a thick blue candle. Above the couch were two small square windows half covered with beer labels advertising Oland Export and Alexander Keiths. A blanket and a comforter lay tangled in a corner.

Helen sat in the red chair near the door. Her anger was like a pit in her stomach. Hard. Condensed. She thought of Warren. She could no longer stand the sight of him. She would turn her head, when they drove to work, and look out her side window so that she wouldn't even see him in her peripheral vision. He had begun to make sounds that she didn't remember him making years ago. Was it possible that he always had and she was just beginning to notice now? If they were something new, what was their purpose, other than to aggravate her? He would make a sucking sound with his tongue on the back of his teeth, and then he would drag it out as if conscious of how it made her nerves bristle and the hair stand up on the back of her neck. And he would burp long, drawn-out, deliberately rude burps, usually in the car.

She looked around the shack, finding relief in the chaos. Beside her chair she noticed a plastic fish tray half full of shingle nails and a box of beer caps. A couple of paint cans were rusting in a corner.

The colours used to paint the beams were appalling: a strong, dark mauve; fluorescent pink; yellow; and even small patches of fluorescent green. The initials HP—her initials—were stuck on the wall, roughly fashioned out of masking tape. Helen did a double take. Rube would not accept that this was a coincidence. She would look for a deeper meaning in it. Helen was sure that Rube had told her what this type of occurrence was called. She tried to remember, but it escaped her. *What fun it must be to be able to float on your dreams and crazy ideas like so much flotsam and jetsam, the way Rube does.* The floor was filthy. No. It was dirty. It wasn't a threatening or disgusting filth; the wind that blew through the place kept it fresh. It didn't smell bad. It was just not clean. Helen sat for fifteen minutes, feeling ten years old, dreaming of playing house.

Finally, she rose and started back. She picked up a stick on the beach and used it to poke at sea urchins and crabs, then dragged it along with her, making a line in the sand. She remembered writing in the sand a long time ago, but she couldn't think of anything that she dared to write now.

A poem began to run through Helen's head as she walked back to her car. She had written poetry in high school but had given it up when Warren came into her life. Now, it was as if the voice of Dr. Seuss were whispering in her ear.

How dare
How dare
How dare you move my chair
and force me to expose myself
before the window bare?
I will not sit
I will not sit
I will not sit in view
where anyone, who's passing by
can witness what I do.

The Gospel According to Pastor Wallace
Mother's Day Eve, 1995

The two men savoured a moment of righteous contemplation before Obie asked, "What do the children think of this Rube woman?"

"They seem quite fond of her. She's their aunt. They don't have any other relatives on their mother's side around here. Oh, I've heard Sean refer to Rube's," Pastor Wallace paused as if searching for a word, "oddness, so I suppose they can see that she's not normal, but Warren got after him for it and told him he wouldn't have any disrespect."

"How old are they?"

"Sean's twelve, and Harriet's, let me think, I believe she's nine or thereabouts."

"It's too bad. She'll have that much more influence over them now. It's hard to control a situation like this." He shook his head sorrowfully. "Hard to control."

Pastor Wallace sat, his elbows on his desk and his head propped on his hands, which were interlocked in front of his mouth and chin. His eyes were thoughtful. "I used to wonder sometimes if maybe Rube really wanted to come to church but just couldn't quite get past the fitting-in period. Wouldn't quite give over to the Lord. Helen tried. She invited Rube to come now and then whenever Harriet was singing." Pastor Wallace stopped abruptly, overtaken by a heinous memory. "She brought that friend of hers once. Gordon." He lowered his voice. "A queer. Made quite a stir."

The Tripper has the elasticity to inflate its ego into an extraordinarily enormous, puffed-out chest. As well, Trippers often feed other birds semi-digested, regurgitated bile until the other bird retches and the Tripper is satisfied.

"Ah, don't you just wish you could die feeling this way?"

"That was a wonderful dinner. I must have gained ten pounds from dessert alone."

"Would you like some more wine?"

"Only if there's more left. Otherwise, I'll have to make do with the glow I've got."

"What a little boy scout."

I poured more wine into Gordon's glass. We were on my deck, stretched back with our feet up like two pregnant women. We'd walked the beach in the afternoon, and now we were poised in readiness for the grand solo performance of the setting sun. The air was warm and the repetition of the waves hypnotic.

I said, "I feel like I'm in my mother's womb."

"Love this amniotic fluid." Gordon held his wine glass up to the light and swirled it gently. The telephone rang. My cordless phone was beside my chair, but I didn't move. I made a face at Gordon.

"Who could that be that would make it worth answering?"

It rang again.

"Perhaps a wealthy millionaire wanting to commission a huge mural for his playroom."

"All millionaires are wealthy, you moron," I laughed, "and besides, I don't want any big commissions right now."

The telephone rang again.

"Perhaps it's Peter Gzowski wanting to interview you."

"I wouldn't know what to say."

On the next ring I picked it up. I could feel my face tighten and my smile evaporate. "No, it's all right. I'll take my van." I looked over at Gordon. He was running his fingertips over his chin thoughtfully, eyeing me like a child who was alert to unfair discipline, summoning his tantrum energy. I looked at the empty wine bottle and said, "Better still, we'll walk." There was a pause. "Gordon's here. He came for supper. I had completely forgotten. I'll see you there."

"We'll walk where?" Gordon asked evenly.

I slowly put the phone down, looked at Gordon, and winced, dreading and delaying the bad news. "Where would you least like to go?"

"We're not going to church," exclaimed Gordon. "It's Saturday night!"

"Gordon, I'm so sorry. I forgot, but I promised. It will only be for an hour."

"Why would you ever promise to go to church?" asked Gordon, incredulous.

"Harriet's doing a reading. Helen says it's important to her. I'm her aunt. It's the kind of thing aunts do. It goes with the job."

"But I'm not her uncle."

"Well, pretend. Helen asked me two weeks ago, before she saw the paintings. I've got to go. It might smooth things over."

"What about the sunset?"

"It'll happen again tomorrow."

"Probably not. Not if I go to church." Gordon's voice had

risen in pitch.

"Think of it as an adventure."

He rolled his eyes and gulped down the last of the wine in his glass. For a moment I thought he was going to sling the glass at the wall like they do in the movies—I was sure he was considering it—but he set it down on the table. "Oh, I suppose." He sighed. "Do we have to leave right away?"

"As soon as I change. I think it's best if we walk. I'm in no shape to drive."

"I'll probably be sober by the time we get there," he whined. "It's a damn shame."

The church was a fifteen-minute hike away. In the distance, six or seven miles to the north, the white houses of Silver Bay shone like specks of hope in the sun, surrounded by a vague dream of land. The church sat on the right side of the road facing a respectable congregation of spruce on the left. The back pew of spruce, which was the closest to the sea, held the less-upright trees.

Gordon said, "I will not sit up front. Do you hear me? If you start heading for the front I'm out of there."

We arrived late. The congregation stood singing a hymn as we entered. I recognized the music from my cemetery days but had never heard the words clearly. We settled into a pew, two up from the back. I opened a hymn book and passed it to Gordon. I was secretly fearing he might sing, but he was still busy orienting himself when the music ended and the sitting-down shuffle began.

A special speaker was announced: Pastor Dexter, imported from Massachusetts. I didn't like the set of his face. My study of portraiture made me want to identify what exactly it was about a face that was responsible for its expression—the subliminal, instinctive impression. In this case, the expression was one of meanness. I couldn't stop staring, analyzing, totally fascinated.

Pastor Dexter began, instructing the congregation to turn

to the first chapter of Romans. I had trouble finding the first chapter of Romans, and I frowned, suspicious of his reasons for not simply giving out page numbers. It was a trick, a test to see who had memorized their bibles and who hadn't. I failed. He was well underway, like a train beginning to chug out of the station, before I found my place.

"'For God is my witness, whom I serve with my spirit in the gospel of his Son, that without ceasing I make mention of you always in my prayers. Serve with my spirit friends, serve with my spirit.'" Pastor Dexter smiled. Sort of. His smile was parallel to his eyes. *That's it! Or at least part of it.* Pastor Dexter stretched his mouth out, but the ends didn't curl up; his cheeks were uninvolved, his eyes flat. *Why bother? It's more like a grimace than a smile.*

"'For I long to see you, that I may impart unto you some spiritual gift, to the end ye may be established.'"

I glanced somewhat nervously at Gordon. His eyes were roaming the congregation, and my heart warmed to him, knowing I would be treated, later, to a witty commentary on the outfits and hairdos. I noticed he was listening.

"'I purposed to come unto you, but was led hitherto, that I might have some fruit among you also, even as...'"

Gordon gave me a quick glance and whispered, "Some fruit among you? How'd he know I'd be here? I didn't even know I'd be here."

I shushed him as I snickered, keeping my head down. I was thankful there wasn't anyone behind us, but there was a couple next to me and an older man across the aisle from Gordon. I looked up at the backs of Warren, Helen, and the children sitting near the front. Gordon took the bible we were sharing and began to browse. He leaned over and pointed to *Professing themselves to be wise, they became fools.* He nodded knowingly. The effects of the wine had worn off a bit, but he was still not to be trusted.

I tuned in to the pastor's voice and tried to catch his drift.

"'...whom God hath set forth to be a propitiation through faith in his blood, to declare his righteousness for the remission of sins that are past.' To be a propitiation, my friends. Propitiation. 'What's that word?' you might ask. Propitiation. To propitiate means 'to win back the favour of.'" Pastor Dexter's eyebrows had been drawn down by the gravity of the situation. He paused, lips pressed tighter than the gates to heaven, to survey the faces before him. Guest speakers could deliver powerfully formidable messages, unshackled as they were by relationships with the individual members of their congregation. It was a heady experience, this lack of inhibition. It lifted and straightened Pastor Dexter's spine, adding a good inch to his stature. "Now friends, by sins that are past He doesn't mean sins that you, yourself, are guilty of having committed last week or last year." Pastor Dexter's wattle wobbled with the importance of his admonition. "Sins that are past are sins that occurred before Christ died. God saved sinners in the Old Testament, and he saved them on credit! He didn't save them because of their sacrifices—their lambs and goats. He saved them on credit!"

Gordon turned to me and muttered, "I've been saved by credit a few times myself."

"Shhh!"

"Christ paid their debts by dying on the cross. He made it possible for God to redeem those that are past and the sinners in the future. Your salvation and my salvation are only made possible by the blood of Christ." Pastor Dexter climbed the topic, his voice getting louder, the tempo building, the emphasis a little more pronounced. "Now it says here in Romans, chapter four, verse five: 'But to him that worketh not, but believeth on him that justifieth the ungodly, his faith is counted for righteousness.' But to him that worketh not—this means, friends, that it's not enough to do good work. You can't earn your salvation by being a nice guy or baking cookies for the fellow next door."

"Damn," whispered Gordon, "I like baking cookies for the fellow next door."

"'Believeth on him that justifieth the ungodly.' The ungodly, my friends. 'His faith is counted for righteousness.' God doesn't save good men, my friends." An edge had come into Pastor Dexter's voice, an irritated, grating, goading edge. He had begun to swoop in a rolling way, flagellating the congregation with words, dragging out the *God* each time he said *Godly*. "Goodness is not the mark of man before God. They're ungodly; they're sinners. The Lord Jesus came not to call the righteous to repentance, but sinners."

Pastor Dexter whipped his voice out in simulated anger, admonishing the congregation, shaming them, blaming and berating them. Gordon's shoulders stiffened and his jaw tightened.

"God sees you as a sinner and you must come to Him as a sinner and you must repent."

Gordon watched Pastor Dexter, transfixed, but with narrowed eyes.

"For God sent not his Son into the world to condemn the world; but that the world through him might be saved." Pastor Dexter shifted quickly from the fast, frenzied talk of a time-limited offer to the hushed cooing of a Don Juan. He was coaxing, enticing, all sweetness and promises. I could imagine candy in his pockets. He had concentrated the energy of the room into a rhythm that vibrated on a low frequency with a power-line hum of straining anticipation. It went on and on, accompanied by a collective drone and the occasional *Yes, Lord* and *Praise God*.

"If you are a sinner, my friend, and you have never known the power of Jesus, if you have never made that commitment to Jesus that in your heart you would like to make, make it now."

Gordon turned, sighed heavily, and said, "Oh, for heaven's sake!" all in one sweep.

"Maybe you've never received the Lord Jesus Christ as

your saviour and you've realized tonight that you are unable to save yourself, that you are a sinner."

Gordon looked at his watch, and I said a silent prayer that Pastor Dexter would soon give up on the sinners and give us some peace. I was aware of the stern glances that had been directed our way from either side.

The collection plate was now being passed. Gordon shot me a quick frown. "What? I have to pay for this?" He reached into his pocket, came out with a dried-up ball of tissue, and gave me a devilish look. I shook my head and passed him a folded five-dollar bill.

"My treat," I said, with a wry smile. Gordon snorted. A big man two rows ahead of us turned and levelled a severe gaze on Gordon and then on me. Gordon leaned my way. "I think I recognize him. He's in one of your paintings, isn't he?"

Pastor Wallace beamed as he introduced, as a special treat, one of the church's own budding soloists, Cindy Hall, "who is here tonight to serve the Lord through song." Cindy rose from her seat and drifted delicately toward the organ. She settled in front of it like a fallen flower petal. She smiled shyly at the organist and moved slightly so as not to block her from the congregation's view—as if any eyes would wander from Cindy, for she was not only talented and modest, but she was also pretty. She wore a white sweater and a cotton jumper of the palest robin's egg blue. It accentuated her lovely amber curls and hazel eyes. Head bowed demurely, she blushed as she waited for the opening chords of her song. When the music began she lifted her face heavenward and opened her mouth to sing like a small fragile bird making virgin chirps. She was, undisputedly, the centrefold of the occasion.

I felt sorry for Harriet. Cindy was going to be a hard act to follow. But when Harriet's time came she was so nervous that it didn't seem to make any difference whom she followed. She spotted me for a brief moment and smiled. I was glad I had come.

Finally it was over. I held onto Gordon's sleeve to keep him from bolting toward the door. About a dozen people were ahead of us in our exit line. We could see, as we approached the vestibule, that Pastor Dexter and Pastor Wallace had scooted down the aisle and positioned themselves in the doorway to gladhand the Godly and collect compliments in their ego baskets.

"What an inspired message," said Gerald Pynes as he shook the pastor's hand heartily.

"I'm so pleased to have been able to hear you speak. Thank you," said Gerald's little wife, blushing as the pastor covered her hand with his.

It was with no small measure of alarm that I realized Gordon would have to pass through this tollbooth in order to get out.

"Our little church is privileged to have you here, Pastor," said a frail, grey-haired man nodding his head vigorously.

Gordon was in front of me. He turned slowly and read the anxiety on my face. A half smile combined with lifted eyebrows made my blood run cold. All I could manage was a firm "No."

The woman ahead of Gordon murmured to the visiting pastor, "You are a man who knows his Bible. God bless you."

I jabbed Gordon's back and, in the most threatening tone I could manage without raising my voice, said, "Don't! Just keep walking."

Gordon stepped forward. I shuddered, afraid that he would take the pastor's outstretched hand. He didn't. Instead he paused in front of Pastor Dexter, turned toward him with a calculated sluggishness, allowed his eyes to wander up and down Pastor Dexter's face, and snarled in a voice that was audible, but just barely, "You ought to be arrested for verbal abuse." Then he moved on, leaving me in his place. Pastor Dexter's eyes bulged. He stood with his hand rigidly extended like a cigar store Indian. I couldn't bring myself to take it.

I could think of nothing to say. We shared a mouth-gaping two-second eternity before I spun away and sprinted down the steps after Gordon. Somewhere in my frenzied mind, the thought registered that it was the first time all evening that the expression on Pastor Dexter's face had not been contrived.

The Tripper's behaviour toward its mate is cyclical, alternating between spirit-breaking dominance and patronizing kindness. Its keen sense of timing, combined with an astute assessment of the gullibility of its mate, allows it to repeat this cycle almost indefinitely.

At times Helen would convince herself she was staying with Warren for the sake of the children, and then after a particularly upsetting example of Warren's arrogance she would decide that she should leave him for the sake of the children. The stress of indecision weighed heavily on her, but like aging store-bought bread loaded with formaldehyde, her mind failed to completely break down. To all appearances her pureness, her whiteness was preserved; it was too bland to warrant closer observation. Her unresolved grievances went unnoticed.

You ought to be arrested for verbal abuse. She never said a bad word about anyone. The two sentences squared off in Helen's mind. Regretfully, she'd missed Gordon's insult, and even more regretfully she'd been exposed to the fury it had elicited in Warren ever since. Word of it had spread like a virus. Gordon's nerve had become a source of twisted inspiration to her. *What would it feel like to speak one's mind so bravely, so honestly?*

Warren had assumed that Helen would share his indignation. How little he knew her! How little she knew herself.

Gordon marched indignantly out of the church and headed toward the road. I was breathless when I caught up with him. "Did you have to say that?"

"I'm sorry, Rube, but I have little patience for that sort of thing. And they take up a collection for that old fool and compliment him on the message! What kind of message was it beyond being a tyrannical rant of abusive threats? It makes you hope there is a hell."

Gordon crossed to the little lane leading to the shore. "Let's walk back by the beach. I don't trust the road. One of these 'good people' might decide to do the 'Lord's work' for Him and run us over."

It had become quite dark, and neither of us had thought to bring a flashlight. We had to pick our way carefully across the ridge of stones at the high-water mark. Once we reached the smooth sand, walking became easier.

Gordon complained. His feet were sinking too far into the sand. The air had become cool and he hadn't brought a jacket.

"Stop bitching. I thought you liked the beach."

"I was in such a good mood before we went to church. Why does it have to be that way?"

"Forget it. It was just something we had to do. Leave it."

"I know, but it pisses me off. Church has become too much of a conjuring act. There's too much manipulation involved. When someone starts to manipulate me, I get my back up."

"No kidding. I hadn't noticed."

"Well, I'm being kind. On a good day, they manipulate. On a bad day, they intimidate."

We walked in silence for five minutes. Then I asked, "Did you notice the cemetery beside the church?"

"Yeah. I didn't really look at it, but I noticed one there."

"That's where I go to church sometimes. I have a place in the bushes. I can hear the music but not the words. The music's not bad."

Gordon looked my way and mumbled, "You're pathetic!"

"I take a lunch and tea, and I lie back and look at the clouds."

"I'd be willing to try it once."

"I wasn't inviting you."

"Then why did you bring it up?"

"I just thought you'd find it amusing."

"I'll tell you after I've tried it."

"You're not going to try it."

"Just one time."

"I've been to church with you once, and believe me once is more than enough! It does make you wonder though, doesn't it? I mean, I wonder what percentage of the words we use actually do any good and how many words actually keep us from communicating."

"I guess it would depend on who you are. If you were Pastor Dexter, I'd say—"

"Never mind Pastor Dexter. You've had enough to say 'bout him. I'm thinking about Helen for example. She's cross with me now, ever since we talked about the paintings. It's when we talk about things that are meaningful that we get into trouble. And yet, I know she loves me." I hugged my sweater about myself. "I can't help but wonder whether or not we might get along better if we didn't talk."

"What would you do? Sit around and smile at one another? Sounds more than boring to me."

"It would be an interesting experiment: seeing if we could spend a whole day together without saying a word."

"The interesting part would be getting Helen to do it. I can't imagine. Remember, she may not be allowed to speak, but she could still glare."

"Words are sort of like hair when you think about it."

"No," said Gordon, "they're like hair when *you* think about it. Words are like words when I think about it."

"Some like them short, and some like them long." I was feeling quite philosophical all of a sudden.

"Pastor Dexter likes them very long," said Gordon, "and probably, if the truth were known, a bit kinky."

"They just grow out of us. We play with them in order to give the impression we want. Our hair is just about the only part of our 'being' that we manipulate for self-expression. We dye them, we shape them, we snip here and snip there."

"Kind of makes you wonder what has happened to all of your hair over the years, doesn't it?" said Gordon. "Think of all those bits of yourself, swept up and mixed in with other people's hair, thrown out, probably in the same place our words have gone—into nothingness. By the way, what did you do with your hair? You didn't throw it out, did you?"

"No, I put it in a bag."

"Good."

"Why good? What does it matter to you?"

"It means I still could end up with a little bit of it."

"How do I approach Helen to get her to try it?"

"Try what?"

"Spending a day together without talking."

Gordon slowed down. His eyes narrowed, and he squinched his face up as if he were trying to pour his thoughts out through a funnel. "You ask her for someone else's phone number and tell her that you're going to ask them to do it. Someone that she doesn't want you to call. Pastor Wallace's wife."

I frowned. "I think I'll just ask her."

"What will she tell Warren?"

"I don't know. I'll have to think about it."

Everyone needs a trusted best friend who can hold your grievances up to the light and help you determine whether they are valid or unreasonable, a friend to whom you can grumble about your husband, children, boss, or co-worker without fear of judgment or betrayal. Helen didn't have such a friend. She had casual, arms-length relationships with other women, but not one confidante. She had Rube. Confiding in Rube was a dangerous business. Rube was impulsive, unpredictable, and often a little too blunt. There were times when Helen secretly agreed with Rube's opinions but dared not admit it. So, when the call came from Rube suggesting an attempt at reconciliation, Helen was relieved. Trust Rube to come up with a crazy idea like not talking for a day!

"Let's call a truce on Saturday. We can pack lunches and go for a hike, like when we were kids. There's only one rule." Here Rube had paused. "No talking. Absolutely no talking. Deal?"

Warren's presence in the kitchen had made her guarded, conscious of everything she said. From his point of view, she was consorting with the enemy.

She limited her response, after an uneasy pause, to, "What time?"

Helen deposited her pack on the table, then turned toward me like a cadet awaiting orders. I pointed to a paper on the fridge. It read, *Even a fool, when he holdeth his peace, is counted wise: and he that shutteth his lips is esteemed a man of understanding.* (I had replaced *he* with *she* and had slashed through *man* and written *woman* above it). Helen smiled.

I was wearing a grey hoodie over an orange tank top. I'd rolled my jeans up above my ankles, and the bare feet showing through my sandals had brightly painted toenails. My hair was no longer embarrassingly conspicuous; in fact, I thought it looked rather cool with my sunglasses. Helen had tied a navy blue sweater around her waist over her white t-shirt.

We took a pleasant, unhurried walk. We passed small houses, which had been distorted over the years by add-on after add-on; the occasional two-storey house; and fish shanties. We stopped to watch a pair of mallards, squat and cumbersome, lift their roast-pan bodies as if on strings and fly over the top of a nearby row of trees. We paused to be sniffed by a German shepherd that had been exchanging pleasantries at the side of the road with a freshly coughed-up Pekinese. We lingered in the middle of the bridge to throw pebbles into the shallow, low-tide river below, then continued on to the beach beside the wharf.

Helen stooped to roll up her pant legs. I ran out onto the sand, threw back my head, and laughed along with the gulls above. Helen watched me, smiling.

The sky was patchy, and the temperature dropped several degrees each time the sun ducked behind the clouds. We poked along, pointing things out to one another and smiling our appreciation back and forth like Japanese tourists. The beach was beautiful and deserted. Tall grasses along the dunes wavered in the wind, correcting themselves in jerky motions, unable to keep from swaying, but unwilling to bend. Parts of the sand shone as if a can of varnish had been swished across it. Halfway up the beach a shallow stream had sculpted itself out of the sand. Its sound was like a tickle to our ears compared to the muffled roar of the waves. We moved back half a dozen steps and, with a running leap, crossed it. Then we dawdled on the other side where furrowed sand stretched for twenty feet like freeze-dried waves. I rubbed my sneaker across the ridges. Helen did the same. It felt firm and yet flexible against my sole. Idly, we watched the waves that seemed to be propelled toward their deaths. Seagulls waited at the water's edge like distant relatives at a wake, hoping for tidbits.

Helen moved closer, but the gulls became aware of her. They lifted slightly into the air, then taxied along just above the waves before gaining altitude and flapping their way to a spot farther down the beach. Helen and I carried on. There was much to admire: rocks squatting in private baths of trembling reflections; thin skims of advancing water pushing their deckled edges before them; logs shelved at high water, waiting for another tide.

We climbed the grassy slope running parallel to the beach. At the top, ten feet from the edge of a cliff, sat a stone house—our destination for lunch. This had been a favourite place during our early years, before boyfriends and husbands had separated us. We sat on the stone halfwall along the side of the porch. I faced north with my back against the house, and Helen faced south with her back to the stone pillar. The view was spectacular. Gulls swooped and dipped below us. Occasionally a fishing boat left the wharf, which was now five miles away, and we watched lazily as it headed out to sea.

Helen didn't seem to miss words. In fact, I think the absence of them allowed us both to be more in touch. We were surrounded by sound, like a baby in its mother's womb. Honest sound. It was sound that required no interpretation, that made no judgment. And yet, it was different than if I had been there alone. The presence of another person, without the baggage of talk, shifted the energy, set up an exchange in which I felt another dimension of understanding. My thoughts no longer chased themselves around in my head as they did on my solitary walks. I was able to step up to the periphery of myself, to move away from the place that concerned itself with conversation or self-analysis, toward the place that was aware of feelings. It felt like a holy place. I turned to look at Helen, and the words *when two or more are gathered in his name* came to mind. If it were only possible to stay in this place; returning to the world of words seemed sinful.

We were less animated on our walk home, separated into our thoughts. Once back at the house, we began to prepare supper. Helen picked up the wine bottle, waved it at me, then set it down next to the two glasses. I handed her a corkscrew and smiled as she filled the glasses and proposed a toast: "Here's to less said and more understood."

The time of silence had officially ended.

I concealed my surprise as Helen filled the wine glasses. I'd never known Helen to drink. We eased back into the world of words over supper before settling out on the deck to witness the sun being swallowed by the sea. Our exhaustion, induced by salt air and exercise, resulted in long periods of comfortable silence. Now and then one of us offered up a memory, like a support for this bridge we were constructing, and the other one nailed it in place. This relaxed version of Helen was new to me.

She said, "I had a dream this week. I planned on telling it to you, but I've forgotten it." Before I could respond, she added, "I know, you're going to say I should have written it down."

I lowered my chin until it squashed against my chest and, in a gruff imitation of Warren's voice, said, "Dreams are about as much use to anyone as the dust balls underneath the bed."

Helen laughed. In a high-pitched, childish voice that I feared was supposed to represent the frivolous nature of my arguments, she said, "Oh, but think about it. Dust balls come *from* us just as dreams do. They're largely made up of skin we've shed, so technically they're part of us."

In Warren's voice, I responded, "Well, when the day comes that I start collecting and examining dust balls, I guess I'll know it's time to start doing the same with my dreams."

A squirrel darted up and down the spruce trees on the north border of the lawn, and a particularly single-minded horsefly buzzed around me as if I were a cow patty. I gave up trying to discourage it with my hand and finally fetched a swatter from the house.

"Do you remember when we were kids, when Mom would send us down to the cellar to get potatoes?" I asked.

"I remember. It was scary. I hated it." Helen leaned her head back and looked at the darkening sky. "I remember what it felt like when the potatoes got low in the bin. It was so dark down there. I don't remember there being a light we could turn on. Do you?"

"Might have been one. I think maybe there was, but it wasn't much help."

"It was creepy," Helen shudders, "reaching down into that bin, not knowing whether you were grabbing a potato or a rat."

I smacked the swatter down next to Helen's leg. She screamed and jumped simultaneously.

"Sorry. Missed it." I smiled, but Helen didn't smile back. We're sisters. She knew the fly was nowhere near her leg. I propped the swatter against the side of my chair. We both sipped our wine. In an effort to repair the fabric of comraderie, I returned to the subject of the potato bin. I said, "Yeah, well, but the longer you stare into the darkness, the more your eyes adjust to it and the more you're able to make out the shapes."

"I didn't stare into it any longer than I had to." Helen frowned at her wine glass. "I guess that's the difference between you and me."

"Oh, but you're brave in ways that I'm not," I offer. "You had kids. You've stayed married."

"Some achievement."

"A practical achievement. Me, I'm off navel-gazing while you're actually adding human beings to the world."

"When you put it that way..."

"Back to the potato bin. I think of it as being kind of like my subconscious. At first it's frightening, but what's down there is still going to be there whether you look at it or not." I settled lower in my seat, swinging my feet up onto a small pine table. The fly had returned. I held my wine glass in my left hand and waved the swatter with the elegance of an orchestra conductor.

Helen snorted, "*Your* subconscious probably does resemble a potato bin."

I glanced her way, guiltily remembering the day I told Gordon that Helen would make a good potato. It seemed like a very long time ago. *An upgrade might be in order—perhaps to a turnip. No, a squash. Something above ground.*

We sat in an amiable silence until Helen, laughing, asked, "Do you remember the pullstring on the ceiling light in the upstairs hall? Remember how I hated to go up in the dark and grope around, trying to find it? I'd reach up and circle my hand round and round, and it would seem like forever until I found it. I'd scare myself by imagining all kinds of things; I'd get myself into a real panic."

"Yeah, I remember. You always tried to make me do it for you." I chewed thoughtfully on my lower lip. "I think it's scarier though to be reaching out in the darkness than to just be sitting still. Maybe it's just that by having your arm out away from your body you're more vulnerable."

"I'd prefer to have a flashlight."

"Of course," I said. Then, seizing the opportunity, I went on, "But your dreams are your flashlight. Studying them can be like shining a light into the potato bin." This wasn't the first time I'd promoted the importance of dreams to Helen.

"Good try," said Helen.

A minute or more passed before I continued: "You know why I think it's scarier to be reaching out in the darkness than to just be sitting still?" I didn't wait for an answer; it wasn't really a question, more a musing. "It's as if, by reaching out, you're asking for trouble. We've been programmed to think that with action we run the risk of being held responsible, of being punished, of feeling guilt. So it seems like inaction equals innocence."

"Perhaps."

I poured our third glass of wine. Helen, not seeming to notice, asked, "Do you miss Robert?"

I said, "No." Then, "Not usually."

"But... you have your art."

"Yeah." I paused. "I don't miss the feeling of inadequacy that I associate with Robert." I shook off the memories and turned to Helen to asked, "You used to write poetry in school. Do you ever write now?"

"No. Who has time?"

"That's too bad."

"I'm getting more now than I used to. Time I mean. I'm taking it, and Warren doesn't like it. In fact, I lied when I said I don't write anymore." Helen chuckled to herself. "I wrote a poem the other day. Want to hear it?"

"Sure. Go for it."

Helen recited her Dr. Seuss poem. Our laughter was partly wine-induced and went on longer than was called for, but it felt good.

Helen stopped suddenly. "Warren will smell the wine on me when I go home. What will I do?"

"Don't worry 'bout it. He spoils too much for you already."

"You've noticed."

This set us off again. Then Helen sobered up. "I don't know what's the matter with me lately, but I'm losing my patience." She paused. "I can stand him less as the days go by."

"Well you've stood him longer than I could've."

"I've tried to look past the little things, to understand his reasons."

"His excuses."

"His excuses," Helen conceded. "It's the little things that really get to you."

I sat with my head tipped against the back of my lawn chair, gazing at the tops of the spruce trees. I asked lazily, "Like what?"

"Like..." Helen pushed out her lips and drew a heavy

breath, as if inhaling from an imaginary cigarette. "Like I can't even get him to put his dirty clothes in his laundry basket. He drops them on the floor in front of it. It sounds like a silly thing, and I'm probably being petty about it, but why can't he drop them in the basket?" She swivelled her head sloppily toward me, trying unsuccessfully to appear sober. "Especially his underwear. He would only have to move his hand another two inches," she illustrated daintily, her fingers pinched together, "and they would drop in the basket. But do you think he will? He drops them in front of the basket so that I have to bend down and pick them up off the floor. It's usually his underwear. It 'furiates me. I guess because it's so damned unnecessary. Sometimes I think he gets a kick out of making me mad." She then muttered almost to herself, "D' I say damned?"

"Yes, I believe you did. Have you talked to him about it?"

"Of course I have." Helen's head wobbled in an attempt at indignation. "That's why it annoys me so much. I've asked him time and time again," she gestured with her glass, slopping a little wine on her sweater, "to put his clothes in the basket, and he still keeps doing it. I think he just likes to make me bend over and pick them up."

"So why do you pick them up? You could just leave them where they are." I shrugged. "If you only wash what's in the basket and he runs out of underwear," I paused, "whose problem is it? If he has to wash his own underwear a few times he'll smarten up."

"But why does he do it?"

"What does it matter why he does it? You don't need to understand him. You'll never understand him, so forget it. The important thing is that he's not listening to you when you ask him to stop, or he hears you and he's just playing some kind of little game. So don't waste your words."

"I suppose if he ran out I could let him borrow some of mine." Helen snorted at the thought.

"I wouldn't start that if I were you. You might be getting yourself into worse problems."

We giggled.

Helen said quietly, "This was a good idea, you know. I hate to admit it, that *you* actually had a good idea. I think I might ration my words fer a while, figure out where they'll do the most good. I'll talk to myself since I'm the only one that listens anyway."

"I have an idea."

"Another one?"

"Why don't you try—and I know this won't be easy—but try to ration your words, like you said, and write them instead of saying them? Use the stupid things he does as inspiration for what you write. Even shit can be a fuel, you know. Only make it funny. It usually is funny, in a way, when you really think about it. Like the poem you just recited. Then bring your words back to me."

"I don't know. The poetry I used to write when I was in high school was stupid stuff. Insipid." She considered my suggestion and frowned with almost comic, wine-induced alarm. "What if Warren found it?"

"Hide it well. Write them in your dream book. Warren would never look there."

"But I don't have a dream book."

"So start one." I got up, made my way inside to the desk in the corner of the living room, fumbled through a drawer, and came back with a book. I handed it to Helen. "You've got one now."

"You never give up, do you?"

"Who was it that said 'words are a form of action, capable of influencing change'? Somebody smart. Can't remember who. But it's true, and the best part is that writing doesn't carry that feeling of guilt that goes with talking out loud. It cleanses you but doesn't drain you. Come on, do it as an experiment. What have you got to lose?"

"My sanity. I'm afraid that if I keep on this way I'll end up just as flaky as you."

"Not a chance!" I laughed. I twirled the wine in my glass and mused over the subject of flakiness for a few minutes. Then I said, "It's okay to be a little bit flaky. There are different gradations of flakiness, you know. You have your 'flirting with flakiness,' your 'fringe flakiness,' and your 'fully-formed flakiness,' and then you have your 'suicidal, over-the-edge, flying-fruitcake flakiness.'"

"Which one are you?"

"I'm moving toward the edge."

"Perhaps I'll flirt with flakiness."

"It would be a place to start."

I closed my eyes. From the open door to my living room I could hear Willie Nelson croon, *Give us your tired and weak and we will make them strong. Bring us your foreign songs and we will sing along. Leave us your broken dreams. We'll give them time to mend. There's still a lot of love, living in the Promised Land.*

I said, "It's funny. When I was with Robert, I was so conscious of what everyone said or what I imagined they said. It was like I was hearing an ongoing commentary on my behaviour, like whispered gossip. It was like I was overhearing fragments of criticism, snippets from neighbours and relatives. Anybody." I altered my tone. "She's not much on housework—have you ever looked under her sink? She says Tupperware parties aren't her thing! Whoop-de-do! Who does she think she is? Too good to associate with the likes of us! Poor Robert. I don't know what he sees in her.

"Then it was as if I broke the sound barrier. I left Robert, and it all stopped. I did the unthinkable, leaving Robert. I said to hell with everyone. I stopped caring. I gave them legitimate things to talk about, and I left them to it. It was as if I had broken the sound barrier and arrived in a hushed world where *she* was replaced with *I*."

Helen's voice betrayed a touch of sorrow. "If only it were that easy. You didn't have kids. Robert wasn't like Warren."

"No," I said. "The harder they are to live with, the harder it is to get away from them. Robert wasn't all bad. He was just stubborn, and I was stubborn too. But he made his own choices. We all make our own choices." I paused. "I had no power to change him, but I did have the choice to refuse to participate. Before I was married, I had no idea I could be such a bitch. A person just crosses a line."

I allowed a couple of minutes to pass before I asked, "So back to you and Warren. What now?"

"I don't know."

"You can't go on this way. There's no need."

"There's no need," repeated Helen. "That's the thing. There's no need for any of it." She sighed heavily. "Warren is involved in something shifty with Kenny Duncan."

My ears perked up. All the serious talk was spoiling my wine buzz. "What kind of thing?"

"Something to do with Kenny's taxes. Warren does his books. I'm not supposed to know about it."

"So how did you find out?"

Helen gave a short laugh before recounting the tale of the camcorder.

I said, "The good deacons have their secrets."

"Yeah. Apparently. I've lost respect for Warren. It's not just about the thing with Kenny, although that just verifies that he's not all that he pretends to be. It's the other things too. It's hard to know what to do."

"It wouldn't be for me," said I flippantly.

"You may think so. But you don't have kids."

"No, but I can't believe you're doing your kids a favour by having them grow up thinking it's normal for a man to treat his wife like this. It'll just go on and on. Harriet will marry a man like Warren, and Sean will become a man like Warren."

"I know. There are no good choices here."

"So don't make the choice. Let Warren make it."

Helen came to life. "Oh, Warren would never choose to leave. Why should he? He knows a good thing. And, besides, it's not Christian. I would end up waiting a lifetime for him to go."

"I didn't mean for him to choose to leave. I meant for him to choose whether or not *you* leave. Tell him that you'll only allow him to hurt you," I made a face, "say three more times. Whatever. Set a figure and keep track. If he wants you to stay, he'll smarten up; if he keeps on acting like a jerk, then he deserves for you to leave. But when he's used up the three times, you've got to be ready to go. Even if he spaces the things out over a couple of months. That's how he's gotten away with so much up until now. He spaces them out."

Helen looked at the horizon. The sun was almost down. She said, "Not lately."

"No, not as much. He seems to be getting worse, but that's because you've dared to stand up to him. Buying the camcorder. He'd even see a small thing like not picking up his underwear as an act of defiance. Up until now you've cowered and scurried around trying not to offend him. He has no respect for you. Neither do your kids. They love you, but they'll only respect you if you stand up for yourself."

Helen released a deep sigh. "You've never talked like this before. How long have you thought this?"

"Almost forever. How long has Warren been around? I remember the way he acted when you were pregnant and when the kids were born. I could've taken him out and shot him. I had to keep out of it because you were so emotional and I knew that it was hard for you then." I shook my head. "But you'll never know how much I hated to see you having children with that man. Women kid themselves when they think that if they smile and pretend everything is fine, other people won't see through it all. Other people see; they just don't let on. They see it in your eyes. If the words that other people have held back over the years ever came raining down on you, you'd be buried. You'd drown. You're too nice." I smacked the fly swatter on the side of my leg. The fly fell to the deck, providing dramatic punctuation to my speech. I was pleased. Helen was speechless.

"You can be too nice, you know," I continued. "I don't try to be nice anymore. Nice people let not-so-nice people get away with things that they should never be allowed to get away with. They let them do it because they're afraid that if they object someone might say that they're not nice. I looked the word *nice* up in the dictionary one time. Do you want to hear what it has to say in Webster's about the word nice?" I made another trip into the house and returned with a dictionary. After settling back into my chair, I began to read in a teacher's voice—albeit a somewhat drunken teacher's voice. "'Nice. Word history: Since its adoption in the thirteenth century, the word nice has developed from a term of abuse,'" at this I levelled what was intended as an emphatic look at Helen, "'to a term of praise, in a process called melioration.'" Again, I looked up at Helen and repeated, "From a term of abuse to a term of praise. That's interesting." I continued. "'Nice is derived from the Latin *nescius*, meaning ignorant, and was used in Middle English to mean foolish or without sense.'" I paused to check Helen's expression. "'By the fifteenth century, nice had acquired the sense of elegant in conduct and dress, but not in a complimentary sense; rather, nice meant over-refined or overdelicate.'" I closed the book. "Do you really want to be foolish and without sense? If people were less concerned with being nice, the con artists and manipulators in the world would have a hard time operating."

Poor Helen. I had harangued her enough for one night. We switched to tea and passed the next hour and a half on safer subjects. By the time I drove her home, a little after eleven, we felt completely sober.

Warren was asleep in bed, postponing any confrontation until the following day. Helen brushed her teeth thoroughly in the hope that the toothpaste would camouflage the smell of wine on her breath.

Helen was startled out of sleep, early Sunday morning, by a nightmare more terrifyingly real than reality itself. In it she watched a huge snake slithering along the edge of a nearby store before disappearing from sight. Helen entered the building and tried to warn the shoppers, but the snake was nowhere to be seen. She descended the basement stairs and continued her search. The floor was crawling with snakes of all sizes and kinds, some contained but most free. She found two caretakers and informed them that one of their snakes was above, possibly in the store. They weren't interested. She was worried about the shoppers, who were unaware of the danger.

Then the dream changed. She was alone and the snakes were in her belly. She could feel them moving around. Something was in the back of her throat creating pressure. She needed to retch but she was afraid to vomit, afraid she would half vomit a snake and it would be caught, half in and half out. She heaved, and the head of a snake came out of her mouth. It tried to turn its head back toward her, but it wasn't out far enough. She could see its tongue flickering like a small flame, and she was afraid to vomit it out further for fear it would turn on her. She was also afraid of choking if she attempted to swallow it. She couldn't scream, so she prayed silently until she heard a voice say, "Don't let anybody feed you snake eggs." The dream was over, but the nausea stayed with her. Warren was breathing easily beside her. Helen decided not to tell Rube—she wouldn't be able to resist painting it.

Helen lay still, recovering. The white mini blinds divided up the grey morning sky like empty lines on a sheet of paper. She rose, shifting her weight carefully so as not to wake Warren; put on her bathrobe; and tiptoed to the living room. Once the dream was recorded, she settled back in her chair and waited, pen in hand, for more words.

Memories of her mother, dead five years now, presented themselves. Children take sides without knowing the facts, without understanding the causes behind the resentment. She wondered who would Harriet and Sean would side with. Which parent would seem the most reasonable? The parent *seen* to be breaking up the marriage would be blamed even if the other parent was also culpable. Helen's mother had lived her life compensating for her husband's lack of responsibility. *She'd* been the sensible one and had resented it bitterly, and now Helen had landed smack in the middle of her mother's mid-life resentment.

A sound from the bedroom made her start; she relaxed, realizing it was only Warren turning over. *Rube would be proud of me. I've recorded a dream already. It must be from all the talk or the wine.*

Helen pressed her head against the back of her chair and closed her eyes. The faces from Rube's painting confronted her followed by the faces from the church picnic tape. They weren't the same, and yet she suspected that, if a video camera caught their every moment, like the eye of God, there would be similarities. There would be hints of the attitude apparent in Rube's painting, and there would be many weaker, more vulnerable moments as well.

This made her wonder what she would look like through the eye of God, how other people saw her. She wasn't sure how she saw herself. Was she like her mother? Surely not! Her mother had had power; she had been in control of most of the family money. Even so, Helen's father had squandered plenty. At least that's what her mother had claimed in her rants. He'd ignored her and read books while she fumed and slammed things around. Helen had promised herself that she would live with more dignity than her mother had. She therefore tried to reason and negotiate instead of demand. It hadn't done much good, but it had always been her preferred method. She didn't want to be like her mother.

She wasn't like her father either. He was the problem. She had been clear on that when she was growing up. The problem was that he was irresponsible. Warren was not irresponsible; Helen would give him that. If anything, he took life too seriously. So how did she get here? She was stuck in between, refusing to be the worst of her mother and rejecting the worst of her father. She feared their weaknesses, but she was not really sure what their strengths had been. They must have had strengths. All she could think of was her mother's management skills, her work ethic, her sense of order, of control. Her mother had drilled it into her that these were her strengths. When had she realized different? Alternatively, were they her mother's strengths and her weaknesses both? It had been her mother's preoccupation with these qualities that had tipped the balance. It had been her insistence that Helen's father needed to change his ways and be more like her.

Helen recognized that she had loved her father more than her mother allowed, and she had felt guilty about it. She had loved her father, but she had married her mother: the dominant one, the strong one. Not the happy one. Not, necessarily, the intelligent one. The dominant one. And yet she had not permitted herself to be her father. He had ignored her mother and indulged himself in his piles of books—he had bought them to spite her, and he read them to avoid her. Then he went off on walks so that she would be powerless when she needed to vent and so that he wouldn't hear her.

Helen's father had always worked and provided adequately for the family. He had been a plumber, which must have been dirty, unpleasant work at times, but he had never complained. He had been a plumber and a philosopher. What could be more practical than a plumber? Why had she been told he was irresponsible? Had her mother lied? Helen suddenly realized that she had chosen Warren because he was different from her father—the opposite. It had never occurred to her before. Helen tried to imagine what it would be like to be married to a man like her father, and in that moment she missed him terribly.

Experts have been puzzled by
displays of irrational, unprovoked aggression
by Trippers toward their mates
and can only conclude, after a great deal of study,
that the purpose of this behaviour is to keep the mate
submissive and uncertain of its own ability.
Often, after prolonged periods of this irrational behaviour,
the Tripper's mate will be unable to function normally.

After showering, Warren returned to the bedroom to dress. He reached into the closet to deposit the underwear he had slept in and noticed the little pile next to the empty hamper.

"You missed some," he grunted over his shoulder to Helen.

"Oh?" Helen, still lying in bed, glanced lazily at the pile of underwear and said, unconcernedly, "Well, put them in the hamper and I'll get them next time."

Warren turned, still buttoning his shirt, and gave her a dark look. He tucked in his shirttails, zipped his fly in one irate thrust, and buckled his belt with all the violent indignation he could muster.

"You're going to be late for church."

Helen shifted in the bed so that he couldn't see her face. "I'll get up in a minute." The situation amused her. She smiled to herself under the covers. She could feel words lining themselves up like shadow dancers behind a screen. They were teasing, taunting, tempting. A poem had begun to incubate.

She sat quietly all through breakfast. Warren was fuming, but she ignored him. At his side throughout the church service, oblivious to his anger, she happily toyed with words: *It's hard for a God-fearing man who has no underwear....* The passages of the bible reading rose like smoke to the ceiling of the church; fragments broke off like ashes and floated down into Helen's poem: "...a more excellent sacrifice than Cain, by which he obtained to keep, to hold, not to be, was translated that he should not see to maintain, yes, to...." Helen grasped the word *maintain*, dropping it in place: *maintain a pure and upright stand....*

It's hard for a God-fearing man
who has no underwear,
to maintain a pure and upright stand
if underneath he's bare,
not to mention what can happen,
if he's gazing at God's sky
and forgets to safely tuck it in
before he zips his fly.

On the following Saturday, in the ordinary home of an ordinary God-fearing family, an extraordinary thing happened. A small pile of socks and underwear that hadn't made it into the laundry hamper went unwashed. A revolution had begun.

Alone in the house after lunch, Helen got down on her hands and knees and scrubbed the kitchen floor. The thought that she could never see herself as others do had begun as an idea and had metamorphosed into an obsession. She imagined how she would look through the lens of her video camera instead of in the bathroom mirror. Finally, Helen loaded her video camera with a blank tape and, setting it on a chair, recorded herself as she waxed the floor, wiped the counter, peeled vegetables, turned this way and that. She slid the tape into the Playpak, popped it into the VCR, and watched herself. She noticed, with a perverse fascination, that she had begun to slouch, that her hairstyle had no real style, that her jeans made her backside look about as attractive as two couch cushions. She was appalled by what she saw, and at first she credited the location for the unflattering likeness. The depressing, mundane, uninspired domesticity of the kitchen was to blame. Then she blamed the light. Too much light was coming from one direction. Every crease, every wrinkle cast a shadow. She looked old.

She rewound the tape and tried again in the living room, but what she saw made her feel worse. She couldn't determine exactly what it was. Warren's chair? The tedious familiarity of the room? She rewound the tape once again, faced the camera toward a blank wall, and pressed record, slowly erasing the shameful images of herself.

At bedtime, Warren glared into the closet. "Helen. I won't put up with this. Do you hear me?" His outrage rivalled that of an emperor discovering the infidelity of his wife. How was it that a man of God, confident in the superiority of his vision over that of his wife and in fact of all females, could stoop to such juvenile behaviour over a little pile of stinky socks?

"I wash what's in the hamper," said Helen.

Warren slammed the closet door. "I've put up with enough from you lately." He threw his watch on the bedside table, dropped heavily to the edge of the bed with his back to her, and wound the alarm clock, before snatching back the bedspread and climbing in. With one final yank of the covers, he became still.

Helen stiffened. She had to in order to prevent her body from rolling into the depression created by Warren's weight. She was sure an animal would never sleep this close to the vibration of an implied threat. They would act upon their instinct to distance themselves from danger. And so would Rube.

Within minutes, to Helen's amazement, Warren was snoring. The tears began. Her throat ached with the pressure of anger and began to swell around the unspoken words lodged there, words that began to drain from her thoughts and arrange themselves like droplets on a clothesline.

She crept from the bed, made her way quietly to the living room, and switched on the lamp beside her chair. She wrote: *On the surface there were signs of resignation, but only in the darkness did I weep. You were there in the darkness. Did you hear me? Did you care or did you turn away to sleep?*

Once again she carefully described all that had happened—what Warren said, how he'd said it, how he'd acted, how she'd felt. She wrote it as if it were a bad dream.

The church interior photo provided me with enough information for my first sketch of the church pews and pulpit; however, the pews were empty. I needed figures—shoulders, backs of heads. I called Gordon and enlisted him as a model, promising a meal in return. It wouldn't be necessary for us to return to the church. I placed kitchen chairs in my living room, spacing them to mimic the distance between church pews. With my camera on a tripod in a stationary position, I photographed Gordon in one chair after another in an effort to gauge diminishing sizes.

When we were finished I popped the cork on a bottle of bordeaux as Gordon hung his jacket on a hook. I tossed a padded envelope on the table in front of him and proceeded to pour the wine.

"What's this?"

"What do you think? It has slides in it. My address is written in my handwriting. Any ideas?"

"Sounds like a rejection." Gordon lowered himself into a chair at the table, reached for his glass, and took a sip.

"Read it."

He scanned the gallery name on the envelope before unfolding the letter and frowning.

Dear Ms. Peckham,

Thanks for proposing your work to the gallery. We considered it together with many other dossiers at a recent exhibition planning meeting. The gallery's program for the next eighteen months will focus on the development of critical and resistant strategies in visual production, particularly in relation to feminist concerns and identity politics. Your work makes a complex statement, however we decided not to offer you an exhibition. We feel that your work might be more consistent with curatorial priorities at anoth—

"What the hell does that mean?" Gordon tossed the letter on the table.

"Your guess is as good as mine."

"'...the development in critical and resistant strategies in visual production....' Don't you think your strategies were critical? Weren't they resistant enough? Ohh, they didn't relate enough to feminist concerns.... But they do, don't they? I mean, many of the issues women have around religion are related to feminist concerns. Identity politics. I may be stupid, but what's that? They say your work makes a complex statement! This letter makes a complex statement! Well, the long and the short of it is, dear, you've been kicked to the curb."

"Again."

He raised his glass. "I can think of no better reason for a drink." In a gentler tone, he asked, "So do you ever wonder why you bother?"

"I wonder all the time." I sat at the opposite side of the table.

"It can't be for the money," he said, gesturing with his wine.

"You've got that right."

"It can't be for the prestige."

"Nope. A hoodlum gets more respect."

"Well, you must be crazy then," he declared with a shrug.

"What else can I do?"

"You wouldn't make much of a nurse."

"How about a demolition expert? I'm in the mood."

"Yeah, I like it. Go right to the opposite side." Gordon looked up at the ceiling and chewed his lip. "Destroy things instead of creating them. You'd get more money."

"I'd have more fun."

"What's the difference anyway? Destroy. Create. Destroy. Create. It's all a matter of how you look at it."

"Both ways, you make a difference."

"That's right. Who's to say that when you paint you're not destroying a perfectly good, clean, white canvas?"

"Lots of people would agree."

"And if you blew up a building, say if it was an old dilapidated thing, you'd be creating a nice vacant lot. It's all a matter of how you look at it."

I began to serve up the food. Gordon had spread his napkin with a flourish and was helping himself to the salad.

"Do you suppose people who blow up buildings—not the demolition experts, but the quacks—do it because they look up at these buildings and are overcome by the thought that they can never create such a thing, so the next best thing is to destroy one?" I asked as I settled into my place opposite Gordon.

"It's an interesting theory. Probably good for a government grant. It opens up a whole other way of thinking. How does one establish what is good and what is bad in creating and destroying?"

"I suppose it would have to be based on whether it does anyone harm or not. Does it cause pain or personal loss?"

"I've seen some art that has caused me pain," said Gordon.

"If bad art were declared criminal, the jails would be full."

"Not mine though," I put in, in a flagrant bid for support.

"No, of course not. Not yours," Gordon reassured me with a wave of his fork.

"What about the kind of pain, like, when you look at a painting that is sooo good that you wish you had painted it and it makes you depressed that you didn't? Should that be criminal?"

"Hell no. That's different."

"Are we so different, do you think? A person needs to make their mark using whatever means they have available. Is this a male and female thing?" I asked. "Women can create in the ultimate way—they can give birth. Men can't. Perhaps that's why they choose, more often than women do, to kill, to destroy."

"You might have something there," agreed Gordon.

I took a drink, rested my fork on my plate, and settled back. "Women, when they're in love, express that love by being willing to give birth to the child of the person they love. Men, on the other hand, express this emotion by their readiness to kill, if necessary, to protect the one they love. Which is worse?"

"Both emotions are instinctive." Gordon, sensing that it might be therapeutic, was indulging me, even encouraging my rambling.

"But does that make them acceptable, understandable? We have laws to deal with people who end people's lives before their time, before they're ready. We've decided that this is criminal. Is it criminal to begin a person's life before you're ready, before you're prepared with the skills to care for them properly?" I had been cutting my steak and now I was using my knife to emphasize my point. "Perhaps it's not good enough to make the excuse that it was an accident any more than killing is an accident."

Suddenly, I clapped my hands together. "I know what I'm in the mood to do! Clean house!"

"Good God. Is that why you invited me over?"

"I'd like to take some of my paintings that I'm not happy with down to the beach and make a bonfire."

"Oh, Rube, really!"

"Nothing good, just some of the complete failures. It'll be good for me."

"It'll be smoky."

"Oh, come on. You'll enjoy it. It'll be a night to remember."

"I have plenty of nights to remember, thank you. And for better reasons."

"Come on. You know you can't stop me now." I was already out of my chair and heading toward the stairs. I called over my shoulder, "We'll have dessert afterwards."

"Oh, all right." Gordon poked one last forkful of salad into his mouth and, while it was still half chewed, said, "But only if I get the last word on what paintings get burnt. I don't trust your state of mind tonight. You'd quite likely burn them all."

"We'll commemorate the failure of my creations with a celebration of destruction."

"Whatever." Gordon picked up our wine glasses and carried them to the studio. He settled into my stuffed chair, and I began dragging large pieces out of the way so that I could get to the smaller canvases and masonite boards that were leaning against the wall.

I pulled out a half-finished scene of the beach and wharf. I had been attempting a spectacular sky on a dark day but hadn't quite pulled it off when my mood had changed and I'd set it aside. "I don't think I'll ever get around to doing the work that's needed to salvage this."

Gordon frowned and pushed out his lips, then gave the painting a dismissive wave and said, "You know better than I do."

I rummaged around a little more. "Oh, I'd love to be rid of this one. I hate seeing it. It's ugly." I turned toward Gordon holding an overworked arrangement of still life objects.

"I'll have no problem seeing that one go," he said.

I tossed it into the centre of the floor with the first one. Then I held up a medium-sized canvas of a figure sitting in an awkward pose. It looked like a ballet dancer with a broken leg.

Gordon hooted. "Whatever were you thinking of? Let's put her out of her misery." It went onto the pile.

The next painting caused an argument. I hated it but Gordon loved it. It was of two small boys sitting on a wharf intently examining a worm from their can of bait. I threw it on the pile, and Gordon pulled it off.

"You're not burning that one."

"Yes, I am. I don't like it."

"It's good."

"No, it's not. His head is too big."

"No, it isn't. It's his hat. He has a big hat on. Maybe it's his father's." Gordon had propped the painting on his knee, half turned so we could both see it. He maintained a tight grip on its edges.

"It doesn't look right."

"I won't participate in this if you burn this one."

"Come on, Gordon. Don't be difficult."

"Let me have it if you don't like it."

"Then I'd have to see it when I visit you."

"No, you wouldn't. I'll hide it before you come over."

"Oh, Gordon. I don't like having pieces of my work around that aren't good."

"But it is good."

"I don't like having my name on it."

Gordon looked at the painting. "But you haven't signed it, so it doesn't matter."

I shook my head. "You're impossible."

Gordon smiled. He leaned the painting against the side of his chair. I moved on. I was less sure about the next few that I put forward. I said, "There're parts that are okay. I like that little bit right there." I pointed to some loose brush strokes in the reflection of a fishing boat. "And those clouds are nice, but there's something that bothers me."

"It falls apart," said Gordon. "All this empty space out here. It takes away from it."

"I could cut that off." I placed a smaller frame on top of the painting, isolating the part that I was happy with from the rest.

"Much better," said Gordon. "We'll let that one live to see another day."

I moved on. In the end, we agreed on six paintings, two on canvas and four on masonite. I cut the canvases from the stretchers with a box cutter so I could reuse them later.

I outfitted Gordon in a pair of my father's rubber boots and one of my jackets. We were able to carry everything in one trip. After choosing a hollow spot surrounded by medium-sized rocks, we made our fire. Gordon balled up the newspaper and covered it with small bits of driftwood. It lit on the first match. We sat on a large rock nearby to wait for the fire to establish itself enough to handle the paintings.

I gazed up and down the shoreline. To the north the breakwater of Brood Bay stretched into the sea, its rocks slapped black and shiny by the breaking waves. Rusty-coloured rockweed curved in an irregular ridge at the water's edge, tinting the receding water dark purple. A thicker ridge of rockweed and kelp lay nearer the base of the bank, brown and dry, deposited there by an earlier tide. Far above the waterline were pieces of silvery driftwood and an empty bleach bottle.

The water directly before us was a dark golden shade where more seaweed floated just beneath the surface, undulating with the ebb and flow. Farther out, salty green waves built up just before breaking. The sun shone faintly from behind thin clouds to the south, and the water, in that direction, gleamed a metallic grey.

I smiled at Gordon. "So. Which one will we sacrifice first?"

He chose the ballerina. Then he said, "No, I think we should start with the smallest. That would be the ugly still life." He placed it carefully on the fire. Smoke curled around its edges. We watched the seagulls drift up and down, seeming to stay in one spot but actually moving sideways as the water shifted back and forth beneath them.

I said, "I wonder if they use their feet as rudders."

"Maybe I'll come back as a seagull."

"Let's not start that again."

Gordon leaned down and carefully took hold of the painting by one corner. He stood it straight up in the fire and placed a rock beside it to hold it in place.

I said, "Helen told me the other night that Warren is up to something shifty."

I immediately had Gordon's full attention. Sounding like a priest in a confessional, he said, "Go on."

"Apparently he's been doing some fancy accounting or something."

"And you're surprised?"

"No. I've seen Warren lie before." I stared into the fire and added thoughtfully, "I'd rather have someone steal from me than lie to me."

"Says the person who's been telling people she's sick."

"I know." I laughed. "Not because I want to. And I haven't said it to many people. Okay, you've got me. What can I say?"

Gordon bent to poke at the fire. "I've known some pretty good liars in my time."

"I have too. Not many, thank God, but a few. Professional liars. You wonder why they do it sometimes. The things they lie about aren't usually important. It's as if they lie just for the sport of it." I looked out at the darkening sea.

"They do it for practice," said Gordon. "To them it's like practising the scales on the piano. A good liar has to practise. You've got to keep the lying muscles supple, ready for an impromptu performance."

"But you'd think they'd realize after a while that they're getting a reputation for it. How can they expect to be believed when they're telling the truth if they lie all the time?"

"Honey," said Gordon, standing with his hands on his hips, "any liar that's worth his salt can make you believe him when he needs to. They may have a reputation for lying, but they go on as if they have a God-given right to be believed. They can tell a lie with more conviction than you or I can tell the truth. And if you want to see somebody act indignant, just call them on one of their lies!" Gordon threw another stick on the fire. "They're like skinny people standing in front of convex mirrors. They insist that they believe in the distortion and refuse to accept that other people don't believe it as well."

"Well, I think Helen has had about enough."

"Good. It's about time. I hope she has the guts to do something about it."

I placed two more paintings on the fire, bracing them against one another. It was starting to get dark. I looked back toward the house to see if I'd left any lights on. I had. I stood staring at the spruce trees at the edge of the bank. They were bare of needles on the seaward side, giving them a dry, dead look, but the sides away from the water were thick and rugged. I turned to look to the north. The wharf lights were on, and Cranberry Point, off in the distance, was beginning to twinkle.

I said, "Do you suppose they've noticed the smoke in the village yet?"

"They'll just think we're roasting wienies."

It was completely dark by the time the last painting was cremated.

Trippers often enlist the help of other birds in their colony to peck at weaker birds when they are down.

I cut the painting of the fishing boats, reducing it from a sixteen by twenty to a nine by twelve; put it in a frame; and delivered it to the gallery to replace the last one they'd sold. I decided to celebrate by eating lunch at an air-conditioned restaurant. Hundreds of August tourists, just off the ferry, kept the Yarmouth traffic at a crawl, and my errands took twice as long as I'd planned. I still needed to make a trip to the bank and to the laundromat. I went directly to a booth and sat down.

A frizzy-haired redhead brought the menu and delivered the message from the kitchen that the day's special was "pitter" bread with curried chicken and a choice of salad or home fries.

"That sounds good," I said, and I chose a salad. I pulled a book from my bag and tried to read while waiting for my food. My concentration was disturbed by voices from the booth behind me. Three women were chatting comfortably, like old friends who ate together often. I was intrigued by their conversation.

"I bought three and put them up as a sort of test to myself."

"I wouldn't be able to leave them alone."

"Yes, but they're in a cupboard up high. I have to get up on a chair to get one." This was followed by laughter and murmurs.

"But, don't you feel so good after you've had one?"

"Hersheys are the best. They are just the best chocolate! I almost always buy Hersheys."

"Yes, but then my doctor tells me that I've got to take off a few pounds."

It had never occurred to me that women their age might hoard chocolate bars and binge on them as a guilty pleasure. I would have guessed their weakness to be brownies or pie, or maybe homemade Nanaimo bars, but not Hershey bars. Then I caught something that surprised me even more. The conversation shifted at the mention of one of their husbands.

"Not a word of this to anyone—promise? He warned me not to say anything, but he's really quite upset."

I paused in my chewing and allowed myself a little smile.

"Warren asked Steve to keep an eye on Helen. They're having problems."

My smile narrowed and my eyes widened. I turned my head slightly toward the voices.

"He's all but positive that she's having an affair, but he hasn't been able to catch her at it. He has no idea who with—probably someone from work."

My fork clattered onto the table.

"She's been acting odd lately, going off on her own, but they only have one car so he can't follow her. She *says* she's going to her sister's, but one Saturday Warren sent Sean on his bicycle to the sister's, pretending he needed Helen for something, and she wasn't there. She had left fifteen minutes earlier."

I stared soberly at my plate, remembering the day Sean had come to the door to ask for Helen. I recalled my concern that he might find it odd for me to be wearing a hat inside the house.

The woman continued, "An hour later when she got home

and he asked her where she'd been, she said that she'd been to see her sister, Rube. No explanation for the extra hour or more. She pretended that her sister was sick so she stayed for a visit. A nice guy like Warren. It's too bad."

"And two kids." A sorrowful sigh. "I hadn't heard anything about it."

"Of course not. Nobody knows. Steve would kill me if he knew I'd mentioned it. It's just that it's hard not to think about it, and I was wondering if you'd noticed anything."

I bristled as the two friends were sworn to secrecy. Studying them carefully as they passed my booth, I wondered which one would betray the confidence first.

It is interesting to note that, though Trippers do not actually clip the wings of their mates, they do attempt to undermine their mate's confidence in their ability to fly to such a degree that flight is confined to a short radius from the nest and for the purpose of food finding only.

Only one week into the revolution and things were about to go very wrong for Helen. Apparently, her prayer for peace, the one she had whispered so as not to wake Warren, had not been heard by God either. Warren announced at breakfast that he needed to go to Canadian Tire, but one o'clock came and he still hadn't left. Helen said, "I was thinking of going for a walk on the beach. If you don't need the car 'til later, I'll use it now. But if you want it now, I'll go for my walk later." Warren made the mistake of not bothering to answer. Imagine his surprise when he heard the sound of the car backing out of the driveway.

Helen sprang from the car with the eagerness of a dog being treated to its weekly run. Something raw was in the air, something resembling the salt of tears after long hours of crying. Thinking at the edge of the ocean was akin to shouting in the wind. It might be hopeless, but it felt so good. Helen walked for fifteen minutes in the direction of the shack. Her chair waited in the open doorway, and she was up the steps and turning to fall back into it before she saw the man lying on the shabby couch. She jumped, and he pulled himself up quickly with one arm on the back of the couch and one on the seat, his face rigid with alarm.

"I am so sorry. I'm… I'm… I didn't mean to intrude."

He said, "It's all right, it's all right. I was just resting a little bit." He pushed frantically at his hair as he rose to his full six feet. His long neck stretched and twisted out of his collar as if designed to extend or reduce his height according to circumstances. He swooped down to the floor for his billed cap, then remembered his cigarette burning in the ashtray and bent to butt it out.

Helen had, by now, moved to the bottom of the steps, but she could hear him saying, "I was just about to leave. If you want to sit a bit, go ahead. I've had my smoke, and it's time I was getting home."

She protested, "Oh no, I shouldn't be here. This is your place. I'm sorry that I disturbed you. I had no business." He stood in the doorway, and Helen backed away from the steps so that he could descend.

"No, no, really. It's just a shack," he said, moving his head back and forth dismissively. "It ain't worth fighting about. If you'd enjoy sitting a bit, go ahead." He was touching the bill of his cap, looking at the shack and away, working his eyebrows like he had no idea what to do with them.

Helen stood, hands in her jacket pockets, unsure which would be more rude, walking away or staying.

"I just knocked it together over time," he said. "It's not much of a piece of work. It's only junk. I can do better when I've got the proper materials. But it's a place to come to and relax. Maybe have a smoke."

Helen studied him surreptitiously. He seemed familiar, but it took some effort to place him. Finally, it came to her. "Did you buy a lawnmower a few weeks ago, a used one for seventy-five dollars?"

"I bought a mower. The fellow was asking seventy-five, but I offered him sixty-five and he took it. Actually, I offered him sixty and he said sixty-five, so I gave it to him." He smiled somewhat sheepishly. "Why d'you ask about that?"

"That was my husband, and I'm afraid you didn't get much of a bargain. I don't know why he did that. If you're not satisfied—if it doesn't work—I'll be happy to give you your money back."

"It works just fine. I've mowed the lawn twice with it already. You're not getting that mower back." He grinned down at her.

Then Helen remembered—Warren had said it was Gladys's husband Cecil who had bought the mower. Yes, this man did look like the one she had watched through the window. Once again, she was struck by how different he looked from how she imagined a wife beater should look. He was a little rough around the edges and not what you'd call intelligent, but he seemed harmless. *It's kind of scary that someone that mean can look so innocent.*

Cecil touched the bill of his cap, turned, and started off toward an opening in the edge of the woods. Helen waited until he was out of sight before going back up the steps. She sat in the red chair for a few minutes, but it wasn't the same as other times. The smell of cigarettes had fouled the air, and Cecil's presence was too fresh. Perhaps it would be better to go a little farther up the shore instead of spending time in the shack. She had never explored beyond this point.

The steep bank presented a problem: there was dirt on the top half and round stones on the bottom half. She eyed the gravel beach below and looked back along the path in the direction she had come. She could backtrack a couple hundred feet to where the land sloped gently or she could take her chances scrambling down from here.

Helen held onto a bush as she lowered herself over the lip, and leaning into the bank, she edged her way down, scuffling for footholds and struggling for balance when the ground failed her. She soon developed too much momentum and staggered dangerously toward the smooth, rounded rocks near the bottom, unable to correct her movements when the rocks started to roll. Her struggle for balance became a frantic, fast-stepped dance that ended when she snapped her ankle and knelt, crumpled in pain. Furious, she spat, "Darn! Darn!" How could she have been so stupid? She imagined Warren's reaction when she tried to explain how this had happened. He'd wanted to go to Canadian Tire.

I bent to the clothesbasket and then reached for the line, bent and reached, bent and reached. Perspiration trickled down my sides as I raised my arms. The air was still, so still. I felt like I recognized it, like I had breathed the same air again and again. I worried that the clothes were going to dry stiff unless a breeze came from somewhere.

The beach must have been full. I hoped to be able to walk it later, maybe even swim. I was so hot. I wanted to jump into the cold waves and feel the salt tingle on my skin, but I had things to do. Maybe later. I picked up a brown plaid cotton sundress and pinned it by its shoulders to the line. It was the last thing in my basket, and I hated to let go of its coolness. After a minute of staring wistfully at the dress, I glanced around, then quickly pulled my T-shirt off over my head, took the dress down from the line, and began to struggle into it. The material stuck to itself and then to me. I laughed as I thought about how funny I must have looked with the wet fabric clinging to my body. Then I wiggled out of my shorts, threw them into the basket along with my T-shirt, slung the basket on my hip, and headed toward the house.

I stopped suddenly. A funny feeling passed over me, out of nowhere. It made me a little uneasy. I decided to call Helen and make sure everything was okay.

Helen stared at the steep bank and groaned. Her situation was impossible. The car might as well have been ten kilometres away. She carefully maneuvered herself onto a large rock so that she could examine her ankle, the first broken bone of her life. Waves continued to form, crest, and break as they had been doing since the beginning of time, but there was little comfort to be had from their continuity. Her predicament was insignificant in the larger scheme of things and yet, in her world, it was catastrophic. Pain was the least of it. Her newfound confidence and determination had also been also broken by her fall. This time, when Warren berated her, he would have reason.

She jerked her head up at the first hint of a sound coming from the vicinity of the shack and listened a moment more before she began to yell, "Hello? Is someone up there? Hello? Can you help me? I've hurt myself." She waited and was about to try again when she saw Cecil come tentatively to the edge and frown down at her.

"Can you help me? Please. I've hurt my ankle."

"What are you doing down there? If you don't mind me asking?"

"I came down over the side too fast."

"What did you do that for? You mean you went down over there? Man alive. Why didn't you go on down to the path?" He pointed farther down the shore, then turned and hurried in the direction in which he'd been pointing. Helen clenched her teeth and sucked in her breath. Hopping wasn't an option on the round stones, and she couldn't put even a little bit of weight on her foot. Cecil made his way toward her, his movements made erratic by nervous excitement. Hands on his hips, he drew a deep breath and winced. "I don't know. Can you walk at all?"

"I'm afraid I'm going to have to lean on you. Then maybe

I can move without jolting my foot so much." Helen pressed her lips together, and her chin quivered.

Cecil was clearly horrified by the possibility of tears. He kept his distance and stood looking—first off to his left, then to his right—working his lips, frowning, and then raising his eyebrows. "You need a crutch. Just you wait here." He started back in the direction he'd come from.

"Don't go. Where you going?"

"I'll be right back," he said with the soft reassurance he would have used with a child.

She was helpless to do anything other than watch him leave. He disappeared; she waited. He reappeared at the top of the bank holding an old blue broom. "Your crutch," he said. He tried it out as he approached her. The plastic bristles were worn almost to stubs and were parted in the middle, making a notch for his armpit. He handed it to Helen and raised his eyebrows as he waited to see if it would do.

She said, "It's not bad, but I could still use some help in steadying myself."

He stood next to her, and she put her left arm over his shoulder and carefully positioned the broom handle a little bit ahead of her. She lurched forward. By the time they'd reached the shack, Helen's foot was swollen. She sat on the steps to wait while Cecil walked back to the house for his ATV. Her watch read two forty-five. Would Warren go with her to the hospital or would she have to call Rube? She dreaded his anger and felt as guilty as if she had transgressed.

Feeling around in her pocket for a tissue, she came up with nothing more than a used, dried-together wad with one small promising loose end. She raised this to her nose, and the air around her face was filled with a flurry of fibres from the disintegrating ball.

Cecil's return was surprisingly quick, but the ride up the bumpy lane was painful. As they neared the house, she could see Gladys putting on her jacket and hurrying down the side steps clutching her purse. Cecil stopped a few feet away from her, and she said, "I tried to call your house, but there was no answer. Warren maybe went out."

"He might just be outside."

Cecil extracted a pack of cigarettes from his breast pocket with a practised swan dive of his wrist. He pushed the pack open, removed his lighter, and offered a cigarette to Helen. He then shoved one between his lips and, with it hanging down like a broken diving board, lit it and waved out the match—a ballet of graceful gestures.

"We'll be going by your house on the way to the hospital. We can check, but it's no trouble to take you in ourselves if he's not home."

"I hate to make you do that. I'll spoil your Saturday."

"Not at all."

"Warren will not be pleased. I told him I'd only be gone an hour, and here it is quarter to three. He wanted the car so that he could to go to Canadian Tire."

"Well, you can't help it."

They climbed into Cecil's truck, Cecil driving and Gladys between them. Cecil held the door for Helen and slammed it after she was in.

"It was so stupid of me, trying to go down the side of the bank. I remember doing that when I was a kid, but I suppose..."

"Even kids break their ankles sometimes."

"Maybe it's just sprained."

"There's not much difference. One's about as bad as the other from what I hear," said Cecil.

They headed off down the road in the direction of Helen's house. "I don't know what I would've done if Cecil hadn't come back. I'd still be down there," she said in Gladys's direction.

"Forgot my cigarettes."

"Thank God."

"You see, there's good things come from smoking too." He grinned at Gladys. "That's what I try to tell her."

"I'm not going to be able to work."

"No," said Cecil. "Looks like you're gonna get a little unplanned vacation. You work for a doctor, don't ya? He ought to understand."

"Understanding's not the problem."

Warren wasn't home, and neither Cecil nor Gladys would agree to let Helen call Rube. They insisted on taking her to the hospital, and in fact they seemed to be enjoying the adventure. Cecil stopped in front of the hospital door, and Helen and Gladys got out.

"Stay here so you can lean against the truck. I'll go and get a wheelchair." Gladys was back in less than a minute. She flipped on the brake and raised the footrests as if she had done it many times before. Helen settled gratefully into the worn leather seat. Her ankle was throbbing badly.

Cecil parked the truck while Gladys wheeled Helen to the outpatient window. Only then did Helen remember that she didn't have her purse—she had no hospital card and no money. Gladys graciously paid for a new hospital card.

"I am so sorry to make you have to do all this," said Helen, "but I have one more favour to ask. Could one of you try the house again to see if Warren's gotten back?"

Cecil stopped at the payphone, and Gladys and Helen continued on to the outpatient window.

The reception room was crowded. Cecil returned from the payphone and sat down next to Gladys.

"Well?" asked Gladys. "Is he home?"

"Yeah." Cecil crossed his arms and worked his lips into an assortment of puckered positions but offered no more in the way of an explanation.

"If you called my sister, Rube, she'd come and wait with me and you could go home."

Gladys wouldn't hear of it.

"Did you think to tell Warren that the car is in the parking lot by the beach?"

"Yeah, I told him."

"He'll probably be able to get someone to drive him there to get the car. He's got his own keys." Helen looked at her watch. "He might still be able to make Canadian Tire."

"Must be something awfully important that he needs at Canadian Tire," said Cecil.

The Gospel According to Pastor Wallace
Mother's Day Eve, 1995

The room was silent except for the sound of chewing. Pastor Wallace picked a piece of date from between his teeth with the end of a paperclip, then said, "The Lord works in mysterious ways. I truly believe Helen's accident happened because the Lord wanted her to stop running around. She broke her ankle down on the shore, on the rocks. Now what was she doing down there? I truly believe it was a sign, a nudge from God. I tried to persuade her in that direction; I dropped by to see her while she was laid up in her cast and read her some appropriate scripture and prayed with her." He paused to be sure the distressed tone in his voice matched the distressed look on his face. "But her fella and her sister had quite a hold on her, between them."

Pastor Wallace's mouth twisted as he remembered the day he had visited Helen with her broken ankle. Rube's arrogance had been typical of her. He'd read scripture to Rube, and she would have done well to listen to it, but he may as well have poured water over a stone, for the amount of good it did. He consoled himself that at least he'd made the effort. He could control what he offered, but he couldn't control how it was received. He smiled. He'd held his own. He'd gone with the right ammunition and had made a few direct hits. She made it hard to pray for her, but he did it all the same. He cleared his throat. "I read to Rube about women's heads being covered when they prayed, and do you know what her reply was?" His tone hardened. "She said she wasn't a sheep and didn't have time for the glory of God." Pastor Wallace folded his hands as if to say *I rest my case.*

Helen's cast gave her a good excuse to sleep in the living room. She'd claimed she was concerned that she'd hit Warren with it during the night. Some days she didn't bother to get up until the house was empty. At first the children brought her cups of tea and checked regularly to see if she needed anything, but by the third day the novelty had worn off and, accustomed to the weight of the cast, she told them she could manage.

I vacuumed, dusted, changed the sheets on the beds, and did my own laundry along with Helen's. Helen fretted about being away from work, but she had been told to stay out of the office. Her replacement was doing fine, and the office was too small to accommodate the clumsiness of someone wearing a cast. Three and a half weeks passed. Helen and I had just settled in the living room with our coffees when Pastor Wallace arrived, clasping his bible to his chest with his left hand as he extended his right, first to Helen and then, briefly, to me. He installed himself in Warren's chair and accepted a mug of coffee before turning to Helen. "So you're laid up for a while. How long do you expect to be off work?"

"A few more weeks."

"I trust Warren is giving you a little extra help around the house." Pastor Wallace exuded charm.

Helen squirmed in her chair and repositioned her cast on the stool. "Not exactly. He thinks that if I'm home all day I should be able to get everything done by myself. But Rube's been helping me."

Pastor Wallace acknowledged me begrudgingly.

"Harriet has been helping too," said Helen.

"Ah, yes," said Pastor Wallace with renewed enthusiasm. "This would be a good opportunity for her to learn a few extra household chores. The Lord usually has a plan, though we often fail to see it right away." He smiled broadly. I squinted and frowned as I tried to decipher what kind of plan would involve Helen's injury. I was new to this game.

"Warren told me about your little accident. Perhaps you needed some time to yourself to reflect a bit on things."

Helen nodded, smiling, but the smile soon faded as he continued in a voice firmed up by the Godly gravity of the situation.

"It's wise to stop and evaluate every so often, to consider what we're doing with our lives and why we're doing it, to re-establish our priorities, and perhaps to recommit ourselves. I'm sure God has slowed you down for a reason."

Helen stole a quick glance at me.

Pastor Wallace's gaze followed. "And Rube. How are you? I heard you haven't been well."

My eyebrows shot up, and I blinked a few times. "Oh, well, yes, I'm much better now. Thank you."

"So do you feel the chemo helped?"

I blurted, "Chemo?"

Pastor Wallace said, "Chemotherapy."

I looked at Helen and said, "I'm sorry. There must be some mistake."

Helen shrugged.

I said, "I don't have cancer, if that's what you think."

Pastor Wallace said, "Have it your way," and looked at the far wall as if to say *What can you do with liars?*

There was an awkward pause before he turned to Helen and asked, "So have any of the ladies from the church been by?"

Helen said, "It's not necessary. Really, I'm fine."

I thought again of the conversation I'd overheard at the restaurant. I'd never had the heart to share it with Helen.

Pastor Wallace opened his bible with the help of a white tasselled marker. His gestures in handling the bible were like Cecil's with his cigarette pack—they had the fluid familiarity of addiction. He said, "If you ladies are agreeable, I'd like for us to bow our heads while I read a prayer from Psalm fifty-one. His tone changed as he began. "'Have mercy upon me, O God, according to thy loving-kindness; according unto the multitude of thy tender mercies blot out my transgressions. Wash me thoroughly from mine iniquity, and cleanse me from my sin. For I acknowledge my transgressions; and my sin is ever before me. Against thee, thee only, have I sinned and done this evil in thy sight; that thou mightest be justified when thou speakest and be clear when thou judgest. Behold, I was shapen in iniquity; and in sin did my mother conceive me.'"

A car turned into Helen's driveway. I raised my head and caught the black look that had taken over Helen's features. Pastor Wallace continued unperturbed.

"'Behold, thou desirest truth in the inward parts; and in the hidden part thou shalt make me to know wisdom. Purge me with hyssop, and I shall be clean: wash me, and I shall be whiter than snow. Make me to hear joy and gladness; that the bones which thou hast broken," at this Pastor Wallace raised a finger and darted his eyes at Helen briefly before continuing, "may rejoice. Hide thy face from my sins, and blot out all mine iniquities. Create in me a clean heart, O God; and renew a right spirit within me. Restore unto me the joy of thy salvation; and uphold me with thy free Spirit.'"

A knock at the door brought me to my feet, but I was waved back down by Pastor Wallace's left hand. He riffled through his bible. "Just a moment. I have something else I would like to read to you." The pages rustled and snapped, and then he began. "'But every woman that prayeth or prophesieth with her head uncovered dishonoureth her head: for that is even all one as if she were shaven. For if the woman be not covered, let her also be shorn: but—'"

"Shorn.... It makes her sound like a sheep," I said.

Pastor Wallace shot me a nasty look and then continued with a well-honed edge in his voice, "'But if it be a shame for a woman to be shorn or shaven, let her be covered.'" He glared at me victoriously. I ran a hand through my cropped hair and frowned. "So what exactly are you getting at?"

Pastor Wallace returned his attention to his bible and, like a lawyer delivering his summation, he continued, "'For a man indeed ought not to cover his head, fore as much as he is the image and glory of God: but the woman is the glory of man.'"

I snorted. I rose again after the second knock and stood looking down on Pastor Wallace. He shifted uneasily in his seat and attempted a smile. I shook my head and turned, throwing back at him, as I left the room, "Here's the thing, I don't want to be the glory of man. I don't have time for it."

Pastor Wallace gathered himself up, as if he were a man of many parts, and left, almost knocking the plate of cookies out of Gladys's hands as he passed her on the doorstep.

"Pastor Wallace's prayer didn't seem appropriate to me," complained Helen when he was gone. "It was like he was implying that I deserved this for being a sinner. There was some part in there about broken bones. Maybe he thought that made it work. Gladys, I'd like to know what you think. Pass me Warren's bible over there by his chair. He said it was Psalm fifty-one."

Gladys delivered the bible to Helen and returned to her place on the edge of Warren's chair.

"What was he talking about with the part about this being God's way of slowing me down and making me think about my priorities? About recommitting?"

I hesitated, tapping a fingernail on my front teeth and glancing back and forth between Gladys and Helen. "I think I might know. There's a rumour." My eyes lingered on Gladys. "Do you know about it?"

Gladys avoided eye contact.

"I heard a couple women talking in a restaurant. I didn't know whether to tell you or not, Helen. I thought it might be best to just stay quiet about it."

Gladys looked at the floor.

"What kind of rumour?" shot Helen.

"I think the women may be from your church. One of them mentioned her husband Steve?"

Helen looked quickly at Gladys and stated, "That would be Freda."

"Well, according to her, Warren told Steve he was almost certain you were having an affair."

"What?" Helen slopped coffee on her sweatshirt. She didn't seem to notice. "Where would he get that idea?"

"I don't know. I guess he said you were out running around a lot. Going off on your own."

Helen's gaze settled on Warren's chair as if it were guilty by association. Her face hardened. "Running around? I can't even go for a walk on the beach." She levelled her gaze on Gladys. "How is it you haven't heard about this, Gladys?"

Gladys squirmed in her seat. "I don't hear too much. I don't like to get involved."

Helen exhaled in exasperation. "I don't know how much more of this I can take, Rube. He's spiteful. He's just being spiteful."

Gladys said, "Well, you know what rumours are like. Everybody's abuzz with them today, and then a week from now they've forgotten all about it."

"No," said Helen, "that's not good enough. There'll always be people that think this is true. Forever. They won't forget about it. And I'll have to live with that."

I said, "And then there was that bit about me having cancer. That must be another one that's going around."

Gladys looked at me quickly and said, "I did hear that one."

"Well, it's not true."

"Somebody must have seen you," said Helen. She narrowed her eyes at me.

I laughed. "At least two people thought my paintings would go up in value if I died. I thought it was odd that I sold two paintings so close together."

Helen's face represented her tangle of emotions—her wide eyes were glazed with frustration and tears while fury dominated her eyebrows and mouth. We sat for several minutes, like stunned passengers after a crash. Finally, Helen turned toward Gladys. "Gladys, there'll probably never be a better time for this, and I probably shouldn't be asking it, but I've got to. I haven't been able to make myself believe it since I met Cecil and saw the two of you together. People say he beats you. It's not true, is it?"

"No," said Gladys, "he certainly does not." There was not even the suggestion of surprise in her voice.

"You knew, didn't you?" asked Helen in wonderment.

"Yes. They've been saying that for years."

"Doesn't it bother you, going to church knowing they're saying that?"

"It did at first," she shrugged, "but what could I do? I like going to church. I think they only say those things because it galls them that Cecil doesn't go. They make out he's an alcoholic too just because he has a beer now and then. I can still go to church and have it mean something to me." She sighed. "That kind of stuff usually comes back on people."

Helen drew in a deep breath. "You're a better person than I am, Gladys. But then things are good between you and Cecil. It's the idea of Warren starting this that I can't forgive. He knows it's not true. He doesn't believe for one minute that it's true. He's just being spiteful."

"So why don't you give him reason to believe it?" I suggested with a wry smile. "It would serve him right. Let him find a few things lying around that aren't his."

Gladys chortled and then, reading the invitation in my raised eyebrows, turned quickly to Helen for assurance that the appalling idea would not be seriously considered.

"Like what?" asked Helen, her voice a mixture of trepidation and curiosity. "A pair of underwear beside the bed?"

"No. No. Things that require his interpretation to make them suspicious. A pack of matches. Maybe cigarette smoke in the air when he comes home from work." I hesitated and, without a hint of my former playfulness, asked, "What's going to become of you, Helen? You're going all to hell."

Helen smiled ruefully. "I have no idea what is going to happen to me. I wish I knew. How I wish I knew."

I slapped my hand on the arm of my chair and announced, "I know! A psychic. I know a good psychic."

Helen shot me a warning look and shook her head. "Don't give me that."

"Why not?"

"It may seem to you that I've lost my mind, but I'm still not *that* crazy."

I said, "There's nothing wrong with psychics."

"No, there's nothing wrong with them, but there's something wrong with the suckers that go to them."

"You said you wish you knew—"

Helen interrupted crossly, "I do wish I knew, but I don't believe in psychics." Then with a shake of her head, she sighed. "I need a good night's sleep. I couldn't have slept more than two hours last night."

"How long are you planning on sleeping on the couch?"

"I don't know."

"A good psychic could tell you." I beamed.

"Yeah. A good psychic could get me kicked out of the house. That's one way of knowing."

"She told Janet that she was going to have something valuable taken from her, and the next week someone swiped her best world atlas."

"You call that valuable?"

"It was worth forty-five dollars."

"So why didn't the psychic tell her to hide her world atlas?

That would have been worth something. What good did it do her to be told she was going to lose something? That's kinda vague."

I said defensively, "Sometimes she's more specific."

Helen waited.

I went on. "She told Janet that she would enter a competition."

"So? Janet could just go out and enter one to make it come true. Did she tell her that she was going to win?"

"Yes, she did. She said she'd win."

"So did she?"

"I don't know. She hasn't heard yet."

"What competition?"

"Well," I shifted guiltily in my seat, "it wasn't really a competition. But it was sort of what you could imagine a psychic mistaking for a competition. She sent a photo to the cancer society and suggested that they use it for posters and promotional material."

"A photo of what?"

"Of me bald with a halo."

"Oh, Good Lord!"

Helen had much to consider as she cut up the chicken, peppers, onions, and mushrooms for supper. So much had happened since she had decided, eight hours ago, after breakfast, to make fajitas. If the food you cook is affected by the spirit in which it is prepared, then these fajitas were toxic. To forgive could be divine, or it could simply be stupid. More and more Helen found herself searching for God in the debris of her life with the desperation of a bag lady in a dumpster. There was something about following the rules that no longer satisfied her spiritual hunger.

More and more, the *correct* thing didn't feel like the *right* thing. In her gut, she knew the difference. She would give just about anything to have a peek at her future, but, she asked herself, would she give in to the temptation to go to Rube's psychic?

Warren arrived home with a bouquet of yellow chrysanthemums. Helen viewed the flowers with a momentary disinterest before turning back to her work at the counter. Would the psychic have predicted that? Probably. There was nothing new or original about a guilty man bringing flowers. Long ago a caveman transgressed, got kicked out of the cave, and noticed some pretty wildflowers, which became his ticket back into the cave. Ever since that day mankind, or, more appropriately, man-unkind, has featured flowers in their attempts to undo damage.

Warren filled a vase from the tap and carried it to the table. He said, "We've been invited to supper Saturday night."

"By whom?" Helen frowned. She could think of no one that she was in the mood to socialize with.

"Dick and Cynthia. I told him I'd have to check with you first."

Helen was quiet.

"Would you like to go?"

"I'll think about it."

Trippers are capable of making sounds that resemble laughter, giving the appearance of being possessed with good humour. The mate does not seem gifted in this respect since it is usually silent at these times. Usually, but not always.

Dick Hemeon sold cars at the local Toyota dealership. His wife, Cynthia, taught fifth grade at Brood Bay Elementary School. Their hundred-year-old home, situated halfway between the church and school, was well maintained—with white sparkling paint and a walkway bordered with pansies and marigolds. Two cars were in the driveway. Helen's heart sank when she recognized the black Acura parked behind Dick's dark blue Camry. It was a regular in the church lot every Sunday. There would be extra dinner guests this evening, Geralyne and Harold Reed. Helen, hobbling on her crutches, followed Warren to the front door. He knocked, then straightened his shoulders and adjusted his belt with a little hitch as if he had just swung down off his horse and was about to enter a saloon.

Dick, a short, chubby man of forty, answered the door. "Keep your shoes on. I'm sure they're not dirty. It's not like it's muddy out there. I kinda wish we'd get some rain though," he said, by way of a greeting. "The lawn's getting all dried out, and I hate to water it for fear of running the well dry." He clapped Warren on the back and then turned to Helen and asked jovially, "How are you making out with your crutches? Looks like you've mastered them pretty well. The girls are in the kitchen so you might want to go on through and join them." Helen flashed him a quick smile, nodded in the direction of Harold in the living room, and made her way down the hall toward a voice that she was sure belonged to Geralyne. Most hairdressers consider talking almost as important to clients as the hair care, but Geralyne was extreme. Loud and seemingly unaware that a proper conversation involved more than one person being allowed to talk, she was sitting on a stool at the island and entertaining Cynthia, who was putting the last-minute touches on the meal. Geralyne paused long enough to shake her head at Helen's cast and crutches and offer, "You poor dear," before continuing to describe the latest antics of her six-month-old terrier. For once Helen wasn't annoyed by Geralyne's prattle; in this situation the talk was appreciated. Helen went to the kitchen table, leaned her crutches against the wall, and sat down. She examined her nails as she listened, conscious that she had never had a manicure in her life, a fact that must be obvious and somewhat shocking to Geralyne. Geralyne was part of the species of modern women who were completely processed; her lifeless hair was a shade of reddish brown that did not exist in nature. She was unattractive but not for lack of effort. Cynthia, on the other hand, was petite and blonde. She and Dick had been married for eighteen years and had two children. At the first opportunity, Helen asked, "Where are Mark and Faylene?"

"Sleepovers."

Helen had begun to relax. Before coming, the idea that this could be a set up, an intervention of some kind, had presented itself. Now she quickly dismissed the thought as paranoia, a carry-over from her frayed nerves and Pastor Wallace's visit. By the time Cynthia and Geralyne had the food on the table, Helen was less alert for signs of judgment against her, from the women at least, and was hopeful that the evening would dispel the rumours about her affair. She knew that if she wanted to convince people things were fine between her and Warren, she would need to show Warren some warmth. She tried to put a few smiles his way as they took their places opposite one another at the table, but it was difficult to meet his eyes. Instead she turned her attention to Harold, a quiet, likeable man who managed the Royal Store in Yarmouth. Helen admired Harold's patience. Geralyne could be fun, but occasionally Helen caught a brief twitch at a corner of his mouth or a quick jerk of his eyebrows that hinted at irritation or, at the very least, acknowledgement that her manners were not endorsed by management. By the end of the main course, Geralyne had wound down and the talk had dwindled. They quietly enjoyed their apple pie and coffee.

As stressful as the evening was for Helen—with her mind busily trying to analyze every look, word, and tone—Warren appeared completely relaxed. He was in fine form.

As if to revive the storytelling, Warren asked, "Shall I tell them about the time we went swimming at Three Island Lake?"

Helen blanched. She knew what was coming. He had done this before. "I don't think they want to hear about that, Warren."

"But it's a pretty good story."

Encouragement came from every corner of the table. Warren began to tell the story, knowing it would be accepted as truth. After all, Helen had all but acknowledged, by her reluctance, that something embarassing had happened at Three Island Lake.

"We were there canoeing," began Warren. "We had fishing poles with us, but I don't remember catching anything. It's a wonder Helen didn't catch a cold though." He grinned at

Helen and slowly set his knife and fork on his plate. "We hadn't gone prepared to swim, you see, and we didn't have our swimsuits with us or anything, and around midday it got real hot. Well we see this little beach, so we paddle over to it and pull the canoe up and get ready to have ourselves a swim." He nodded and smiled as if enjoying a fond memory. He looked from person to person as he talked, pausing to meet Helen's eyes each time his gaze passed her. "Helen doesn't want to wear wet clothes in the afternoon, and there doesn't appear to be anyone around, so she strips off buck-naked and goes—"

At this point Warren was interrupted by Helen's protests. "I did not. I didn't take all of my clothes off."

"Yes, you did, honey." Warren tipped his head and met her glare. His lips were in the shape of a smile, but it was the cruelty that he was enjoying. "Now let me get on with my story," he said slowly.

"No, I didn't, Warren. If you're going to tell the story, tell it right."

"She's embarrassed," said Warren as he looked from one attentive face to the next around the table, "because we weren't married then. Look, she's blushing. If I remember right, she did a little blushing that day too." He chuckled.

Everyone laughed and said "Ohhh" as they looked at Helen.

"Anyway," continued Warren, "after a while she got out of the water and was just bending down to pick up her panties when—"

"Warren, I had my pants on and a T-shirt. You're just making this up."

Warren studied Helen's red face, her pleading eyes, begging for him to stop. It had become quiet around the table. He continued evenly. "She was picking up her panties when we heard a twig snap and the sound of someone coming quite close to the beach."

"You're doing this to embarrass me. You're not funny."

"Then why is everybody laughing?" Warren glanced again around the table. The laughter had dwindled to a few awkward snickers.

"Tell them that's not the way it happened."

"It's okay, Helen. We're among friends. These guys have probably skinny-dipped before at one time or another. So this guy comes out of the bushes, and here's Helen standing with one leg in her pants and almost falling over cause she's trying to get the other leg in fast and she keeps losing her balance."

All eyes were turned on Helen. Her discomfort was funnier than the story itself. And then it wasn't. The women made feeble attempts to stop Warren, so convinced were they that the story was true.

Helen threw up her hands, sat back in her chair, crossed her arms, and scowled at Warren. She imagined herself picking up a rifle from beside her chair, levelling it on Warren, and holding it just long enough for fear to register in his eyes before pulling the trigger. Slime would splatter against the wall behind him, and she would announce to the bulging eyes and slack mouths around the table, *And that, my friends, is the end of the story.*

But Helen didn't have a gun. She would have to drop a bomb. With a sense of intense calm she said, "Warren loves to tell a funny story even if he has to make it up and present it as the truth. His capacity to lie for the sake of a laugh always amazes me, especially for someone who calls himself a Christian!"

Warren's eyes blackened. Slowly, the rest of his face congealed into a smirk. He looked around the table as if enlisting support before saying, "I guess we can't blame Helen for being embarrassed by my telling this story, but it's only in fun. Have a sense of humour. If you can't laugh at yourself, what can you laugh at? Be a good sport, dear."

"You're right," said Helen. "Tell us another story. How about the one about Kenny Duncan?" She looked at Warren and waited. "You know, the one about him and the tax man."

Warren's expression narrowed; his eyes darted about, chasing thoughts, and then settled in frozen alarm. His face—eyebrows, forehead, upper cheeks—seemed to gather, as if puckered by a drawstring.

"I don't know what you're talking about."

Breathing around the table became suspended until Geralyne smashed the brittle silence with, "'Kenny Duncan and the tax—?" She was cut off by sharp stares.

"Talk about being caught with your pants down! And to think it was all on the advice of his accountant. Shocking, wouldn't you say, Warren?"

Cynthia hastily offered seconds of dessert and coffee, but the dinner party was over.

Cleanliness is next to godliness. If you want to be close to God, get down on your knees... and scrub your floor. It usually works for me. Self-imposed humility (how can anyone hand scrub a floor and not feel humble?), with a small but healthy dose of self-satisfaction (a floor thus scrubbed is the cleanest). In my thinking, using a mop is the equivalent of putting a minister between yourself and God, but then I often get carried away with things.

My mental processes while scrubbing were halfway between thinking and praying. The practical part of my brain (the left side) was distracted by the physical act, leaving the creative part (the right) to problem-solve. Pastor Wallace clearly considered me dishonest. The grapevine had gotten wind of my baldness, interpreted it to mean cancer, and felt resentment toward me for misleading them when it hadn't been my intension to lead them anywhere. It made me think about intention. *Are we responsible for consequences that we don't intend? Can we lie without saying a word?* I decided long ago that words are an inflated currency, and that more often than not they are used to distract from the truth. The handicap of thinking in words gives language an undeserved credit rating. Thankfully, I am somewhat bilingual: I think in words and images.

I pulled my bureau out away from the wall, exposing a buildup of dust and grime that filled me with a mixture of revulsion and shame. These emotions were soon replaced, after I wiped the area clean, with a virtuous satisfaction. I leaned back on my haunches and smiled. Now I understood why Christians took a particular interest in people like me. To them, I was like the dirt in the corners. They saw in me the potential to make themselves feel proud. The person who saved my soul would be celebrated. How could they know that I was as incapable of playing along with them as they were of pole dancing?

Helen had been accumulating grievances toward Warren for many, many years. The collection had become too large to conceal. It had been swept under every carpet and allowed to build up behind every bureau. There were no more places to hide it. Like dust, each speck alone was insignificant; it was the accumulation that gave offence. On the evening of the dinner party, Warren contributed the last speck of dust and instigated a domestic apocalypse.

On the way home, he demanded an explanation. "What makes you think there is anything to tell about Kenny Duncan and the tax man?"

"I don't think, I know," answered Helen.

"You bitch."

"You made up that whole stupid story about me, and you did it just because you get a kick out of humiliating me in front of other people! Consider yourself lucky that I didn't tell the story myself!"

"Yeah, you just try it and see who believes you. You just try it!" Warren's voice cut through the air like a scythe.

"It would be interesting to find out who would believe me," said Helen, trying to insert more strength into her voice than she felt.

"I asked you how you know about it, and you'd bloody well better tell me!"

"Go to hell!" snapped Helen, looking out into the darkness. She felt both charged and alarmed by what she had done. Words came, like insects flying toward the windshield. "You bastard. You hateful, lying bastard! Give me a straightforward thief who admits what he is any day over a parsimonious fraud like you."

Helen could not face going to bed with Warren, so she settled in the living room. Once she was certain that Warren was in bed, she pulled her book from beneath her chair and began to write. *Holy lies, purified by your saintly saliva. Have you no fear of the God...?* She scratched it out. She was incapable of putting humour in the poem, as Rube had suggested. It had been several days since she had even attempted to write for Rube. What she came up with now shocked her.

He grinned like an inbred fool
one hand beneath the table
watching her
as he talked of her nakedness.
It didn't matter that it was a lie
or that she wasn't laughing.
It's called, "fun for one,"
"hillbilly humour."

Warren rose from behind his desk and closed the office door. He dialled Kenny's number.

"Ken. You by yourself?"

"Just a minute." Warren waited as Kenny left his house and got in his truck. The door slammed. "Yeah. What's up?"

"We've got a problem." Warren paused.

Kenny asked warily, "What kind of problem?"

"Helen knows."

"How could...? Shit, Warren, you didn't tell her?!"

"No, I swear. Not a word. She found out from somewhere else."

"That's... Where would she...? Who'd tell her?" Kenny's voice was slowing as if his batteries were going dead. "Nobody knows but us and the old lady. She doesn't know the old lady, does she?"

"I don't know how she could. She's never mentioned her. I mean, if she were a patient of Dr. Romaine's, it's not likely she'd get around to talking about her electrician to Helen. She wouldn't connect me to you. Nah, she knows from somewhere else."

The line was silent as they both thought. Then Warren asked, "Who'd you tell?"

"No one."

"Well somebody out there found out about it, tied me in with it, and filled Helen in."

"Can't see how. I swear to God, Warren. She must've found out from somewhere else. It's got to be the old lady. What did Helen say anyway? Couldn't you just ask her how she knows?"

Warren grunted. "You don't know Helen."

"Well, what did she say?"

"Just something about you and the tax man."

"Out of the blue?"

"Yeah. She was mad at me. She wanted to shock me. We were at Dick and Cynthia's."

"She said it in front of them?"

"Yup."

"That's all she said?"

"Yup."

"Thank the Good Lord."

The line was silent.

"You've got to shut her up, Warren. She's your wife. I don't want this around. It don't look good. Can't you just," he hesitated, "come down on her a little hard or something? Get a little mad?"

"She's stubborn."

"If she knows then who else does?"

"I'd bet her sister." Warren stopped, chose his words carefully, and then went on. "In fact, there's a chance that that's where she found out."

"Why'd you think that?"

"Her sister's... Well, let me put it this way: it wouldn't be the first time she knew something that she shouldn't have."

"I don't follow. What are you talking about?"

"She's weird. She's into stuff. You remember when Wallace caught her in the church? She's half witch."

Kenny's voice wavered. "You mean you think she's psychic and that's how she knows? For the love of Jesus! What else does she know?" Kenny sighed. "No, I don't believe in that stuff. There's got to be another way."

"It wasn't long ago that Randy saw her burning paintings down on the beach. Her and her friend there, like they were sacrifices or something. Could be she makes bargains. I don't know." Warren's speculations had gone too far, and he was now pulling back in embarrassment.

"You've got to get it out of Helen. Whatever way you can. Before it gets spread around."

The flight of the Tripper is feeble,
of short duration, and almost uncontrolled,
possibly because of their tiny hearts and
inadequate sense of direction.

Some men are born to be pall bearers. The duty encompasses all of their favourite features and interests. They get to wear a suit, be rigid and sombre, and carry a heavy burden in front of a gathering of people. Warren made an excellent pall bearer. He practised at home, replacing the coffin with a burden of anger and righteous responsibility. As the man of the house, the onus was on him to keep his family on God's path. This was not an easy task; at times it required corrective measures.

On Tuesday evening, after supper, Warren announced that he and Helen were going for a drive and it would be up to Sean and Harriet to clean up the dishes.

Helen followed him to the car reluctantly. They drove in silence. She cracked her window as if to reduce the pressure and waited for Warren to begin. He pulled into the park where they had had the church picnic and stopped with the car facing the beach. Helen stared ahead at the water. The tide was halfway out.

Warren asked, "Do you want to go for a walk?"

Helen looked at her cast. "No."

Warren grunted. "I forgot."

The water gleamed, brittle and frigid. A cluster of sandpipers skittered about at the leading edge. Helen's stomach was tightening, but her mind was super clear as she waited for Warren to begin. It occurred to her that this, her special place, might be forever contaminated by the conversation that was about to happen.

Warren said, "We've got to talk."

"Okay."

Silence. "So what do you have to say for yourself?"

Helen looked at him and then turned her head slowly toward her side window. She didn't answer. He had no idea how far away she was from the day when that kind of question would make her shudder. She shook her head.

Warren asked, "So?"

"If you want to ask me something, Warren, make it a clear question."

Feeling the intensity of Warren's glare, Helen silently willed him to go ahead and hit her. She stared ahead, allowing the waves to push time forward, measuring, like the hands of a clock, the pulse of the earth.

Finally, Warren asked, "So what were you talking about? This business about Kenny?"

"That's not what we *need* to talk about."

"I think it is."

What would life be like if Warren were able to simply sit here beside her and rejoice in the beauty of God's creation, the breathtaking wonder of the light on the ocean, the grace of the seagulls, the gentle progression of the clouds across the sky? What would it be like if he were able to give up the need to control? If he could just relax? Surely God never intended for life to be a struggle full of so much angst and obligation.

"Helen! I asked you a question."

"Are you more concerned about this business with Kenny than you are with us, our relationship?"

Warren issued a theatrical exhale. "You're tinkering in areas that are none of your business, Helen. A person can get in trouble that way."

"Oh?" Helen looked directly at Warren. He met her stare for a minute, then turned to scowl at the dashboard.

"Warren, I'm tired of having you humiliate me in public. The other night, it wasn't the first time."

"Oh, I was only joking. You know that." Warren tapped the steering wheel. "It didn't get nasty 'til you made it that way."

"That's not true. The whole thing was nasty. What you were doing to me was nasty. And here's the worst part: you enjoyed it." Helen stopped. A car had pulled into the parking lot, and she was hoping it was no one they knew. Two teenagers bounced out and, slamming their doors, set off, hand in hand, up the beach.

Helen continued, "I don't know why you enjoy it, but you do. And it's something we're going to have to look at if we're going to go on."

"What do you mean if we're going to go on? What kind of thing is that to say?" Warren's fingers were flexing and gripping the steering wheel, flexing and gripping, suggesting the kind of preparatory warm up athletes go through before their practice.

Helen looked down at her hands and examined her nails as if she were considering their need for polish. She was stalling for time, calculating the risk of what she was about to suggest. She felt as if she were initiating something, even though the *something* had started long ago and she was just acknowledging it. "I think it's time we went for marriage counselling."

"Marriage counselling." Warren was incredulous. "I'm not going to go for marriage counselling. I'm a counsellor myself. How would that look?"

"That doesn't mean anything. We're still all screwed up, and we need counselling." Helen was strengthened and somewhat fascinated by her sense of relief. Truthfully, she felt beyond the help of counselling, but she had recognized the value of suggesting it.

"One of us is screwed up," said Warren.

Helen's smile had nothing to do with humour. She nodded her head in agreement. "True."

"I brought you here to talk to you about this business with Kenny."

"So talk to me. What do you want to say about Kenny?"

"I want an explanation. Why did you threaten Kenny with Revenue Canada?

"When did I threaten Kenny?

"You said something about Kenny and Revenue Canada. What were you talking about?"

"Lack of respect. That's what I was talking about."

"Respect!" Warren spit out the word indignantly.

"Yes, respect. You don't treat me with any respect, and I find it more difficult every day to respect you, what with all the lying and everything."

"That's your problem! I am the leader of our family. Don't you forget that. I didn't ask to be a man, to have all the responsibility, but that's the way it is. The Bible makes it very clear who the leader is in a family and that they are to be treated with respect."

"Leaders don't have to bully."

"When have I ever bullied you?"

"Right now."

"I'm trying to make you see some sense."

"You're trying to avoid talking about the party."

"You're exaggerating. As usual."

"I am not exaggerating. You made that story up."

"Can't you take a joke?"

"That wasn't a real joke."

"Everybody else laughed."

"At my expense. If it had been something that had really

happened, it would have been different. It still wouldn't have been okay to humiliate me, but I could have considered it poor judgment. But you were lying, and you wouldn't admit it. I can't forgive you for that." Helen looked at the side of Warren's face. "You made it look like I was the one lying."

"You're making a big deal out of nothing."

"Lying isn't nothing in church. Why is it nothing when you do it?"

"I wasn't lying. I was teasing."

"You lie, Warren. Think of who you're talking to. I know. I know better than anyone what you do. You lied when you told me the lawnmower didn't work."

"That was none of your business. You concentrate on the inside of the house and leave the outside to me."

Helen sighed in resignation. "You make it impossible for me to respect you, and then you order me to treat you with respect. Warren, I mean this. I'm getting close to the end." She shook her head. "I don't feel like I love you anymore."

Warren turned toward her and said, plaintively, "We didn't have any problems until Rube moved back."

"Rube's got nothing to do with this."

"Well, you're acting more like her every day."

"Thank you. But there's not a lot for us if this is the best you can do at discussing things. Can't you see that I'm trying to do something here?"

"Ah, Helen. Now, honey, you make too much out of things. It's just your nerves. You bring your stress from work home, and then you get yourself all upset. You know I love you. I was just trying to have a good time at the party. Why don't we just say lesson learned and forget about it?"

"I'm not forgetting about it. I want an apology, and I want you to admit to the others that were at the party that the skinny-dipping didn't happen."

Warren drew back and snorted, "I'll apologize when I've made a mistake, not when I haven't done anything wrong!"

Helen said quietly, "Warren, I think I can stand maybe three more of these kind of incidents, but after that I'll consider it *your* decision that one of us moves out."

"You would do that to our family, to our children?"

"No, Warren. *You* would be doing that to our children."

When Warren reached for Helen in bed that night, she rolled over, turning her back to him. She was deciding whether or not to move to the couch when she felt his hand cupping her breast. She pushed it away, but it returned, staking its claim on territories up and down her body. She cringed when he entered her, then lay still, waiting for his snores, thinking of the bedroom she'd had as a girl. She remembered the little plastic tray she'd had on her bureau with three covered dishes, pearly pink plastic, for bobby pins and elastics. She thought about the shelf on the wall full of teddy bears and the brush and mirror set that Rube had given her for one of her birthdays.

She remembered what it felt like to be able to close her door and know that no one would come in without knocking.

The Gospel According to Pastor Wallace
Mother's Day Eve, 1995

Pastor Wallace leaned forward in his chair, rested his elbows on his desk, and began rubbing his hands together in a slow wringing motion. He frowned dramatically and worked his lips in and out of puckers as if struggling with a deep thought.

Pastor Obie waited.

Pastor Wallace stretched his fingers out straight, and then ever so slowly brought his hands together in a "here is the church" formation. He leaned his chin on his outstretched thumbs. The effect was spoiled somewhat by the "steeple" of his forefingers pushing upwards on his nose, enlarging his nostrils and giving him a pig-like appearance.

Pastor Obie scarcely noticed, so intent was he on discovering the matter behind these tension-building theatrics.

Pastor Wallace maintained this pose for several minutes, staring soberly at his desk, and then he rolled his eyes upward and looked sternly at Pastor Obie from beneath shaggy eyebrows.

"What do you know about psychics?" he asked.

Pastor Obie's head jerked in surprise. "Psychics?"

"Yeah, have you come across any?"

"No, not directly." Pastor Obie hesitated, but his face opened like a time-lapse lily before closing down again. His initial intrigue was complicated by a memory of one time when, while on vacation, he had laid down his palm for a woman claiming to be a fortuneteller. He didn't know what had made him do it. She had obviously been a fraud. He said, "I've had the odd person from time to time claim to have had an experience." He paused. "They were convinced that they had been given foreknowledge of something—usually isolated incidents. I find that if you don't make much of them they tend to die down. I'm sure there're all kinds of rational explanations that could be given. Not that these are irrational people, but that maybe they're under a little stress. I've never had anything directly like that myself."

Pastor Wallace said, "I'm back to thinking 'bout Warren's sister-in-law, Rube. Warren mentioned that she dabbled in the occult; he said she sometimes knew things that she had no way of knowing. Said she'd told Helen things. At least he thinks she told her. Wouldn't elaborate but said Helen knew something that she shouldn't have, couldn't have known. When Warren asked her how she knew it she said she was psychic, that Rube was teaching her how to be. This was before they separated. Warren didn't know what to make of it. Kind of gives you the willies. Makes you wonder just what they know. I don't like it at all. If God had intended for us to be able to read one another's minds he'd have, he'd have..." Pastor Wallace searched his mind for what he wanted to say. "He'd have given us more sense. I mean another sense."

Pastor Obie scratched the side of his neck. "World would be in a real mess if we could all read one another's minds. I don't believe it. I think she found out about whatever it was some other way."

Pastor Wallace looked doubtful. His head nodded slightly as if in agreement, but his eyebrows took a severe nosedive.

Janet made the arrangements. Helen had been adamant that she would not risk being seen entering a psychic's house, so the plan was for the meeting to take place in Janet's apartment.

Helen expected the woman to have a New Age look—dangly turquoise earrings and Indian cotton or, at the very least, black clothes and bangle bracelets. Fran Brampton wore a pink sweatsuit. She appeared to be at least fifty and wore her greying hair short and wavy. She looked as ordinary as a back door.

Fran settled on the sofa with books on either side. Her tape recorder waited to be fed in the middle of the coffee table. She said, "Sit down," indicating the other end of the couch. "Did you bring the dates?"

As requested, Helen had prepared a list of birth dates for the people in her life. The list was in her pocket. She said, "I'd rather you just talked to me a bit first to see how much you can tell me without them."

"Fine." Fran stared for a minute at a carton of books at the far side of the room. She then raised her gaze to where the wall met the ceiling. "You're married."

Helen said, "Yes."

Fran bobbed her head slowly. "You have two children."

"Yes."

"I think a boy and a girl."

Helen nodded.

Fran said, "But you're not happy." This statement did not have the same tentative tone as the previous ones. Fran went on. "Your parents, are they both deceased?"

"Yes."

"What were their birth dates?"

Helen told her, and she wrote them down. "Bad match. They weren't happy. Your mother died first?"

"Yes."

"Your birth date?"

Helen provided it.

"And your husband's?"

Helen handed her the list.

Fran pushed her lips out as she considered the dates. She consulted one of her books, running her forefinger across the chart. Helen noticed that her nails were bitten and looked sore. "I see your husband as being rather solid. Would you describe him that way?"

"Yes," said Helen wryly. "That's a good word to describe him."

"I see that it's both good and bad. Umm. He's dependable but, umm, rigid."

"Yes."

"You're worried about your son. It's almost like you want him to be a little more like your father."

"Yes." There was a note of surprise in Helen's voice, as if she had only just now realized this.

"There's something... people around you that would put pressure on you, kind of an ugly thing. Don't feed into that energy. It's something that you're attracting to yourself right now." She paused as she consulted her book. "It will continue for about another six months. Then it'll be as if a cloud has been lifted. Umm. Have you felt that yourself? It's almost as if there's secrecy surrounding you. I see it here in your sister's chart and in your husband's and in yours. It's kind of amazing."

Helen shifted her position, unsure whether a response was required of her.

Fran went on. "There's something, umm, coming up around a hospital, umm. I can't tell you who. It shouldn't be anything too serious."

"I work in a hospital."

"I don't see you as a healer."

"I'm not. I work in a doctor's office."

"I see someone as a patient."

"I broke my ankle not too long ago."

"I can see that. No, this is coming up. But don't worry about that." Fran leaned back into the cushions, shifted, then pulled one out from behind her back and tossed it on the floor. She wiggled into place. "That's better." She closed her eyes and tapped her thigh for a minute, then turned and looked at Helen. "You've known your husband in a past life, you know."

Helen avoided meeting Fran's eyes.

"I believe in more than one lifetime. You were together in Australia. I see you as a guard. It was a penal colony, and he was a convict." Fran's eyes narrowed, and she frowned. "Umm and once in the south. He was your father in that one."

"I don't believe in past lives."

Fran shrugged indifferently and said, "Many people don't." She reached into a little cloth bag beside her and rattled some small smooth stones. Then she pulled her hand from the bag and examined the contents. "A change is coming up. A big change. You have a rough patch ahead. You have something built into your chart that says you're meant to shed some burdens this year. This is coming up. It's your starting point for this year." Fran's eyes closed. She leaned her head against the back of the couch. It gave Helen a chance to study her more closely, to wonder who this person was when she wasn't being a psychic. Did she have a husband? Children? Did she believe in God?

"I see a blue house. Do you live in a blue house?"

"No."

"Does anyone you know live in a blue house?"

Helen thought for a minute. "No, I can't think of anyone."

"Well, I see some of this negative secrecy mess around a blue house. Oh well. We'll leave that. I see a bird feeder outside a window, and I see you happy."

It was Helen's turn to shrug.

Fran went on in this fashion until the half hour was up. Then she clicked off the tape recorder, popped out the tape, and handed it to Helen in such a matter-of-fact way that it made Helen feel foolish. She'd just been ripped off thirty bucks.

The contents of the session, once strained through the cheesecloth of Helen's skepticism, were pretty thin. She had sorted all of the information into categories: she's reaching, that could apply to just about anyone, we'll wait and see about that one, and so on. Fran had been dead on about details like the number of children and whatnot, but Janet could have filled her in on that stuff. Helen didn't really know Janet well; their only contact was through Rube and then not often, so it was easy to be suspicious. She pocketed the tape and rejoined Rube downstairs in the bookstore. On the way home, it occurred to Helen that it might be judicious to not keep the tape at her house. She gave it to Rube, saying, "You can listen to it if you want."

Rube listened to it at the first opportunity she got. It all made sense to her except for the part about the blue house.

Mates of Trippers are seldom seen with other birds unless they are preoccupied with food-finding or unless the Tripper is present. Mates are not allowed to sing.

I knew nothing of the dinner party and the ensuing fight until I stopped in at Helen's house to check if she needed anything. She said, "Yeah, I need to get out of this house. I'm climbing the walls." The last week of her work leave was passing too slowly for her liking.

"Come on over."

"Can I stay overnight?"

I couldn't have been more surprised by her request. "Sure. Of course. Is everything alright?"

"Just need a break."

Gordon joined us for the evening. Helen was coerced into letting him sign her cast. He wrote, *Lucky you. I love getting plastered!* We ate pizza and discussed Helen's session with Fran. She agreed to let Gordon listen to the tape. He leaned forward on the table, his head resting on his chin and his finger tapping his lips as his eyes moved around, sometimes pausing on Helen, sometimes on me. Helen's eyes were steadier. By now she was familiar with the results of the session. Now and then she stole a glance at Gordon, but seldom at me.

Gordon frowned when it was finished and muttered, "Interesting."

A deck of cards appeared. We decided on rummy. Gordon's first insults were towards me—a strategy to ensure that Helen didn't take offence when he began directing his jibes in her direction. His risks at card play were extravagant and his losses were many and thoroughly mourned, but his cards were laid with the flourish of confident royalty. Over all, his process of losing toothpicks was uninhibited. It was infectious. He accused Helen of cheating, so she cheated. He challenged her to bet money, so she threw a five-dollar bill down on the table and lost it to him. He slapped her hand when she reached to draw an extra card and giggled at the shocked look on her face. Gordon left at ten thirty. Helen and I went to bed shortly after. She slept soundly on my cot, in the kitchen, three feet from the wood stove.

The pain had begun in the afternoon. Harriet complained to her father after supper. He looked at her blankly. An hour later she told him that the pains were getting worse. He said, in a reprimanding tone, "Now look, Harriet. You're just doing this because your mother is away. It won't do you any good. It won't bring her back, so do something that will take your mind off it. Don't you have a book you could read?"

Warren was sprawled in his recliner, watching television. His eyes remained on the screen as he spoke to Harriet, but his thoughts were on neither her nor the golf game. Ken, who he'd asked to sort of observe Rube's house from the beach side, had just reported in.

"So what did you see?"

Gordon had arrived with a pizza. Ken had moved closer and had crouched outside a window. "That friend of Rube's was there. They kind of huddled together listening to something. It wasn't music; it sounded more like people talking. I couldn't hear what it was. They looked serious though."

"Didn't you hear anything?"

"They didn't talk loudly enough. I had to be careful. What would I have said if they'd seen me?"

"Well that doesn't help us much."

"If you want more than that, hire a detective. Oh, I just thought of something. He wrote something on Helen's cast. You may want to check that out."

Warren said, "I've got to go." Harriet was standing before him once again. "Can I call Mom at Aunt Rube's?"

"No. I don't want your mother disturbed."

Harriet returned to her room. An hour later Sean appealed to his father, saying that Harriet was in a lot of pain. Warren sighed heavily. "Alright," he pointed the remote at the television, "we'll make a trip to the hospital." He pressed the power button. "There."

Harriet was operated on for appendicitis later that night. Warren promised that her mother would be there to see her first thing in the morning.

Rube dropped Helen off at her driveway. When she got inside, the house was empty. Helen wandered from room to room, like a mother cat whose kittens have been shifted to a new location. She gave Rube ten minutes to get home before she dialled her number.

"No one's here. There isn't a note or anything."

Rube said, "Relax. They're allowed to go out."

"Why didn't they leave a note?"

"Because they're coming right back. It's not the middle of the night. It's normal for people to go places.... It's only ten thirty in the morning. Have a cup of tea for God's sake."

Helen called Rube again at noon. "They're still not back." There was silence on the other end of the line. Then Rube said, "Sounds to me like Warren's just being inconsiderate. He wants you to worry. I'm sure everything is fine."

Helen washed the dishes and settled on the couch with her cast propped on the coffee table, cushioned by a bedroom pillow. She turned on the TV. It was almost two when Warren called. His first angry words were, "Look, aren't you going to come to the hospital?"

There was a pause. Helen's back straightened. Panic began to set seeds throughout her body. "What are you talking about? What's going on?"

"She's asking when you're going to come. She doesn't understand. I don't understand."

"Wait a minute. What's wrong? What's happened to her? Do you mean Harriet? Is she all right?"

"Your own daughter and you won't even visit her in the hospital?"

"Warren, what are you talking about? What's the matter with you?"

"You might say it's just an appendix, but it seems pretty important to her. She's asking for you, and I think the least you could do is to take a few minutes to visit her!"

At this, he hung up. Helen stood with her mouth agape. *He's flipped. He's gone right over the edge.* He had been talking as if he couldn't hear her.

I drove Helen to the hospital. I shrugged when Helen told me about the telephone conversation, saying, "Try to figure Warren out." I debated over whether I should wear a hat. Unsure, I grabbed a billed Gap cap, leaving Helen to make the final judgment about whether my hair was respectable. She didn't seem to notice.

Helen said, "Nothing he said connected with what I was saying. It didn't make sense."

I let Helen out at the entrance before parking. A group of wheelchairs were clustered to the right of the foyer like employees gossiping on break. I commandeered one for Helen.

As we left the elevator, Helen caught fragments of a conversation coming from the nurses' station: "...been throwing up, poor thing. Her mother hasn't been in...." It ended abruptly as we approached. Helen's inquiries at the desk brought about a swift change from the unmistakable tone of disgust to one of reserved embarrassment blended with unkind judgment.

We found Harriet in a ward, propped up in bed, frowning into a teen magazine. A blonde girl who Helen guessed to be seven or eight years old was staring at a television set that was suspended above her bed. Next to her, a form appeared to be sleeping with its back to them. The third bed, the one beside Harriet, was empty, its sheets and blanket as smooth as the first snow. Harriet's head jerked in their direction when they entered the room.

"Where were you? Why didn't you come? I've been waiting."

"Honey, nobody told me you were in here. I was at Rube's. You know that. I got home this morning and no one was there. Your father didn't leave a note or anything." Helen kissed Harriet on the cheek. "He didn't call me until a few minutes ago. I came right away." She smoothed a few of Harriet's stray hairs back away from her face and tucked them tenderly behind her ear.

"Why would he do that?" It was clear by her tone and sharp look that Harriet was accusing Helen of lying.

"I don't know. You'll have to ask him. How are you doing?"

Harriet didn't answer immediately. She was being expected to undo her anger too quickly. It had been hours, and she had worked herself into a state. Things didn't make sense. The idea that her mother might not have known about her attack and subsequent operation hadn't occurred to her. She needed to consider the possibility. Accepting it required that she also accept her father as capable, for some reason, of not telling.

"I'm okay. No thanks to you," Harriet added. She slung her magazine down. They took my appendix out, you know. You wouldn't believe the pain I was in last night."

"Last night? You came in last night?" Helen cast a sharp glance at me. "Warren knew where I was. Why didn't he call me?"

"Punishment perhaps?" I suggested, making a face.

"For what?"

"Enjoying yourself? I hear it's a sin."

"I'm thirsty," said Harriet. "It's so dry in here."

"I'll get you some water." I ventured down the hall in search of the kitchenette. By the time I returned, Harriet had forgiven her mother. I offered, after another fifteen minutes, to give Helen and Harriet some time alone together. I asked Helen to walk me to the elevator, and then, when we were out of Harriet's earshot, I said, "I think I understand the weird conversation you had with Warren."

"You do?"

"Yeah. Look where the payphone is—right beside the nurses' station. His end of the phone call was for the benefit of the nurses!"

There were four blue houses between Brood Bay and the town of Yarmouth. I had never paid them any mind before, but now I counted them and wondered. I packed my paints and my portable easel into my van and knocked on the door of the blue house closest to Brood Bay. No one was home. I moved on to the second blue house. An elderly man opened the door. I said, "Excuse me, but I'm an artist and I was wondering—would you mind if I did a painting of your house?"

He snorted, then answered gruffly, "As long as you don't expect me to buy it."

I said, "Oh no, of course not." I thanked him and trudged off to set up in a field to the north of his house. I didn't bother to start a painting. Something told me this wasn't the place I was looking for. According to Helen, Ken had referred to a woman on the videotape. I spent ten minutes doing a sketch, packed up my gear, and set off for the third blue house. In the back of my mind was the worry that there could be dozens of blue houses on all of the side roads between Brood Bay and town.

My knock was answered by a woman looking to be in her early seventies. She eyed me sharply through thick glasses and squinted as I made my request, as if reducing her eyesight improved her hearing. She wore a man's flannel shirt thrown over a blue polyester sweatshirt. Her hair looked homemade both in colour and cut—orangey tufts with grey roots. But she was agreeable in an abrupt way, declaring, almost tersely, "I'm Gert. I don't mind if you need to use my bathroom or if you'd like a glass of water. Feel free."

I settled at the far, unmowed edge of a wide lawn. The house had little appeal as a subject. A large window had been punched into the wall next to the driveway, and a veranda had been removed, leaving evidence of where the roof had once joined the house. Concrete steps now sat in its place. A confusion of containers, chosen for their ability to hold dirt, littered the area around the back door. Fifty shades of green sprouted, spread, and trailed out of them, spattered with a disorganized conglomeration of blossoms. A badly weathered lawn chair sat, like a throne, in the midst of the jumble.

I sketched directly on my gesso-primed Masonite with a soluble colour pencil before roughing in my colours with oil paint. I then worked on the sky, catching glimpses of Gert at the window every ten or fifteen minutes. *Good, she's interested. She'll want to chat.* When forty-five minutes had passed, I rose and stretched, moving my body this way and that, going through various tai chi positions. Gert appeared at the back door.

"Would you like a cup of tea or coffee? Water maybe? Or something?"

I smiled. "Sure, I need a little break."

I followed Gert into the kitchen. An old oilcloth covered the floor, its pattern worn away from too many decades of travel back and forth between the sink and the stove. A stack of *National Geographic* magazines climbed almost as high as the arm of a rocking chair that sat next to the window.

"You can sit there." Gert motioned to one of the chrome chairs at the table, plugged in the kettle, then turned, her hands on her hips, and asked, "What'll it be?"

I said, "Tea please," guessing that it would be the easiest to make.

Gert tossed two bags into a stained Pyrex teapot, then faced me as she waited for the water to boil. Her hands were once again on her hips.

"How's it coming? The picture."

"Oh, good. It's a nice day to be painting outside. A few too many bugs though."

"Yeah, well. I prefer to be outdoors in nice weather digging in the dirt or something."

"I noticed that you like to garden. I'm putting all your planters in my painting. They'll add colour."

"Yeah, they will." Gert opened a plastic bag of sugared doughnuts and dumped half of them on a plate. She plunked it down without ceremony in the middle of the table. "Can't imagine why you'd want to paint this old house though. It needs work."

"So does mine, but it's a roof over my head. As long as it keeps me warm and dry that's the main thing." I threw out a line, fishing. "It costs so much to get work done now."

Gert snorted, "Tell me about it."

I waited, thinking that Gert had been hooked, but her attention had turned to the boiling water. She concentrated on filling the teapot, switched the burner beneath the pot on low, and then turned, rubbing her wrists. "Arthritis." Gert sat down on the opposite side of the table.

I faked concern until I felt I could change the subject back to the house without being rude. A metal disc covered the chimney hole above the electric stove. I nodded toward it and said, "Must have been an oil stove here at one time. Or wood?"

"Yeah, oil. Used to be a room heater in the sitting room too. Then we put the furnace in. It's good, but I miss the stoves. I like standin' next to heat. George wanted the furnace."

"Is George your husband?"

"Yeah. He's been dead for ten years."

"Oh."

Gert moved to the stove, but I jumped up and said, "Let me pour that for you—your wrists."

"Er, thanks. He died of a heart attack. Right there." Gert pointed to the rocking chair next to the window.

"It must have been a shock to you. Did you find him?"

"I found him. Who else would?" She shot me a sharp look.

We sat back down at the table.

I waited a minute before asking, "How do you manage without a man around to," I paused and flicked my hand, "do the repairs and things?"

"I do what I can. Some don't get done. I hire some."

I said, "It costs a lot to hire things to be done now. I can't believe what they get by the hour."

Gert sipped her tea. "Need to get someone you can trust. I used to get a fella lived over the way, handy doing all sorts of things. George never was that handy. Donald always did most of the..." Her voice trailed off.

I asked, "Used to?"

"Dead," Gert stated as she shoved the doughnuts toward me.

"Oh."

It had been years since I'd eaten a sugared doughnut. Gert tugged a napkin from a ceramic holder decorated with black cats and offered it across the table. I placed it next to my cup and set my doughnut in the middle of it. I tried again. "I need to get someone to go up on my roof. I've got a leak around my chimney." This was a lie, but Gert would never know. Gert just shook her head as if offering condolences. I waited, and then asked, "Do you know anyone that's good at things like that?"

Gert puckered her nose and pushed her glasses in place. She seemed to be thinking about it. Half a doughnut later she said, "No."

I was beginning to think this was the wrong house. I'd have to finish the painting up quickly so that I could move on to the next one. When I had drained my cup, I asked, "How about sitting in the lawn chair so I can put you in my painting?"

Gert threw her head back and guffawed. "You are crazy. I knew it. You are crazy."

I laughed. The change in Gert had been immediate. I coaxed, "Come on. You should be there with your flowers."

"It's not close up, is it?"

"No, you'll only be this big." I measured an inch with my thumb and forefinger.

Gert said, "Even that's enough to spoil your picture." She chuckled again as she rose to put the empty cups in the sink. When Gert reached for the doughnuts, a pamphlet that had been lying beneath them caught my eye. It was from the Jehovah's Witnesses. Gert noticed the direction of my gaze. She snatched up the pamphlet and tossed it in a little metal garbage can beside the table, then looked me up and down and said, "Don't know what you're inclined toward religion-wise, but I've little use for some of them."

I said, "I pretty much keep away from all of them."

Gert stared at a place on the wall and nodded with thoughtful deliberation before cocking one eyebrow and declaring, "Can't trust someone just because they go to church. No guarantee from that."

Bingo! I am in the right place. I sat back down.

Gert outlined her story slowly, calculating the accuracy of her marks before laying them down. With some prompting from me, she filled in the details of how Ken had tried to take advantage of her. She said that when she had proved to be brighter than he expected, he had made threats. It was not a pretty story.

Like fat on the surface of a cooling stew, bitterness covered the good bits of Helen's family life and destroyed her appetite for marriage. She wanted something to happen, something dramatic that would spring the cage door wide open. She wanted it, but she didn't hope for it. Hoping had begun to feel like an immature pastime, an emotion from the past. Anger, however, settled nicely about Helen, filling empty places, feeding her imagination. Anger kept her going.

School started without Harriet. The house took on the atmosphere of a convalescent home with exaggerated displays of consideration. To Harriet, Warren was contrite, but to Helen he offered no apologies. Helen's cast finally came off, revealing skin as white and withered as old peeled potatoes. Helen sat on the couch with her leg stretched out on the extra cushions, stroking the sickly skin with morbid fascination. Harriet wrinkled her nose. "Eew, that's gross."

"I wonder what people look like after six months in solitary confinement without light," mused Helen. "They must be this pale."

"They probably wouldn't be shrivelled," said Harriet. "They'd at least have air. Your leg didn't have any air."

"You're right."

They were waiting for the Oprah Winfrey show. Helen's

coffee steamed on the table next to her. Harriet jiggled her glass of tropical fruit juice, clinking the ice. Three minutes to go. Oprah was the high point of their afternoon.

Without preamble Harriet blurted, "I don't understand why Dad didn't tell you about my operation. He said he'd call you."

Helen paused, soberly considering her options before answering. "Your father is a hard man to understand. I don't even know why he does things."

"Was he mad at you or something?" Harriet had set her glass down.

"Perhaps."

"He makes me mad sometimes."

Helen delayed her next words, like a skydiver at the open door of a plane. "He makes me angry quite often," she paused, "and I'm getting tired of it." She looked over at Harriet. "He doesn't have to be the way he is. I don't like having you and Sean think this is normal."

There was a long silence.

"I'm thinking of leaving him."

Harriet looked at her quickly. "To go where?"

"To get a place of my own. Our own. An apartment."

Harriet's pupils dilated. "How can you do that? You can't just do that."

Helen sighed heavily. "Why can't I? If he can choose to act the way he does, I can choose to leave. It won't be easy for any of us, but we'll work it out. You could spend time with both of us. If I go." Helen shook her head and raised open hands in a gesture of discouraged failure. "I'm so tired of being angry all the time."

Harriet said, "She's on." She pointed to the television. Helen realized that she was holding the remote, and she turned up the volume.

During the first commercial break, Harriet said, "Why does he have to be that way?"

Helen answered, "Good question."

I presented Helen with the painting of the blue house after Warren went to work. She looked at it and said, "What an ugly house."

"Yes, but did you notice what colour it is?"

"Blue would be my first guess."

"Yeah. And remember what the psychic said about a blue house?"

"Oh for heaven's sake. So the psychic mentioned a blue house, and you ran out and found one to paint. Do you think that's going to impress me? What's that supposed to prove?"

"Do you know who lives in this particular house?"

There was sarcasm in Helen's voice. "Obviously I don't."

"A woman who hired Ken to do work for her."

A look of incredulity passed over Helen's face. "The son of a gun. How do you know that?"

"I started checking out the blue houses. There aren't that many of them." I shrugged. "An artist can do that. People talk to artists."

"Okay, but... how did she know that? Fran, I mean."

"I don't know. That's just how this psychic business works. I told you she's good."

"Unbelievable. So, what did this woman say?"

I crossed my arms and settled back into the easy chair somewhat smugly. "Ken overcharged her for the work. Almost double what he'd quoted her. She hadn't gotten the quote in writing. He claimed that it was necessary, but she'd been keeping track of how much most things cost and their hours. She knew he was gouging her, so she asked to see the receipts." I laughed. "He showed them to her, and she noticed that he was listing, on his invoices, the taxes in the wrong order." I shook my head. "You wouldn't know it to look at her, but she's one sharp cookie. Anyway, she checked to see if Ken was even registered to pay taxes, and he's not.

Apparently, he works under the table. She asked him about it because the taxes alone on her job were several hundred dollars, and he got really high and mighty and told her to mind her own business. Bad move. Baaad move. If you'd met Gert." I laughed. "She's a crusty one. She said she threatened to report him, and that's when things got nasty."

"I'm surprised that she didn't report him anyway."

"She thought about it. Almost did. But he had mentioned, when he was doing the work, that he had kids. She worried about the kids. Said it wasn't their fault that they had an asshole father. What if he went to prison or something for tax evasion? What would that do to the kids?"

"Hmmm, I suppose. And deep down, if he bullied her... when you live alone..." Helen's voice trailed off.

"I guess he pointed out that she didn't have many smoke detectors in the house, said she should really look into getting some. They'd be helpful if she ever had a fire in the night."

"Wow." Helen shook her head. "Well, I'm not really surprised. That's sort of what I figured happened based on what I heard on the tape." Helen narrowed her eyes. "Are you sure you didn't plant that bit about the blue house on the psychic, that you didn't find out who she was some other way?"

"I swear."

"Then it's amazing." Helen looked like a curtain had gone up on a new play. "I want to listen to the tape again. I've forgotten a lot of what she said. Now I'm kind of curious to know."

The last car payment was due in October. With the car paid off, Helen reasoned, it would be easier to leave. She'd sold the camcorder and kept the five hundred dollars in an envelope in her purse. Warren, however, began to look at new cars in

September. He drove slowly through the lots after picking Helen up from work. She tried to discourage him, but he didn't listen.

Helen knew it was time to leave Warren when, on a Friday night near the end of September, he took a car for a test drive and told the salesman that he'd be back for it the following week, after he'd arranged financing. She made one more attempt to reason with him. He told her to leave the vehicle department to him. She asked if she could leave paying for it to him as well, but he didn't answer. The following day, Saturday, Helen sat alone in her kitchen. The empty day stretched ahead. Shiny surfaces glared at her, hard and reflective. She went into the living room. The faded drapes reminded her of Rube's dream about upsetting Warren by uncovering a window. That dream reminded her of another one from the previous night. She pulled her book from beneath her chair and recorded it before calling Rube. "What do you make of this? I dreamed I was walking down the street with another woman and we noticed a beautiful white bird. I think it was a seagull, only it was bright white, almost sparkly, and it was showing off for us like the planes do in an air show, turning over and over in the air. I said to the other woman, 'I wish I could fly,' and she took me to a building across the street. It seemed like she was a research scientist or something and I had donated a rare bumblebee to them for studies. Anyway, she tells me that they have discovered that the bumblebees have very simple brains and though they are able to fly, they are only capable of two functions other than flying. What do you think it means?"

Rube hesitated. "What do you think it means?"

"I don't know. You're the expert."

"It's your dream. I can only guess." Rube hesitated before suggesting, "I'll tell you what I think, but I could be wrong."

"Fine. Go for it."

"Well, I think I heard somewhere that bumblebees shouldn't

be able to fly—what with the size and shape of their bodies compared to their tiny little wings—but they don't know that they can't fly, so they do it anyway. They just flap their wings that much faster and harder, and they do it. I think it's telling you that if you want to fly you can. Don't think too much about it. Just do it."

"That's what I thought. Thanks."

Helen examined the living room. Harriet's sweatshirt was slung over the back of the couch, Warren's socks were in a ball in front of his chair, and a banana peel (she remembered Sean eating a banana the previous night) lay on the coffee table. She wandered down the hall to the bedroom; sat on the edge of the bed, on her side by the wall; and stared down at the carpet.

She expected to cry, but her eyes were dry. She looked up at the open closet. The sight of her clothes touching Warren's repelled her so much that she stood and pushed them apart before picking up the phone on the bedside table and dialling a number she had memorized from an apartment *For Rent* sign. Two minutes later, she was once again sitting on the bed, this time considering her options for getting to Yarmouth to keep the appointment she had just made.

Taxis were not part of her normal life, and she dialled the number with an uneasy suspicion that normalcy would soon to be a thing of the past.

The apartment had been vacant for over a month, and Helen had, more than once, pressed her face to the glass of the front window, feeding her imagination, memorizing every detail. A duplex, it was snugly situated on a narrow street of houses whose fronts were smack up to the sidewalk. One stone step was all that was needed to reach the front door. With their low foundations, they appeared to be kneeling face to face with the houses across the street. In spite of the close proximity to the neighbours, Helen imagined she would have more privacy than she'd had in years. The feature that attracted her most was the secluded yard at the back, small but enclosed by a high board fence.

The front door of the apartment stood wide open. When she entered she experienced an almost fearful reverence, fearful because of the enormity of what she was doing and reverent because she was entering her dream.

The stairs were exactly where she had imagined them. This gave her an inordinate amount of satisfaction. She called out, "Hello!" A woman appeared immediately from the direction of the living room and introduced herself as Barbara. Barbara was tall and slender, in her late thirties, and she had short dark hair. She wore a long-sleeve, navy blue sweater, jeans, and white runners.

"It's frost-free," she said, pointing to the refrigerator, which sat with its doors propped open. "The rent's four hundred, heat included. The same furnace heats both sides of the duplex. You would be required to sign a year-long lease." Barb had clearly done this before. Many times. She scrutinized Helen. "Do you work?"

"Yes, I'm a receptionist for Dr. Romaine."

Barbara nodded her approval. "You could walk there from here."

"Yes, I know."

"If you decide that you're interested, I'll need for you to fill this out." She produced a sheet of paper from a manila folder and laid it beside a ballpoint pen on the kitchen counter. "It's an application form. I'd need references. I'll wait outside. Take your time."

Helen said, "Thank you," and glanced around the kitchen one more time before passing through the archway to the living room. The walls were apartment white, the carpet a gold twist, dated but obviously cared for and in reasonably decent condition. She surveyed the back yard, taking inventory of the rose bushes and flowerbeds. Upstairs she discovered three bedrooms, small but adequate, and a bathroom.

She returned to the living room and paused at the window, trying to work up the nerve to move forward. She considered the possibility of going home and continuing on as if nothing had happened—in the short term it would be the easiest solution—but then the memories of Warren at his most obnoxious slithered in. Warren, across the table, lying and enjoying her humiliation; Warren speaking to her in a tone designed to diminish her; Warren turning the nurses against her by pretending she had refused to visit Harriet in the hospital. Her expression hardened as she lingered in the frustrated fury that these memories inspired. She milked them for anger until, with shaking hands, she was able to fill out the application form, find Barbara, and declare with resolve, "I want it. As soon as possible."

Barbara scanned the application, then Helen's face. "Separation?"

"Yes."

"Been there. You need it now?"

"Is that possible?"

"I think I'd be safe in making an exception for you."

Helen pulled the envelope of camcorder money from her purse and counted out four bills.

"I'd need an extra two hundred as a damage deposit."

"Fine." Helen wrote a cheque.

I was having difficulty keeping my mind on my work. It was time to begin a new painting. I'd chosen a dream from my collection, but so far I hadn't been able to get a sense of direction from it. My thoughts wouldn't focus. My mind wandered to the approach of winter and my dwindling bank account. My unpaid tax bill had been on the kitchen table for so long it was smudged with jam, and my van had started making disconcerting noises. I'd spent half a day sitting in my old studio armchair waiting for inspiration, yet I still had no idea where to begin.

In the dream I saw a man in a church waiting to rehearse a play. He was afraid of being in the church alone and began to pull down the window blinds. People arrived with knives. One of the knives had the words *push* and *pull* carved into its handle. I was terrified and tried to sneak out of the church. The dream ended.

I had nothing except for the lines from Blake that I'd already chosen to go with the dream:

And mutual fear brings peace.
Till the selfish loves increase.
Then cruelty knits a snare
And spreads his bait with care.

I considered the words *push* and *pull* from the dream. I have long been aware that the process of painting had both a push and a pull to it. Usually when I begin a painting I feel pushed forward by the fresh enthusiasm and hope for the new project. About a third of the way along, when the painting fails to resemble what I had envisioned, the fresh hope starts to become stale. For the next third, it's necessary for me to plug away, doing the work, putting in the time, until finally I begin to feel the pull of the finish. The push and pull of the dream, however, had a different meaning. I considered many possibilities. The words on the knife were like instructions to the user: push the knife in, but if you really want to cause injury, be sure that you pull it out again. If a knife (or any object used to puncture) is left in the wound, it will plug the hole and prevent bleeding. *But what does that have to do with religion?* Perhaps, for religion to work, there should be both a push (a desire for a spiritual element in one's life) and a pull (something about a specific religion or church that attracts one to it). The other symbols—the window blinds, the man rehearsing a play, the fear—hinted at a dangerous, deceitful act.

In terms of colour, the fear could be illustrated with red, orange, and black. The sense of danger created by the presence of knives could be arrived at with lots of pointy, sharp edges and angles. I felt weary, unable to summon the confidence to begin. *Perhaps I should leave this one for later.* I sifted through the remaining dreams and came across something less dramatic. In it I was thinking about sculpting out of clay. I saw a clay head that my ex-husband had made. It was of Jesus. I started to work on one, not of Jesus but of a man from my past. My memories of what he looked like were vague, making it difficult. More of Blake's poetry came to mind:

Didst close my Tongue in senseless clay,
And me to Mortal Life betray.
The death of Jesus set me free:
Then what have I to do with thee?

Helen dozed off, warmed by the patch of sunlight, and slept deeply for several hours, conscious all the while of being in the apartment. She felt temporarily safe and continued to lie in her place on the floor even after the change in temperature began to register on her body. Eventually she was disturbed by the sound of rain and sat up. Barb had said heat was included in the rent and the furnace heated both sides of the duplex, so why would she be cold? She found the thermostat. The furnace kicked in immediately like a vote of support for her presence. She moved to the vent beneath the window, slid open the grate, and sat leaning against the wall above it, luxuriating in the warm air blowing up her back. Her mind wandered to Warren and the kids; she wondered if they were home yet and checked her watch. It was not her intention to cause the kids to worry. She could only hope they would think she had gone to Rube's. She doubted Warren would bother to call Rube until tomorrow. He was too stubborn for that.

The window onto the backyard was low enough to see out, even from her place on the floor. She liked that. She could live here. This was going to be her place. She had crossed the line and was on the other side. It had not been so difficult.... But then there was still so much to undertake. The patter of rain massaged her thoughts and made them pliable, allowing a certainty to form, a certainty that, whatever difficulties might lie in store for her, this was where she had to be. She would have been sorry when the rain stopped if her stomach hadn't been growling with hunger. After waiting to be sure the downpour was over, she decided to walk to the store. Her jacket was wrinkled from her nap, but it didn't seem to matter.

Her wristwatch said it was six thirty. The foggy air tasted fresh and sweet, like cotton candy. Puddles dotted the sidewalk and street like shiny scatter mats. It felt great to be walking. The two blocks to the store were not enough to get the stiffness out of her muscles, so she passed it, deciding to circle the block before buying her food. It would be a cold supper tonight; she couldn't risk running into someone she knew in a restaurant.

The absence of shadows lent the streets a gentle, subdued atmosphere, one that contrasted sharply with Helen's heightened awareness. She was aware of the sound of her own footsteps and picked up the faint scent of a woman's perfume as she passed her. The streetlights came on, and the windows turned orangey yellow. The wet sidewalks shimmered a pale peach. She caught glimpses through open curtains, snapshots of evening: a man pressed back in his lazy boy recliner; a woman slouching at her table, shifting papers—probably bills. Another woman stood at her kitchen counter, reminding Helen that she would have nothing to do back at the apartment. She ducked into the library and quickly chose a book—*The Sea, The Sea* by Iris Murdoch. Then, with her stomach growling, she went to the store and purchased a sandwich, chips, a can of pop, juice, cinnamon rolls, a bunch of bananas, a toothbrush, toothpaste, a package of emergency candles, and matches.

A rush of power surged through Helen as she unlocked her door for the first time and hung her damp jacket on one of the hangers that had been left behind in the closet. A streetlight outside her kitchen window provided enough light for her meal. When she had finished she screwed a candle into the hole of the pop can and lit it. Then, deciding one candle would not be enough to read by, she added another to the top of the can by dripping wax into a blob next to the first and sticking the candle in it.

The living room windows were fitted with blinds. She pulled them down. She was a little concerned that the candles might fall over on the carpet, so she set them just inside the kitchen door on the linoleum. Then she lay down on her stomach on the carpet with her book, close enough to the candles that she could read by their light. They reminded her of the two candles at her wedding that had represented the two lives being united. After their vows, she and Warren had each taken their candle and used them to light a single one; then they had each blown out their own. It was one of the silly traditions that spring up around weddings. Warren had complained that it was foolish, but he had done it to please her. The two candles before her now were equal in height and, though one sometimes flickered higher than the other, they burned quite evenly.

It was a bright, sunny morning and I had just begun to make sketches for the “clay” painting when Helen called.

“Rube, are you doing anything? Can I come by?”

“You mean now? It’s Sunday.”

“I need to talk. Can you come and get me?”

"Sure. I'll be there in a few minutes."

"Rube," Helen hesitated, "I'm not home."

"Where are you?" I was a little quick and sharp with my question, but that was just a sign of my surprise.

"In town. At an apartment."

"Whose apartment?"

"Mine."

I couldn't think of anything to say.

"I'll tell you later. Can you come over? I need to talk."

"Sure. Of course. Hel... are you okay?"

"Yeah. I'm okay."

"Give me the address."

"Twenty-three Scott Street."

Helen answered the door seconds after I knocked. I walked into the empty apartment, handed her a Tim Horton's coffee and, waving one of the blueberry muffin bags, asked, "Have you had your breakfast?"

"Sort of."

I looked Helen up and down. "You been here all night?"

"Yeah." Helen laughed. "Pretty bad, eh?"

"Fight last night?"

"No. I came here after lunch yesterday."

"Does Warren know where you are?"

"No."

"It's a wonder he hasn't called me." I checked out the kitchen and then walked slowly into the living room as we talked. "So, you did it! How do you feel?"

"Shaky."

I gave her a clumsy hug, holding my coffee out to the side.

"Yeah, well." I shrugged. Of course she was shaky. She had just jumped off a cliff. It was my job to steady her, be the warm blanket that soothed her shock.

"So, Warren doesn't know where you are? What about the kids?"

"They're at sleepovers. I wasn't planning to do it now. It

just happened. I'd noticed this place, the sign, but when I got out of bed yesterday morning I had no idea that today would be the day. Have I made a mistake?" Helen's head tipped back and she closed her eyes. "Please tell me I haven't made a mistake! I don't know what to do now. Look," she gestured at the empty room, "I have nothing!" Tears had sprung into her eyes.

"It's okay," I reassured her. "It's going to be okay. I'll help you with the next step. We'll get your things. In the meantime, you can show me around. It's nice so far."

Helen wiped her eyes and with a little laugh said, "This is the living room. Obviously."

"Facing south—perfect."

"See the little yard out back?"

"Yeah. And fenced in."

I followed Helen up the stairs and from room to room. I said, "It has a good feeling to it. I think you could be happy here."

The strangeness of the place was already beginning to wear off for Helen, but she knew the hardest part was yet to come. "I don't know how I'm going to get my things out of the house. And I have to talk to the kids."

I said, "That's where other people come in. You've made the first move. It's the biggie. The rest will happen."

"But how?"

"I'll call Gordon. But first we should make a list of what you'll need from the house. Have you given it any thought?"

"Yes. I don't need too much. I can make do."

"Do you have a pen and paper?"

We settled in the living room on the carpet with our backs up against the wall, drinking our coffees and making the list. I said, "Do you have any money? How did you pay for the rent?"

"I sold my camcorder. I wrote a cheque for the damage deposit. I'll transfer from my Christmas account into the checking on Monday to cover it. I can cash in my bond for Christmas."

"Go to your bank on Monday and have your name taken off the joint account. Open one in your name only."

"Oh, come on Rube. I don't think—"

"Are you doing this or not? Warren might be good about you leaving for a few days, but as soon as he realizes you mean business he'll play dirty. Don't keep a joint account. He can use it to cash anything that's in your name. You've got to play smart." I looked at my watch. "Wait a minute. Warren will be going to church in half an hour. What do you say we go to the house and get your clothes and things then? You can sleep at my house for a few nights. We'll go for the furniture later."

The house was empty. We paused inside the door. Helen looked like she was losing her resolve. I asked, "Where do you keep your garbage bags?"

"I don't know."

"What do you mean you don't know?"

"I mean, the kids." Her voice had become shaky.

"Don't think. Just do what you have to." I opened and closed the drawers all along the kitchen counter. I pulled out a package of garbage bags and said, "Come on."

Helen followed me down the hall. I said, "You can't stop now. You know you can't. Get your stuff from the bathroom. I'll start with your closet."

Helen went into the bathroom obediently. I moved on to the master bedroom. I opened the closet doors and looked down at the hamper and then at the floor beside it. Nothing. I couldn't hear any sounds coming from the bathroom. There should have been sounds. Helen's determination needed to be jump started. I lifted, by the very tips of my fingers, a pair of Warren's underwear. My face puckered with repulsion as I dropped them beside the hamper. I called to Helen, "Could you come here for a minute?"

Helen appeared in the doorway. I pointed to the shoes on the floor of the closet.

"Do you want me to take all of these or are there a few that would do for now? We could get the rest when we come back."

Helen looked at the underwear, then at the shoes. In a rock-hard voice, she instructed, "Those black heels... and those... and the brown ones. I've got my sneakers. That'll do."

I nodded. "Okay."

We stuffed five garbage bags. Once we had started, Helen would have liked to fill the van, but I looked at my watch and said, "Let's get out of here."

After lunch, I called the house. Helen was nervous about phoning for fear Warren would answer. As it happened, Sean picked up the telephone. I said, "Sean, it's Aunt Rube. Your mother is here with me. She needs to talk to you and Harriet. Would you be willing to come over here for an hour or two if I come and get you?"

"What about?"

"I think it's best if you come here and talk to her."

"What will I tell Dad?" Sean sounded unsure, his voice plaintive.

"Tell him you'll be back by two."

"Where will I tell him I'm going?"

"Tell him you're coming to my house."

"What if he says no?"

"Tell him your mother says yes."

There was a pause. "What time?"

"In five minutes."

"Okay."

Helen chose to wait at my house, thankful I was steadily moving things forward. She felt herself enter a zone in which she postponed all feeling. She was doing what she had to do. Step by step. The thought of the apartment gave her comfort.

Harriet and Sean looked wary as they trailed into the house

behind me, still wearing their church clothes. Harriet had replaced her good shoes with flip-flops, and Sean scuffed in with his shabby old sneakers untied. Their mother was waiting at the kitchen table. The children stood fidgeting until I suggested that they sit. Harriet shoved a pile of magazines aside, making room for herself on the cot, and Sean slouched into a chair at the table, picked up a pen, and began doodling on the edge of a flyer.

Helen stole a quick look at me, drew a deep breath, and said, "Things are changing now. It's going to be a rough patch for all of us, but once we're through it, things will be better."

Silence.

"I've rented an apartment in town."

Sean's head came up and his mouth dropped open, but he didn't say a word.

Helen continued, "I would like for you to spend part of your time with me and part with your father. We can work out the details."

Silence.

Harriet huddled on the cot, hugging her legs and resting her chin on her knees. She stared dully at the side of the wood stove.

A part of Helen was shocked at the enormity of what she was doing; another part continued explaining to her children that their home would never again be as it was. She did it calmly, without tears, she who had always been weak and prone to crying.

Harriet and Sean, sleeves stretched over their wrists, were both sneaking swipes at their eyes and cheeks. I asked if they would like something to drink.

They answered, almost in unison, "Yes, please."

"Pepsi?"

They answered, "Yeah, that's good" and "Fine, thanks." Their voices were thick.

I reached under the cupboard to fetch two cans. I turned to Helen. "Hel?"

"No, thanks. I'm okay. Well, maybe just a little in a glass out of their cans."

"Do you guys want yours in a glass or in the can? I can put ice in it if it's in a glass."

"That's good."

They had begun to collect themselves. Sean asked, "You're not ever coming home?"

Helen looked at him, and for the first time her eyes filled. She swallowed. "You'll have two homes. I'm making another one somewhere else." She paused and added, "You can help me."

"But what about Dad? You're married. You can't just go off somewhere else." Sean expressed dismay on his father's behalf.

I said, "I have an idea. Why don't we take them to the apartment? Would you guys like to see it? I think it might help."

Harriet and Sean looked at each other and then down at the floor. Then they looked at their mother. She was watching them hopefully. Sean said, "No," and then frowned slightly. "Have you got furniture in it already and everything?"

"No. It's empty."

"I can't believe you. How could you do this?"

"It's not just me that's *doing* it. Your father is also responsible."

"How can he be responsible if he doesn't even know?"

"He made choices that put me here. He wasn't willing to try."

"Well, what are you going to do? What will you sleep on?"

Helen smiled weakly. "I'll take a few things from the house, and Rube," she nodded in my direction, "has said she'd loan me a few things."

"Will Dad let you?"

"Sean, I own the things in our house just as much as your father does."

"Yeah, but..." he said doubtfully.

Harriet hadn't spoken. Helen looked at her. Harriet had

had some warning of this, and though she seemed shaken, she had a head start on the adjustment.

I said, "Well, what d'you say we go to town?"

Later, after the children had been returned home to Warren, Helen and I tried to figure out whether it had been a wise decision to show them the apartment. They had been uncomfortably quiet, and the situation had become very awkward.

I said, "It will be better once you get a few familiar things in it."

We went to the house on Tuesday night for the furniture. Helen had called Warren on Monday to announce her intentions. She'd said, "I just wanted to let you know that I will be coming with a truck tomorrow night for some things."

Warren had said, "Oh, yeah? I thought you already took your things."

"Only my clothes. There are other things I need."

The line was silent. Warren's anger pulsated in her ear. She continued, "So you can be there if you like or you can leave—it's up to you."

"Just like that?"

"It hasn't been 'just like that.' You chose this, Warren."

"What did I do?"

"I'm not getting into this now. I'm on my lunch hour."

"Just tell me. What did I do? You said three more things. Well name me three things that I did."

"You didn't do three things after that."

"So?"

"So then, I guess I lied."

Trippers are, by nature, predatory.
At first glance they appear to be clever songbirds,
but on closer observation it becomes apparent
that much of their hunting and killing is not only for
the sake of providing food, but also for entertainment.
Certain passive, non-predatory species
are their favourite targets. Ornithologists agree
that these demonstrations of aggression are for the purpose of
establishing their dominance and servicing their egos.

Even though Warren and Gordon had seldom actually been in one another's company, their contempt, each for the other, was significant. To Warren, Gordon stood for extreme flagrant disrespect of the Bible and a conscious, evil compulsion to disobey it. To Gordon, Warren stood for the kind of arrogant, smug, self-satisfied bully that made his skin crawl. I had become the conduit through which their venom had been exchanged. I had noticed, early on, that any mention of Gordon tended to immediately infect Warren with a fever of moral offence. Mention of Warren to Gordon had various effects, partly due to his mood at the time and partly due to the nature of the tale. He bristled at accounts that described dominance over Helen or the children, and he poked fun at accounts that exposed Warren's pomposity.

It was fair to say that they had become arch enemies, even before the unpleasant episode with Pastor Dexter.

Gordon had an advantage over Warren in that he, Gordon, liked and respected both Helen and me and, from all appearances, we both returned the sentiments. Gordon came from a species whose members needed to be wary of predators and warn one another. He was familiar with the airborne corruption of hate, and he had spent much of his life recuperating after episodes of contamination. Given the circumstances, it's no wonder that Gordon was willing to provide an Avis cube van for Helen's move. He was proud to be the driver.

He arrived at my house a little after six. I had made pasta, and we ate it in ten minutes flat. It took another ten to load the few things I had agreed to loan to Helen: a fold-up cot, a lamp, a bureau, and an old drop-leaf table. Helen's hands were shaking as she stuffed her list into her jacket pocket. I gave her a reassuring smile and shoved a stack of cardboard boxes into her arms. "Put these in the van." I grabbed my pile of newspapers and garbage bags, and we were off, the three of us crammed into the front of the van.

Warren's car was parked in the driveway when we arrived. "Okay, he wants it to be this way then," said Gordon as he backed the van in behind it. Then he opened his door and climbed out. I was in the middle. I nudged Helen. Her hand was on the door handle, but she had lost her nerve.

Gordon walked around the van, opened her door, and, looking up at her, said, "Remember, Helen, we'll only be taking a small fraction of what is rightfully yours." He added, "By law."

She still didn't move.

"He can't stop you. He knows that, and I doubt he'll even try. He might just want to intimidate you. But what's new about that?" Gordon tried a half laugh. Helen was still staring at the dash.

I said, "A couple of hours from now we'll be carrying the stuff into your new place. Focus on that." I gave Helen a little push to get her started, and we climbed out.

Helen opened the back door and passed through the porch to the kitchen. From there she could see Warren in his recliner pretending to watch TV. Gordon and I followed her, loaded down with boxes. Helen asked Warren, "Where are the kids?" He didn't answer.

I said, "Why don't you go see if they're in their rooms? Gordon and I can start in the basement while you talk to them. Give me the list."

Helen knocked lightly on Sean's door. He said, "Come in." He sat cross-legged on his bed, scowling at his TV.

She said, "Rube and Gordon have come with me to get a few things. Extra things that I can use in my place."

Sean continued to stare straight ahead.

She said, "My chair and bureau and the old couch in the basement. A few dishes and things."

"Whatever."

"I know this is hard for you, Sean, but please don't be angry. I have to do it."

"Yeah."

"Rube will come for you on Friday after school, and you can spend the weekend with me."

No answer.

"I'll have a phone in a few days, so we'll be able to talk whenever you like."

"Okay."

She didn't know what else to say, so she ended with, "I love you," as she backed out, closing the door. She found Harriet sitting on her bed with her schoolbooks. Helen said, "Hi. You okay?"

Harriet looked at her with aged eyes and said, "Yeah, I'm okay."

Helen sat on the edge of her bed and smiled at her. "I'll sure be glad when tonight's over, but it's got to be done."

"I know."

"I'll call you as soon as my phone gets connected."

She got up and was about to leave the room when Harriet said, "Mom?" Helen turned. Harriet was looking at her. "Why didn't you and Dad ever go for marriage counselling?"

Helen drew a long breath. "Your father didn't think it was a good idea."

"Maybe he'd go now." There was a note of pathetic hope in her voice.

"It's too late for that."

Harriet looked back at her book. "I was just wondering."

Gordon and I had finished in the basement and were scanning the list, trying to decide what to take next when Helen joined us. She suggested her armchair in the living room. She said, "I'll start packing my good dishes." Her hands shook as she wrapped the china in newspaper. Gordon winked as he passed by, carrying her chair. She plundered the cupboards, throwing anything that she thought Warren could do without into a box. Gordon and I went by, carrying her bureau. On our next pass through the living room, I removed a painting from the wall. I had given it to Helen, and though it wasn't on the list, I wanted Helen to have it. Gordon picked up the fig tree. It wasn't on the list either. He couldn't resist giving it the slightest little shake as he passed Warren's chair. We were almost finished, and he was beginning to feel brazen.

We left exactly one hour and fourteen minutes after we arrived.

"Things can only get better from here," said Gordon. "Your new life has officially begun." The twenty-minute drive to town served as our de-briefing period. Helen was exhausted and dreading the thought of going to work the next day.

Gordon parked directly in front of Helen's front door and threw open the back of the truck. We had it unloaded in short order. After the last box had been carried inside, Gordon returned to the truck for the bottle of wine he had hidden behind the seat. He held it up to Helen proudly. "Would you like to drink a toast to your new beginning?" It was impossible for him to camouflage the excitement in his voice.

We settled in the living room with our tumblers of wine, Gordon and I on the couch and Helen in her chair in front of the big window. The room was strangely quiet. Gordon was suddenly afraid of saying the wrong thing. He settled for, "I wish you the best." Then he added, "You deserve it."

Helen smiled sadly and nodded.

Gordon delivered us back to my house a little after nine. It had been decided that Helen should sleep there for a few more nights to give her time to unpack and stock up on groceries.

Like the Albatross, the Tripper is virtually grounded without a lot of wind. The comparison can be taken further.

Warren surfaced from his nightmare gasping for air. The excitement of driving a fast car was still with him—the thrill of the steering wheel in his hands, the gas pedal beneath his foot, the turns of the mountain road. The power.

The racing car had responded immediately each time he'd put his foot down as he tested its acceleration and handling on the curves. The speedometer had crept up and up until it became difficult for him to hold it on the road. He knew he should reduce his speed, but he didn't. Couldn't. He had to know its limits. Then he lost control.

The wheels hit loose gravel, and though he struggled desperately to regain the pavement, his momentum was too great. As he left the ground behind, Warren swallowed his stomach. He hadn't realized, until the moment he went over the edge, that the kids were in the back seat.

The cool sheets next to him, on Helen's side, made him feel ill. A week had passed since she had left. Her absence affected his sleep. Sometimes he had nightmares, sometimes happy dreams about their early days. In either case, waking was hell.

Reluctant to begin each day, Warren would stare at the

ceiling as soon as the first grey hints of daylight began to define the shape of the bedroom window. He stared until the crack directly over his head became visible; then he would push back the covers and swing his legs over the side of the bed. The dreams weighed on him like a heavy woollen coat. He wished, these days, that he smoked. It seemed like the perfect way to start his day, sitting and puffing, touching the smooth white skin of the cigarette, feeling it on his lips; it gave him an excuse to stare at nothing. Warren prayed instead.

He would swallow his pride and plead with her to come back. He would appeal to her compassion for the kids. He would try to do better. However, he wavered in his resolve as he remembered the notebook Helen had left behind. He wished now that he hadn't read the words, the dreams that weren't really dreams, and worst of all the poems.

It had been left on the living room floor, unseen by Gordon when he picked up Helen's chair and carried it out the door. Warren's eyes had settled on it, and for a few minutes he had been so paralyzed by the chair's absence that he hadn't thought to wonder what it was. But then, just as he heard the sounds of Gordon's feet on the back steps, he'd snatched it up and shoved it down the crack between the cushion and the arm of his recliner. Later, long after the rental van had backed out of the driveway and the sound of its engine had faded into silence, Warren had remembered the book. Only then did he realize that the living room had grown dark. He had to switch on the lamp next to his chair in order to read.

He scoured the book like a detective searching for clues, only to find the mystery compounded. The handwriting was, without a doubt, Helen's. If this were not so, Warren would have found it impossible to believe the words belonged to her. He opened to the pages containing the two poems written after the dinner party. He read the first one:

Holy lies,
purified by your saintly saliva.

Have you no fear of the God
that you wield like a sword,
that you claim is all seeing
and all knowing?
If you believed in your horror story of hell,
you'd piss yourself in fear
instead of mocking God's goodness
and fabricating his wrath!

Warren paused a few minutes, read it again, and then went on to the next one:

He grinned like an inbred fool
one hand beneath the table
watching her
as he talked of her nakedness.
It didn't matter that it was a lie
or that she wasn't laughing.
It's called "fun for one,"
"hillbilly humour."

Warren closed the book, turned off the lamp, and sat for a long time in the dark. He was terrified at the thought of being left to himself.

Gordon snooped through my mail while I served up generous portions of apple crisp and ice cream. "Not too much for me. I'm on a diet."

"Since when?"

"Since five minutes ago. I ate too much rappie pie. My stomach feels like I just swallowed a five-pound bag of potatoes, which I probably did. So… what's happening with Helen and the power tripper extraordinaire and the little old lady he ripped off and everything? I need an update."

"As far as the old lady goes—her name is Gert, by the way—nothing has happened that I know of. I'm not sure what to do. I'd like to help her, but I'm not sure how to do it."

"I'd like to meet her. She sounds like a real gem."

"She's real."

"Show me the painting again. I kind of liked it. It was a riot of colour if I remember right. How often does one get to say riot of colour? I think it might look good in my kitchen. And if we could screw Warren over good for the sake of the old dear it would bring me happiness by association."

I set the painting on the kitchen counter, leaning it up against the cupboards.

"How much?"

"I don't know, Gordon. Whatever you think is fair. I need any money I can get. You know that. And it's not a painting many people would buy. Although I must say I'm pleased with the relaxed, loose quality that it has. It must be because I wasn't trying too hard. My mind was on my mission."

"Would a hundred and fifty be enough? I wouldn't bother to frame it. I'd just hang the canvas on the wall."

"It's a deal."

"Now, what are we going to do to make sure that it's a happy association? Any ideas?"

I sighed. "I've been so caught up in Helen's move that I haven't thought any more about it."

"I'd really like to see Gert benefit. Maybe get a little extra work done by Kenny for not turning him in."

"And how will we make that happen?"

"We'll ask nicely on her behalf."

"Right. Plan B?"

"I'll threaten him."

"Yeah. You're scary, Gordon. That's sure to work."

"I'll pretend to be a lawyer."

"That would be rich."

"So, when do I get to meet her?"

Warren drove straight to the apartment from work. He was encouraged when he saw the location. He couldn't imagine Helen wanting to live there for long. She would want to come back. He would make it easy for her. It was a little game. A mid-life thing.

Helen opened the door after the second knock, but when she saw Warren she appeared ready to close it again.

He said, "Can I come in for a minute? We need to talk." She stepped aside reluctantly. He glanced around the kitchen, then jumped right in with, "Helen, I want you to come home. We want you to come home where you belong."

"I can't." Helen backed up against the counter on the opposite side of the kitchen.

"Sure, you can. People will understand. Lots of couples have problems."

"No. I can't come back, Warren."

"Yes, you can." There was tenderness in Warren's voice and in his eyes. "We can work this out. We're a family. We're supposed to be together. Come on back, Helen."

Helen shook her head. "It's beyond that now. I don't love you." She turned toward the sink and ran a little water on the dishcloth. "I can't pretend," she said and began to wipe the counter. "I don't want to live with you feeling the way I do."

Warren came up behind her and tried to remove the dishcloth from her hand. They struggled over it as they argued.

Warren asked, "What about the kids?" He kept his eyes on her face, watching for signs of weakening.

Helen yanked at the cloth. "What about the kids?"

He wouldn't let go. "What about how they feel? Are you going to put your feelings before how they feel?"

Helen's chin came up. "Yes, I guess I am."

Warren was clearly shocked. Helen gave a final yank,

and the cloth snapped from his weakened grip. She began scrubbing the counter.

"You don't care how much this hurts them?"

"I didn't say that." Helen moved a teapot and wiped behind it.

"You said you care more about how you feel than how they feel." His voice was getting louder.

"I didn't say that. I care about how they feel, and I care about what kind of messages they're getting." Helen turned toward him and stopped scrubbing. She said, "They're watching all the time, learning every day. What they were learning when I was living with you is that it's okay to treat your wife like a," she paused, searching, "a piece of shit."

The look of disbelief on Warren's face made her want to use more crude language, but she didn't. "They were learning that it's okay to lie and it's okay to bully because then you can go off to church and pat yourself on the head and say *What a good boy am I*. You're not a good boy, Warren. You're sick. You have pushed me to my limits, and you made the choice to push me to my limits. You chose for me to leave you. You could have stopped at any time, but you wouldn't stop because you had to know my limits. Well, now you know. Are you satisfied? Was it worth it? Because it's a funny thing about limits—you can't know what they are until you've gone beyond them. Once you've gone beyond them there's no going back. It's like crossing a line." Helen suddenly realized that she had been shaking the dishcloth at Warren. She threw it in the sink and put her hands on her hips.

"Well, you could come back if you wanted to," said Warren bitterly. "Rube's planted all this in your mind. It might feel good now to be footloose and fancy free and to leave me with all the responsibility, but your day will come. You'll have to face your maker and answer for walking out on your husband and your children."

"And you'll have to answer for bullying your wife until she

left," Helen headed for the kitchen door still talking, "for stomping out the love that we started out with," she went into the living room and circled it, like an animal marking her territory with her scent, "for pushing me out the door, and for pretending to be this nice generous guy to everyone while you're being crooked and dishonest." She stopped in front of her chair.

"I did not bully you." Warren had moved out into the hallway. "A man has to be firm sometimes, to have authority over his household. It says so in the Bible. A lot of responsibility rests on his shoulders for his family, something you could never appreciate."

"Bullshit! I shared as much of that responsibility as you did. I earned as much as you and I did ninety percent of the housework, and you treated me as if I were a ward in your care. No," Helen threw up her hands, "worse than you would have treated a ward."

"Maybe I seemed a little harsh at times. I'll try to be better about things. You'll see. A marriage doesn't have to end just because it's come to its first bump in the road."

"This isn't the first bump. It's the last, the last of many." Helen flopped back in her chair.

"Now, Helen, this would be no way to end after all these years. It wouldn't feel right."

"That's where you're wrong, Warren." Helen braved a laugh. "The funny thing is, it does feel right. In fact, I've never felt more honest in all my life."

"That's just the devil working through you, Helen. Why hath Satan filled thy heart?"

She said quietly, "You can shove the devil up your ass, Warren. Those tactics aren't working anymore. You couldn't tell the difference between good and evil if your life depended on it. You've used up all your brain cells memorizing your Bible, and all you're capable of doing now is spitting out parts of it like a bloody vending machine."

"You're going to roast in hell."

"You hope."

"I know that deep down inside you know that this is wrong."

"No, Warren. What's wrong is people like you using the church for a cover, taking advantage of the good people there that have been drilled into believing that they shouldn't think ill of their 'brother.' They can think ill of everyone outside the church, but they can't take a good look around them. That would be ungodly. It's like a little microcosm that's very attractive to people like you. The good people in the churches need to learn to recognize the manipulators and to boot them out, not to encourage them and protect them."

"Since when have you become an expert on churches? It looks to me like you don't even have a church anymore."

"My church goes with me, Warren. It has nothing to do with the building."

"Well, I wouldn't get too smug just yet. It's not just the church that has things to say about mothers who desert their children. The law doesn't look too kindly on unfit mothers either." Warren had his hand on the doorknob.

"Or on tax evaders and their accomplices."

He turned and walked back to the living room. "What?! Are you back on that again? Do you want to have it out about this business with Kenny? Tell me then, miss smarty: what would happen if you're hauled into court for slander? How would you like that? How do you plan on proving all this foolishness you've been mouthing off about?"

"I guess I'd play them my video."

Warren looked like he'd been whacked in the face with a plank. It took him a minute to form the words, "What video?"

"The one of you and Kenny discussing it in the park the day of the church picnic." Helen smiled as if she wasn't feeling fear. "And don't worry, Warren. I've been smart enough to make copies and put them in safe places."

Outside on the sidewalk the shrill laughter of a young girl

followed by the giggling of at least two other feminine voices broke the silence.

Warren turned and left, slamming the door behind him.

"Ken. Can you talk?" Warren was standing in his kitchen rubbing the back of his neck then smoothing his hair back, over and over.

"Yeah. I'm on my way to town. Did you find out anything?"

"Yeah. It's not what I thought. I mean... how she knew. It wasn't from Rube or any of that psychic baloney."

"I didn't think so. I don't believe in that crap."

"Do you remember when we talked about it at the church picnic?"

"Yeah," said Ken with uncertainty, "but there wasn't anyone around. Not within hearing."

"The darn camcorder. It was sitting on the table. It was on. I didn't know it. It got our voices talking."

"Shit!"

"Do you remember exactly what we said?"

"No."

"Me neither."

The line was quiet, and then Warren said, "Pray to God it wasn't much. I doubt that we used names."

"I don't think she could prove anything with it. She probably just got our voices."

"That's what I'm thinking. I was fooling with the camera before you came up; I had it pointed toward the water and sat it down that way I think. I doubt that she could prove it was us."

"No, she wouldn't have gotten pictures of us, just our words." Kenny's voice didn't sound too sure, but he continued on. "She couldn't prove that it was us. Not with just words. It was enough for her to guess a little about what was going on, but—"

"I wish I knew," said Warren.

"Any chance of getting back in her good graces?" asked Kenny.

"Not likely," said Warren with a mixture of sadness and sarcastic irritation.

I took Gordon to Gert's one evening in mid-October and introduced him as the friend who had purchased the painting of her house. Gert's lack of response appeared to be her attempt at good manners. If she had spoken she would undoubtedly have said, *There's one born every minute*. Instead, after a lengthy and somewhat awkward hesitation, she said, "Come in."

What followed was a repartee that could have been taken on the road and billed as the Gordon & Gert Show. They proved to be a good match for one another. An hour later, a plan had been hatched. If all went well, Gert would have new gutters above her doors, a pane of glass replaced in an upstairs bedroom window, a new mailbox post, and a new doorstep. Gordon shook her hand before leaving as if he actually were a lawyer hired on retainer instead of a partner in petty crime.

Helen's apartment came together, little by little. Helen was surprised by the kindness of the people around her. She had braced herself for condemnation; instead she felt understood. There were unpleasant incidents, to be sure—people from Brood Bay who avoided greeting her, turning away in the mall or on the street, and coldness from certain patients of Dr. Romaine—but apart from a temporary sting at the time of each slight, it didn't really bother her. Word of her separation, passed around the various doctors' offices in the hospital, had effected a change in behaviour toward her, especially among people who were, themselves, divorced. She began to feel like she was being initiated into a club, the League of Marital Exiles or something. They recognized one another by that look in the eye, the look of successful escape from failure, of proud humility, if there could be such a thing. She felt as though her admission to being human and imperfect endeared her to some people, especially those outside of the church. She was a changed woman. She was alive. Where once she had felt closed down and barely functioning, she now felt a low-grade excitement over the simplest things. The tightness of her budget did not make her feel poor; she was challenged by it. She fluctuated between a giddy confidence about her new self-sufficient state and a momentary panic, more physical then emotional. But the important thing was that she *felt* when for years she hadn't felt much of anything other than anger and bitterness. And guilt.

Helen wished that she could accept Warren's apologies and promises as if they were genuine. It would have been nice to believe Warren loved her so much he was distraught at the thought of losing her. There were parts of their relationship that she remembered as being warm and comforting in a localized way, like a hot water bottle. The other parts, however, were cold and brittle enough to make her snap. What was she to make of them? Was there a way of bending them to make them fit in with the image of a great love? Did other women find ways of making indifference and selfishness appear consistent with love?

One day she found a letter from Harriet on her pillow that described how much Harriet missed her presence in the house—how she laid on her bed and listened to Helen's favourite tape, how she kept one of Helen's shirts under her pillow because the smell made her feel close. Reading this, Helen cried in frustrated despair. And yet she knew that she did not have the choice to do anything other than what she was doing. If she tried to go back to Warren, after this taste of life, she would shrivel up and die. She resolved to make it up to Harriet and Sean in other ways.

Sean was angry, silently angry. Helen understood this and kept reassuring herself that if they could make it through the winter, spring would start to turn things around.

"Hello, could I speak with Mr. Kenneth Duncan please?"

"May I ask who's calling?"

"My name is Edmund Kowalchuk, and I'm with Stark, Stone & Parsons. However, I'm calling today on behalf of a relative rather than in my professional capacity. I, ah, thought perhaps if I spoke directly with Mr. Duncan, we could come to an understanding that would make litigation unnecessary. When do you expect him?"

"Ah, Mr. Duncan's not in at the moment. Would you like to leave your number? I could have him call you."

"I'm very busy, and it would be difficult for him to get through to me. Perhaps I'll try tomorrow. If Mr. Duncan's not in then, it would at least be helpful if you had discussed with him a time when we could speak. Or perhaps he has a cell phone?"

"I'm not allowed to give his cell phone number out. Could you tell me the name of your relative? I'm sure he will want to know."

"I think it would be better if I spoke directly with Mr. Duncan. I'll call again tomorrow."

Gordon hung up the phone with a flourish. "How did I do?"

"Fine as long as you're sure you blocked the number."

"Of course I did. If they have call display and she saw your number, I would have been able to tell by her voice. No, she bought it. I would love to be a fly on the wall when she passes that message on to Ken."

Poor Ken. Poor, poor Ken.

"Ken, it's Warren. I've got something."

"Hold on. I'll step outside."

Warren could hear a door open and close and then Kenny's voice saying, "Okay."

"I found the tape. It was under the edge of the mattress. I was changing the sheets. She forgot to take it with her."

"No offence, Warren, but she's not too bright."

"She said that she'd made copies though."

"Oh. So what's on it?"

"I don't know. I haven't been able to watch it or listen to it or whatever. I need one of those things that you put it in to play it on the VCR. You got one?"

"I don't know what you're talking about."

"It looks like a regular VCR, but the little tapes—the kind that go in the camera—fit into it. Do you know anyone that's got a video camera that'd have one you could borrow?"

Kenny said quickly, "The guy across the road."

"Get it and bring it over. If you can. No one's home. We can do it now."

Fifteen minutes later they settled in front of Warren's TV, leaning forward. Warren pushed play. Helen appeared almost immediately, sitting on the couch in the shack.

Kenny asked in astonishment, "Where is she?"

"I don't know."

Helen picked up the ashtray.

"She doesn't smoke, does she?"

"Nah. I know that. She wouldn't smoke. Those would have to be someone else's."

"So who's," Kenny hesitated, "who's she with? Who's got the camera?"

Warren was quiet. Helen was staring straight at him. He shivered. That so-familiar face with the eyes of a stranger. He watched her lie back on the couch. The realization that she really did have someone else in her life closed over him.

Suddenly Helen was on the beach, arms spread. Kenny grunted. "She's nuts, Warren! She looks like she thinks she can fly!"

Mr. Edmund Kowalchuk was able to convince Ken that the misunderstanding over taxes on the bill of his aunt, the aging and vulnerable widow, Gertrude Doucette, could be straightened out without undue embarrassment or negative publicity if Ken took care of a few small, inexpensive, extra jobs that his aunt needed done. And, of course, the bill itself would need to be adjusted to take into account the distress the situation had caused Gertrude. Mr. Kowalchuk reminded Ken that, though Gertrude was of sound mind, she had a temperament often found in elderly people, an unpredictable spirit that might cause her to do something rash and unfortunate such as phoning Revenue Canada.

Ken had the work completed before the ground froze, God love him.

It was a long winter. At times the fresh excitement of her new situation faded into emotional weariness, but Helen kept on. She survived Christmas. She was sure the first Christmas would be the worst. She survived birthdays that were awkwardly divided up between the two homes. She survived.

She felt the seasons as if for the first time. She was like a five-year-old on the first morning when the backyard was covered with snow. She sat in her chair beside the window, parted the two geranium plants on the sill so that she could look between them, and stared in wonder. She celebrated the first leaves on the lilacs and the rose bushes, and as soon as the frost was out of the ground she turned over a small plot for a lettuce patch, maybe a few radishes, perhaps some parsley.

The apartment began to look like a home. Dr. Romaine donated three old kitchen chairs and a box spring and mattress for a single bed. Rube painted the chairs a grey blue. The built-in bookcase in the living room gradually began to fill up, and the plants began to multiply. Helen felt blessed.

She'd been in her apartment two months before she dared to investigate the churches that were within walking distance. The thought of Christmas without church was depressing, so she made note of the times of services and tried the two closest to her. It was difficult, at first, to walk in and choose a pew without feeling conspicuous—like everyone knew she had "abandoned her family" as Warren put it—but, by Christmas, her anxieties were overridden by the spirit of the season.

The field had not been my first choice as a venue for displaying my paintings. I had submitted six proposals throughout the winter to various public spaces, universities, and art centres. Both the size of the paintings and their subject matter made them unsuitable for commercial galleries. By spring, defeated and sick of having the fourteen cumbersome canvases underfoot, daily reminders of failure, I had begun to search for a storage location. Most childless women of thirty-seven are concerned with the ticking of their biological clock, but my "babies" had been born and fleshed out only to be mothballed.

The idea for a temporary "plein air" gallery in a field was suggested to me by Gordon and Janet. They had admired my dedication and witnessed the sacrifices necessary for me to complete the project. More importantly, they believed in *Stations of the Cross* and thought it criminal for my paintings to be stored away without ever being offered for public viewing.

I had appealed to Gordon and Janet for storage suggestions, secretly hoping one or the other would offer their attic. We were attempting to paint Gordon's kitchen at the time, a process made nearly impossible by his preoccupation with the names of paint colours. His sensitivity to such nonsensical things tried our patience.

His first choice had been Wild Parsley, but by the time he had rolled it out on one wall and it had dried sufficiently for the effect to be accurately gauged, he had decided Wild Parsley "lacked conviction." He shook his head. "Nope." He declared, "Wild Parsley was definitely a mistake."

I turned to Janet in exasperation. "Didn't I tell you? I knew he only chose that colour because of its name." She jumped agilely from the stepladder, tossed her brush onto a garbage bag in the corner, and took a mug from the cupboard. "Damn it, Gordon! You know better."

She poured herself a coffee and shrugged. "Hey, I offered to help today. If the kitchen isn't painted at the end of the day because Michelangelo over here couldn't decide on the colour, then that's not my problem." She ran her hand through her spiked grey hair. "Whose idea was it to cut in the upper wall first? I hate that. It's my least favourite part of painting a room, and now we have to do that whole section again."

Gordon said, "I'll be back by the time you're done your coffee," and, grabbing his keys, he darted out the door. Fortunately, the hardware store was only five minutes away. When he returned he was cradling another can of paint, and with shaky hands he began to pry open its lid. "You're going to love this colour. You're going to love it!"

"What's its name?" I asked, my voice laced with skepticism.

"What does it matter?"

"What's its name?" I repeated.

Gordon turned to me and, with the pathetic joy of the

besotted confessing their beloved's name, gushed, "Fallow Yellow."

I groaned. "Gordon!"

Gordon rolled Fallow Yellow onto the wall opposite the partially dry Wild Parsley, stood back, and asked, "Ahhh, how long does it take for paint to dry? Maybe it will look better when it's dry."

Janet and I did a double roll of our eyes and sighed. "Let's have a look at your paint samples." We spread them out on the counter. "I kind of like Withered Leaf," said Janet.

I wrinkled my nose. "Too dull."

"Quince?"

"Too grey."

Gordon had hoisted himself up onto the counter and was offering an ongoing montage of expressions to no one in particular as the names were read. He screwed up his face at Olivette but raised his eyebrows hopefully at Jamaican Dream and Green Banana. A wild protest erupted from him when Janet and I agreed on Colonial Buff. "I am not into things colonial. You know that. It may be a past life psychic scar or something, but that name conjures up images. The buff part would make me feel... eew, like I was inside someone who was naked whenever I was in my kitchen."

"Colonial Buff it is," I said. I think if we mix Wild Parsley and Fallow Yellow together with just a touch of black or dark brown we will have it. Gordon, we need a bucket and a stir stick. Do you have any black or brown?"

Gordon claimed the right to name the newly mixed paint something other than Colonial Buff. He chose Beach Mat. I said, "Whatever," and proceeded to roll it on the wall.

Gordon said, "It would be a damned shame if you put your paintings in storage before anyone's seen them. There must be a place somewhere you can hang them, even for a day."

"A barn maybe," I grumbled, the strain of discouragement edging my voice with sarcasm. Gordon smiled at the patch of

Beach Mat on the top of my head and asked me when I had inadvertently brushed against the wet paint. It contrasted with my short dark hair. It matched the smudge next to my mouth.

"A barn would be better than nothing. Except for the lighting," said Gordon in a voice somewhat breathy from exertion. He was carrying an extra fifteen pounds, and his job at Avis car rental didn't provide enough exercise.

"Out in a field maybe," I said, with the detachment of an adult humouring a child. "There's plenty of light there."

"Well, why not?"

"I was just kidding."

"Hey, there are some beautiful fields along the shore just up the road from your place. Who owns them?"

"Gordon!"

"Why not? Who owns them? They're lovely."

"Some Americans."

"Write to them. What do you have to lose?" Gordon had stopped painting and was waving his brush around dangerously.

"Right." I took the brush from his hand. "Fix yourself a cup of coffee, Gordon. You need caffeine. Or something."

Gordon moved over to the sink to wash his hands.

He said enthusiastically, "I'll write a letter for you. You'll just have to sign it."

"Oh yes. I can see it now. 'Dear Sir, I am writing to inquire about your fields. I would like to have the use of one of them for a day so that I can turn it into an art gallery.' These people might end up being my neighbours someday, Gordon, if they decide to build on their land. No need to make them think I'm crazy."

"Well, here's your chance to get acquainted."

Janet had been painting the edge beneath the upper cupboards, working quietly and meticulously. She straightened up and twisted back and forth to get the kinks out. She turned to me and in a somewhat hesitant voice said, "I think it's a good idea. Really. I can imagine your paintings hanging on wooden posts throughout the field, with the sea behind them. The novelty of it alone would draw people. You've done them for a reason, Rube, and it wasn't so that they could go into storage."

I looked at Janet, and I too began to imagine my paintings in the field. I said, "I've always liked the field that's closest to the edge of the water. It's peaceful there. But if I hung them on posts, they would swing around in the breeze. They might get damaged."

"We could make crosses," said Gordon. "They wouldn't swing around if they were hung on crosses."

I narrowed my eyes at Gordon, unable to suppress the devious little smile that tweaked the corners of my mouth. "Crosses. That would work. Yes, I suppose we could."

The fourteen white crosses became a dramatic spectacle even before the paintings were attached. By six thirty on Mother's Day Eve, we had pounded the last cross into the ground, slung our tools over our shoulders, and walked through the fields back to my house, singing like labourers at the end of the day.

It was sort of a celebration of failure mixed with an anticipation of possible disaster. It made us giddy. It connected us with our souls in a way that success and good fortune never could. We smiled at one another across the old wooden table. The edges of Gordon's mouth worked as if pushed from within by willful words trying to escape.

"What?" I asked.

"Nothing," answered Gordon, still smiling. He shifted his gaze to the hand pump beside my sink. I stared at the side of his face.

Gordon raised his glass and proposed a toast. "May tomorrow be a day we remember forever with pleasure and satisfaction."

"Thank you, Gordon," I said. "Now, what are you smirking about?"

"I've invited someone else tonight."

"Here? Tonight?" I asked.

"It's okay. You know him. I invited John. I ran into him the other day, and we had coffee. I knew you wouldn't mind."

"John? Of the pot luck last year? Sexy John?" I cast a panicked look around my kitchen and ran a hand through my hair simultaneously.

"Ah, don't worry about your appearance." Gordon examined his nails before flicking an imaginary speck of dust off his shirt sleeve. "You're not exactly his type."

As if on cue John's car pulled into the driveway. I noticed the light go on in Gordon's eyes. Janet's eyes met mine. Our mouths hung open. As I turned back to Gordon, I thought, *Things will never be the same. I'm going to lose him.*

Gordon said, "We need to set another place. And Rube, get this junk off the table. We'll need to pull it out from the wall."

He hurried to the door.

John was every bit the gentleman that I remembered. I couldn't help feeling a twinge of jealousy, but I was unsure of the cause. Perhaps I was jealous of both men, of Gordon for having the attention of this very attractive man and of John for winning over my best friend, Gordon.

John said, "Congratulations, Rube. I can't wait to see your work," as he handed me a bottle of riesling.

"You'll be impressed," said Gordon. "Our Rube has done us proud."

"How much has Gordon told you?" asked Janet, as she rattled in the cutlery drawer. "Did he tell you what they are about?"

"Of course I did," said Gordon. He was scooping the last of the papers from the table.

"Yes, and they sounded interesting," said John. He stood near the door, out of the way, as we scurried about making the changes necessary for an extra guest.

Gordon passed him a glass of wine before snatching up a

dishcloth and wiping the table. "Where is your tablecloth, Rube? Surely you have a clean tablecloth we could put on here."

I handed Gordon a heavy cotton tablecloth. He flapped it open with the finesse of a professional waiter. "I tried to sell John on the one of the little boy smashing the stained-glass window with the kneeling bench," Gordon shook his head, "but he wouldn't go for it."

John laughed. "Well, for one thing, I wouldn't have room for it."

"I've got my eye on the bald woman in church." Gordon winked at me. "She reminds me of someone I know."

I pulled the casserole from the oven. "Well, I'm glad enough to have them done. And after tomorrow they'll be out of the house. Janet's letting me store them at her place. I'll finally be able to think of other things."

"Doesn't it make you sad?" asked John.

"Not really. It was something I had to do, and now that I've done it I feel... right with myself, you know?"

Janet had the table ready and said, "Gordon, if you would get the salad out of the fridge behind you, we'll be all set." She directed John to his place at the back of the table, and we settled into our regular places.

"It's a shame for them to be put away," said John.

"Well, I can always take them out again. At least I'll get to show them for a day. That's more than most get."

"It's a lot of work for a day."

"It's not about the day even, or the work. It's about me. How it affects other people is secondary. I needed to work through a few things."

"Religion is a touchy subject."

"Yes, as touchy as sex."

"Oh," said Gordon, "as touchy as sex. I like that. A lot of priests would agree with that one."

I quoted, "'And priests in black gowns were making their

rounds, and binding with briars my joys and desires.'"

"With briars, no less," said Gordon. "Ouch!"

"You're talking to a good little Catholic boy here," said John.

"Oh, I'm sorry," I said. "I didn't mean to offend—"

"No. Actually, I'm a lapsed Catholic."

"Lapsed Catholic. I love that expression. Like your inspection sticker has run out or you've gone past your expiry date." said Gordon. "Best before nineteen seventy-four."

"Why don't you ever hear of lapsed Anglicans or lapsed Jews or lapsed Baptists? Does that mean that they have an indefinite shelf life?"

"Perhaps it just doesn't matter to them if they get stale. I don't know," said John.

Gordon snorted. "Well, I kind of wish I'd been a Catholic. I think I'd enjoy being lapsed. It has a nice sound to it." He set his fork down as if this interested him more than eating. "I've never really been anything, so I can't lapse unless I lapse into it somehow. Is that possible?"

"I don't think so," I said, looking at Gordon. "Especially not in your case."

"Oh, I know. It's not that I don't think about religious things. Where are the rolls, Rube? I brought a dozen rolls. You always forget the rolls. I bet you haven't warmed them up either."

"Oh, God. You're right, Gordon. I'm sorry." I jumped up from the table. "I'll put them in the oven now. It's hot. They'll be warm in a minute."

"Religion affects people like alcohol. Or at least that's what I think," said Gordon. "If the person is mentally stable, it can have a positive effect. If they're not, it will magnify whatever qualities they have." He tipped his wine glass to his lips and continued, "There's a saying that alcoholics treat family like strangers and strangers like family. Some people that are addicted to religion do that as well."

We chewed thoughtfully.

"I think we instinctively know when something's not right," said Gordon. "We were given instincts and intuition for a reason. We were given a sense of humour for a reason too."

"'To the imagination, the sacred is self-evident,'" I quoted, suddenly.

"William Blake again," said Gordon.

"We've replaced intuition with rules," said John.

"Rube, the rolls!" Gordon jumped up and rushed to the oven.

"Religions teach us that to be good we have to override our natural instincts, and that's wrong. It is detrimental to evolution," said Janet. "If you have someone sitting next to you, and your instincts are screaming that they are a crook, or whatever, and you have someone telling you that the crook is your 'brother' and you've got to treat him better than maybe someone down the road because the crook goes to church and the other guy doesn't—"

"Well," said Gordon, "I think we have the ability to be spiritual, church or not. Telling someone that they have to go to church to be spiritual is a bit like telling birds they have to pay to fly in a plane."

A patch of evening sunlight spread across the table beside Helen's chair, touching her teacup and then sliding down over her lap to illuminate the pages of her bible. She opened it randomly, as she sometimes did. It was a peculiar act of faith. She always said a prayer first, asking that she would find guidance on the page. She had been staring at the bird feeder outside her window. It was an early Mother's Day gift from Harriet and Sean. Helen smiled, remembering the eagerness with which they had presented it to her before going off with their friends to McDonald's. She suspected Rube might have been involved somehow. Helen thought of Rube and her paintings. She thought of Warren. Poor Warren. Tomorrow would be her first Mother's Day away from him. She pictured him eating alone at their kitchen table. A melancholy guilt constricted her throat and threatened to spoil the peaceful promise of sunset. And so, she turned to her bible for comfort and prayed. "Please God, give me a sign. Am I right or wrong to have made this move?"

She closed her eyes and thumbed the edges of the pages until directed by impulse to open the bible. And she read. Judges 17:6. Micah had taken silver from his mother, but then he had confessed and she had blessed him and given it back to him. He had then melted it down into graven images, hired a priest, and congratulated himself that now God would treat him well because he had his own priest. There were no repercussions from the initial act of theft. He had stolen silver from his mother and come out smelling like a rose. Helen thought, *this has nothing to do with Warren and me.*

She moved even further up the page and read the chapter before it. It was on the same page, so it was fair game. It was about Samson and Delilah. Samson had a weakness for women that caused him to confess the source of his strength: his hair. This led to the loss of his strength (as well as the loss of his vision) to the Philistines. Helen thought of Rube and smiled. She had a weakness for men, but her strength was not in her hair, it was in her vision. She gave up her hair for the sake of her vision. Helen was also interested in the fact that eleven hundred pieces of silver changed hands in both stories.

Helen thought again of the part about Micah. She turned to the Book of Micah and read more about him, wondering whether the matter of his dishonesty would ever be addressed. No. Apparently not. Micah had gone on to be considered a man of God, a prophet no less. When Helen came to Micah's summary of true religion, she stopped. *What doth the Lord require of thee but to do justly, and to love mercy, and to walk humbly with thy God?*

She closed her bible and sighed. *I guess I'll have to be satisfied with that as my message.*

The Gospel According to Warren
Mother's Day Eve, 1995

While Pastor Wallace and Pastor Obie bemoaned the tragedy of Warren's life, he was enjoying a home-cooked meal before attending the Orphans in Africa service. Warren had been invited to the home of a single lady from his church. In fact, at the very moment that Helen opened her bible, he was appraising Gloria from his place at the table as she bent to remove a roast from the oven. The bow of her flowered apron rested prettily on the upper rounds of her buttocks. He had often wondered, watching Gloria as she sang in the church choir, why she had never married. She was not a beauty, but there was nothing about her that would give offence, and she had other virtues that men such as Warren appreciated. She was thoughtful. Tomorrow would be his first Mother's Day without Helen, and knowing that it would be difficult for him, Gloria had invited him to supper. Warren closed his eyes and breathed in the aroma of roast beef.

"That's just about my favourite smell in the world."

Gloria smiled gratefully. "Do you cook?"

"I manage. I'm learning. Now that barbecue weather's here, I'll do much better."

"Things are just about ready. I'm going to set the dishes on the table so you can help yourself." She scooped the potatoes into a large bowl.

"You're making so much washing up for yourself," said Warren. "I can help you with the dishes when the time comes."

"Oh, no. I don't mind. I like doing dishes. Really."

"You don't have a dishwasher."

"There's only me most of the time, and I don't dirty many dishes."

"We don't have one either," said Warren. "Harriet helps Helen." The error registered in his eyes, and he corrected himself. "Used to. Helps me now. It's good for her." He looked down at his shoes then, remembering, added, "Of course, Sean has his chores too."

"Children need duties," said Gloria.

"Have to learn responsibility somewhere," said Warren.

"They certainly do."

Warren said, "It's quite a responsibility, raising kids in a world like this one. It scares me to think of what Helen will let them get away with during their time with her. Sean's at a difficult age, especially for a boy. He needs direction, firm direction. He gets ideas into his head. Perhaps it's a mistake to let them go to the public schools. I would rather have had Helen homeschool them, but she was determined to have a career. I hate to be old fashioned but..." He hesitated, studying Gloria's face each time she turned from the counter to place a dish on the table until he satisfied himself that she was sympathetic. "When your kids are mixing with all kinds of other kids—some that are getting the worst kind of upbringing—well, it's an influence on them, and you have to be firm to counteract it. Like, for example, Sean decided he wanted to get his ear pierced, and I said 'Now what kind of a pansy thing is that to do?' And I put my foot down, and there was the worst fuss because Harriet wanted to get her ears pierced too and I don't mind so much with a girl, but I was trying to be fair. It might be a small thing, a little pin prick in your ear, but it's the start."

Warren scanned Gloria's kitchen with the calculating eyes of an antique dealer at a widow's door. The appliances and canisters were avocado green. Warren remembered the ceramic canisters he and the children had given Helen. They had matched the wallpaper in her kitchen, and that was where the kids had intended them to stay, but Helen had packed them up in a matter of months and taken them to a strange kitchen along with all the rest of the stuff that she'd claimed was hers. Warren's eyes darkened. Helen's kitchen had been pretty, but did she appreciate it? No. And here was Gloria buzzing around making the best of this ugly little spot. She had never had a husband to give her nice things. Here and there he noticed objects of quality—the china on the kitchen table, the crisply pressed linen tablecloth and napkins—but they had a look that suggested inheritance.

"Your mother," Warren hesitated, "she's gone?"

"Yes, she passed away on February 27th, 1989. That would be a little over, let me see, six years now. Doesn't seem possible."

"And your father?"

"Oh, he went before her. Heart attack. He was only sixty-three."

"I'm sorry."

"Thanks. Well, that's the way it goes." Gloria cut slices of butter and tapped her knife on the side of the pot to drop it onto the hot carrots.

"Your parents?" she asked.

"They're still alive."

"Around here?"

"In Hebron."

"That's nice."

"Helen's are both gone."

"Yes, I remember Helen's folks."

"Kinda odd."

"I didn't know them that well."

"Her mother went first."

"That must have been hard on Helen's father. Men seem to have more difficulty adjusting than women."

Warren sighed. "That's for sure." He examined his hands,

saying almost under his breath, "Rube helped take care of him. That's what brought her back home."

"Where was she before that?"

"Living in Halifax. She was married. A nice fellow. She complained about taking care of his father, and then what does she do but leave him and come here to look after her own father. And his father didn't even live with them. Lived next door. She just wanted an excuse." Warren sighed again in weary disgust.

"You can't help wondering how things would be if this or that hadn't happened," said Gloria.

"I could give a good guess where Rube's concerned. My home wouldn't have been broken up."

Warren shook himself and smiled at Gloria. She blushed. This reminded him of Helen at sixteen. The first time she cooked for him, she'd worn a blue angora sweater and a grey skirt. He hadn't thought of that sweater in years, but now he could see it clearly. She'd worn an apron as well. They'd been playing man and wife, sort of. It had been sexy. It was a sad memory, her cooking for him, trying so hard. But then she'd gotten upset over something that he couldn't recall. She was like that even then. The meal hadn't been very good, but she'd tried.

Warren remembered the young Helen with her hair in a ponytail like Harriet's. He gave thanks that Harriet was old enough to fix her own hair. Warren remembered watching Helen brush Harriet's hair when she was little. She'd stand behind her chair saying, "Hold still. Just another minute," opening her hair-filled hand to allow another thrust of the brush through it, scooping, stroking, tugging at snarls, with flicks and twists of the wrists, drawing the strands into a perfect point of communion with the elastic. And then, just when Harriet could bear no more, she would free her. It wouldn't be long before soft wisps worked their way out to lie on her bare neck as the end of her ponytail switched saucily back and forth.

Warren's eyes and throat began to fog, and he suddenly wished he were at home alone. He saw himself as a sentimental family man, and there's nothing sadder than a family man without his family.

Warren asked, "You ever been to my house?"

Gloria looked at him quickly. "Why no. I know where you live, but I've never been inside."

"I thought maybe you'd been there to a baby shower or something. I worked hard for that house. A lot of men would have drunk the money away, but I wanted my family to have a nice home, and I worked hard to provide it. And now it's empty. It's not the same. It's disheartening to work that hard for a woman and then have her just walk away from it all. Just walk out and leave you holding the bag. Leave you with the bills and the empty spaces everywhere where the furniture she took used to be. It's depressing for the kids. I'd understand it if I'd treated her badly, but I treated her like a queen." He sighed. "Maybe that's where I went wrong. I treated her too good. I don't mean to speak ill of Helen—I'm only saying this as a compliment to you as I can see what a giving person you are—but Helen had a side to her that was kind of selfish. She could be downright unreasonable at times. It got worse over the last year cause she seemed to just let go and stop trying to control it. Went a little crazy spending. Even bought a camcorder. Do you have any idea how much a camcorder costs?" Warren shook his head. "They don't come cheap. And then once she got it she hardly ever used it. It was just a whim. You seem to me like a woman that knows how to manage her money. You should try to stay that way. Don't underestimate it as a quality worth admiring. And I'm not just speaking as an accountant; I'm speaking as a husband too."

Gloria turned away quickly in a flurry of blinking eyelashes. She stared down at the countertop.

Warren then adopted the bearing of a hurt and disillusioned

man. “Helen lied to me,” he said. “I’m sure Rube put her up to it. She’d never lied to me before. She told me Rube was sick, and then she started going over there a couple times a week, coming home with a bag of dirty laundry. I felt kind of sorry that Rube was that sick. I should’ve known, but you don’t want to think badly of people, you know? Helen took groceries to her too. Every week. It’s not like we had extra money to feed another mouth, but if Helen felt it was her Christian duty then I wasn’t going to argue with her. Family’s family even if you don’t like them. I don’t know if that’s when she started with the man or if that came later. I suspect it was or why would she have started all this business of needing to go to Rube’s? It was her cover so that she could get time to be with him. And Rube was in on it. That’s the kind of person she is.” Warren frowned at a new thought. “I wonder if the groceries were for Rube or for him. He’s probably some bum that’s been eating out of my cupboard. She’s lucky I’m not a violent man—that’s all I can say.”

“Praise God you’re not.”

Warren wondered how well Gloria would understand his financial difficulties. To all appearances, she had what she needed, though there was no evidence of extras. Sometimes that could be deceiving though. Her attention might be so taken up with spiritual things that she didn’t consider frivolous material goods. As an accountant, he was well aware that you couldn’t tell what a person was worth by their possessions.

Warren appreciated Gloria’s naïvety. He even went so far as to wonder if she wouldn’t be better suited to him than Helen had been. Gloria wasn’t as strong willed as Helen. She reminded him of someone. He squinted as if the expression of pained effort would help him figure out who. Then he snapped his fingers suddenly, startling Gloria. *Winnie Earle.* That was who she reminded him of. Winnie Earle.

Gloria moved back and forth between the counter and the

table, placing the bowls in the middle and the platter of beef next to Warren's plate. Warren began to plan what he would say if she asked him to say grace. He was ready when she sat down, folded her hands, and said, "Warren, would you?"

"Heavenly Father," Warren sighed long and grievously, "we thank you for this day." He had changed from his regular speaking voice. Words were now emphasized to various degrees as though he could suddenly choose between bold, italics, or underline. *Thank you* was given an extra push with his tongue. "We thank you for giving us another spring and the hope that comes with it." The word *hope* was given a little twist like it was an original idea, implausible perhaps but put in because Warren was such a brave soul. "We thank you for the way in which your love finds opportunities to heal us in our most trying times and for the hands that have so generously prepared and offered this lovely meal in your name. Amen."

Gloria's "Amen" sounded suspiciously close to "A man."

Mother's Day. Janet and I began to load the van at seven thirty with paintings wrapped in old blankets and packed between pieces of carpet underlay. A special trip had to be made for two paintings due to small areas that were still wet from last-minute touchups. All in all, it took three trips for the art and then a fourth for the table and food. Gordon and John worked in the field, screwing an extra eyelet into the back of each frame so that the paintings could be secured at their bottoms. By nine twenty the sun had burned the dew off the grass and our spectacle was complete. The paintings (stations) were spaced ten feet apart, connected by paths that had been mown through the long grass. Strains of "Für Elise" drifted from beneath the billowing white cloth on a table laid out with fruit, vegetables, crackers, dip, and a large bowl of punch.

At nine fifty, a 1987 metallic gold Acura hatchback paused at the roadside, inched forward, backed up, and, after numerous hesitant adjustments, finally came to rest, like a dog circling a spot before settling down for a nap. A vision in puce emerged, albeit a somewhat blurry vision due to many layers of semi-sheer polyester. Gordon, who had looked up from his work in eager anticipation of the first arrival, whistled under his breath. The figure made her way up the path in sandals clearly more suitable to civilized surfaces than to pastureland. She was neither young nor beautiful, and her attempts at gracefulness fell short. Her orange hair was professionally cut with a stylish sweep to the side, but her clothing, failing to disguise her size, merely made the boundaries vague, like a politician's layers of deceit. She approached the table and, without actually making eye contact with anyone, introduced herself as Elvira Madigan and murmured something about a desire to perform a dance that would "calibrate the vibrations for this wonderfully momentous occasion." She then moved on toward the paintings, raising her arms in munificent blessings and twirling awkwardly. A white cow in the neighbouring field eyed her benevolently.

I had been touching up the peacock feathers in painting number eight when I glanced up and whispered under my breath, "Who the hell is that?" I wiped my brushes hastily, packed my paint tubes, and was halfway back to the white table when Helen arrived flanked by Harriet and Sean and carrying a bouquet of tulips and daffodils.

Helen tipped her head in the direction of the bumbling apparition and asked, "You know her?"

I responded with an unqualified, "No."

Sean watched with fascination, the ghost of an involuntary smile haunting his lips even as his brow formed incredulous furrows.

"I wish I had my video camera now!" laughed Helen.

Janet had pulled her camera from beneath the table and was

adjusting the zoom when we all heard the sound of another car parking on the road.

Gordon said, "Okay, there are too many of us bunched up here at the table. It will make people uncomfortable. Come on, kids. Let's take a hike."

Janet followed along the path with her camera, Helen began filling glasses with punch, and I waited nervously, pamphlets in hand.

By the time Pastor Wallace and Pastor Obie arrived, thirty-four people were moving from post to post, marvelling over my vibrant colours and luscious execution in low murmurs. The hushed breaking of waves offered background music to the gleeful crying of gulls and the mutinous bellowing of cows. Thankfully, this mostly drowned out the calibration of Elvira Madigan, and she could only be heard from the table behind which Gordon stood, a place he was to hold for most of the afternoon. Gordon had pulled his socks up over the bottoms of his pant legs after it was discovered the field was infested with wood ticks, and he could think of little else. He eyed the cable TV cameraman nervously, concerned that his fashion faux pas would be exposed publicly.

Roughly ninety people had viewed the exhibit already. Brenda Dugas, reporter for the *Tri-County Chronicle*, had arrived at ten thirty and never left, so rife was the place with potential for award-winning journalism and photography. She conducted many brief interviews and snapped two rolls of film, her excitement mounting as she captured images of three goth art students from the high school. They were standing in front of a painting of a naked woman, who was crouched in an almost fetal position, behind and in the shadow of a huge cross. Brenda spread her jacket on the grass at the edge of the field on the shore side and settled in, judging it wise to collect candid shots through her zoom lens from a low vantage point.

Pastor Wallace nodded severely at Helen as he passed the table. He surveyed the occupants of the field, recognizing at least a half dozen from his church. Three children ran across his path, almost tripping him but not seeming to notice. Their mother, a slender woman with tight jeans and a long dark ponytail, was absorbed in station number seven. She hadn't checked on her children in at least fifteen minutes. There was something about the painting of a little boy smashing the stained-glass windows with a kneeling bench that felt almost like a memory. Short frantic barks from across the field failed to penetrate her concentration. A handsome German man was trying to warn her children away from his little beagle. The dog snapped at the outstretched fingers, and a child screeched and turned away, face contorted. Brenda's camera clicked.

Janet sat behind the table, blatantly observing Pastor Wallace through the zoom on her camera. She said, "I wish I could read lips."

Gordon reached beneath the table for yet another sip of vodka and orange juice; then he dipped a cracker into the guacamole and pointed with it toward the German man before stuffing it into his mouth. "Who's he? Does anyone know?"

I said, "Never seen him before."

"Cute dog."

"Yeah, very cute dog."

The roar of approaching motorcycles drew our attention. I said, "They're here."

Gordon looked toward the open gate of the field. The engines of six motorcycles shut down one by one. Black leather emerged from the dust. Helen's gaze shifted toward Pastor Wallace and back again. He was staring at the newcomers with the smug satisfaction of a lawyer who had just made his case. Helen couldn't keep the edge out of her voice. She asked, "Who are these people?"

"Friends. They just look different in leather. They're harmless. Aren't they, Gordon?"

Gordon was smiling mischievously. He rubbed his hands together.

I continued, “It’s the weekend. They ride their motorcycles on the weekend. Really they’re just ordinary people.”

Gordon’s head had dipped below the edge of the table. He quickly released his pant legs and, taking it upon himself to act as escort, went off down the path, bikers in tow.

“What is he up to?” asked John to no one in particular.

Gordon, who seemed to have completed his mission, turned abruptly and began to backtrack.

“What was that all about?”

“I was just making sure they were aware that a couple of ministers were in attendance.”

Six pairs of eyes and two zoom lenses became riveted on the bikers as they made their way toward the purveyors of hell and damnation.

The second movement of Mozart’s Piano Concerto No 21 issued from beneath the table, accompanied by a satisfying plop as the white cow lifted her tail and executed a movement of her own.

Two of the bikers stopped at the first painting. The group continued to reduce itself by two as they passed each station, the better to view the work. It came to pass that the last two—Mark Spinney, a six-foot-three, two-hundred-and-twenty-five-pound auto mechanic who refused to shave on weekends and his wife Sherry, a rather robust girl who clerked part-time at the liquor store—came up behind Pastor Wallace and Pastor Obie as they stood before the painting of a bald woman sitting on a church pew wearing a white terrycloth bathrobe.

“I say she’s hungover,” declared Mark gruffly. “It’s Sunday morning, and she’s bin partying Saturday night. The head’s cool though.”

“I don’t know. I think she shaved her head to get back at her old man and he threw her out. That’s why she’s not dressed.”

Pastor Wallace turned and smiled uncomfortably. His eyes met Pastor Obie’s, and he asked, “Shall we move on to the next one?”

"Oh, don't let us hurry you," protested Mark.

Sherry reached forward and caressed the paint of the bald head.

"Ah, I don't think you're allowed to touch the paintings," warned Pastor Obie.

"Oh, but I love to touch things." Sherry ran her hand slowly over the bathrobe as if celebrating every nuance of texture, as seductively as a lover.

Pastor Obie opened his mouth as if to speak, but then he thought better of it and turned instead to make his way to the next station. They were soon joined by Mark and Sherry and were forced to watch, in disgust, as Sherry experienced the surface of that painting through her fingertips.

On the seventh station, Sherry noticed a dead fly stuck in the wet paint of the peacock feathers. She tried to remove it with her fingernail but succeeded only in smearing Cereulean blue on two of her fingers.

"That is why you shouldn't touch paintings. Now look what you've done. You've damaged it!" said Pastor Wallace in righteous indignation.

"Well, people shouldn't put wet paintings in public places," said Sherry defensively.

Once again Pastor Wallace opened his mouth to object further but, at the sound of Mark cracking his knuckles behind him, reconsidered. He looked at his watch and, feigning surprise at the time, indicated that they (he and Pastor Obie) should move along more quickly. The last few paintings were given the meager attention of a retail manager taking inventory; ten minutes saw them through to the end.

They approached the food table, confident that the organizers would be eager to hear their reactions.

Pastor Wallace smiled evenly at me. "Perhaps you would be willing to make a little presentation to the folks at church to explain the meaning behind your paintings here. Help us to understand them better."

Helen busied herself by collecting the leftover food on a single plate. John stood with his hands in his pockets, looking in the direction of the cows across the fence. Gordon watched with narrowed eyes from behind the table.

I said, "I can't really explain them other than to tell you that they illustrate dreams that I had."

"Yes," Pastor Wallace paused, "but you could interpret them for us. Isn't that what you do, interpret dreams?"

I edged my voice with patience, a civilized detail, like the crocheting on a stand cloth. "The point of the paintings is that the images be interpreted by the viewer. The meanings people get from them will depend on their beliefs and their experiences."

"I'm sure we would be interested to know what they mean to *you*," countered Pastor Wallace, folding his arms across his chest and spacing his feet apart. "You are the artist. You are the dreamer. They were your dreams."

"It doesn't matter what they mean to me. I am offering them to be used as catalysts for others to examine their own beliefs."

The three vagabond children ran up to the table and proceeded to grab as many squares and cookies as their little hands could hold. Gordon, noticing a tick on the pant leg of the smallest boy, leaned forward to pick it off. Pastor Wallace stiffened. His mouth twisted in a cynical smile. It took considerable effort for him to pull his attention away and return his gaze to me. He continued, "They are provocative images. I am sure they can be taken many ways. We wouldn't want to have people getting the wrong impression from them." A hairline whine had developed in his voice. "A little guidance would be helpful. A little guidance is all I'm asking for."

"There is no wrong impression," I explained. The civilized patience in my voice had begun to fray. "If every person who looked at them today saw something different, then I would be happy. That would be good. I don't deal in right and wrong. It's not my business."

A flock of geese passed overhead in a squawking, honking calamity of sound. All faces turned upward, and the bird shadows swept across them and across the table, darkening the white cloth in an almost biblical moment. Mark and Sherry's approach from behind went unnoticed.

"Well, right and wrong is *exactly* my business, and I felt it only fair that you be given an opportunity to defend your work."

Sherry held her two cerulean blue fingers up behind Pastor Wallace's shoulder and smiled at Gordon, raising her eyebrows in inquiringly. He winked and nodded yes.

"Defend it against what? Whom? Am I going to be under attack?" I asked.

"We are peaceful, reasonable people. Of course you are not under attack. We are interested. You can't fault us for being interested."

Sherry put her hand on Pastor Wallace's shoulder, offering solace. "Of course you are a peaceful, reasonable person. You are, after all, a man of God." She dragged her fingers down his jacket before lifting them off.

Pastor Wallace swung toward her in surprise, then allowed his gaze to wash over each of them in turn, baptizing them in his revulsion. He finished with Helen, saying, "We will pray for you." He and Pastor Obie turned in unison, as if they had rehearsed their exit, and walked away. Two streaks of blue, like footprints from a bird that had tracked across a clear blue sky, adorned his left shoulder. Janet's camera clicked.

When the paintings had been taken down and stored in Janet's attic and the crosses neatly stacked behind my shed, Gordon, Janet, and I popped the cork on a bottle of champagne and toasted one another. I presented them each with a small gift. I handed Janet hers first, saying, "For you, Janet, some word clippings." Inside was a small book made of handmade paper. "Just some things I jotted down while I was working on the series," I said.

Janet looked at me and said, "Thank you."

"And for you, Gordon."

Gordon ripped the paper off, and just as he was about to lift the lid, I said, "Some hair clippings."

Gordon gave a yelping laugh as he peeled back the tissue paper and saw my hair.

At this point in my story, you might be wondering why Warren neglected to attend my art show. We were also somewhat surprised by his absence. Several days passed, in fact, before we heard about what might be called a "collection plate indiscretion" at the Mother's Day Eve, Orphans in Africa Service.

But first I would like to mention an interesting fact of nature. The shadows cast by predatory birds, as they swoop to attack, serve to alert small animals of danger; this is something that one should always keep in mind.

Trippers can appear to walk upon the water, but unlike the Shearwaters, renowned for this trait, for the Tripper it is merely an optical illusion.

Pastor Obie, having done his best to describe the difficulties facing a country that had lost a large percentage of its mothers to AIDS, moved toward the old red velvet chair behind the pulpit next to Pastor Wallace. He had himself looking serene in no time, sort of posed, portrait-like.

The time had come for the collection. Warren and Kenny rose in unison and fetched the offering baskets. Warren took the left side of the church and Kenny the right. They executed their duties solemnly, passing the basket to the person nearest the outer aisle and watching it go from hand to hand down the line and back again. No one looked into the basket. That was considered to be bad manners. They quickly added their offerings and kept the baskets moving like buckets at a fire.

The sun had hunkered down in the sky, and suddenly it blazed in through the open door, lighting up the front of the church in a glorious way. The congregation stared in open-eyed rapture. A large shadow formed as Warren stepped in front of the open door to wait, head bowed in reverence, for Kenny; it spread itself larger than life on the front of the pulpit and up the wall behind it, folding itself over the mouldings, head bent half on the wall and half on the ceiling like a giant trying to fit in the confined space. This shady incarnation of Warren amused the congregation as they watched the silhouette of his every move. They stared in open-mouthed disbelief as the shadow of the hand dipped into the shadow of the offering basket and then disappeared beside the shadow of the pant pocket. Two shadows blurred together as Kenny joined Warren. They turned and walked together up the middle aisle.

Pastor Wallace opened his eyes, stood up, and moved toward the pulpit like a man who was accustomed to having his every move observed. He rested one hand on each side of the lectern and drew a deep breath, puffing out his chest and straightening his back. He gazed down upon the forty-five faces and saw forty-five mouths hanging open. They looked like birds in a nest waiting to be fed.

In what felt like a moment of inspiration, Pastor Wallace consulted the concordance for an appropriate reference to birds. This departure from his planned sermon was an unprecedented breach of his own rules. He turned to Psalm 124:7, frowned thoughtfully from one corner of the back wall to the other, then began, "'Our soul is escaped as a bird out of the snare of the fowlers: the snare is broken, and we are escaped.'" He stopped and broke yet another of his rules by venturing a look directly at the faces before him, a move he regretted immediately. Expecting to see expressions of adoration—this is how he had always imagined his congregation—he was shocked to be greeted with mouths that were still agape, foreheads crumpled into frowns. Silence filled the church.

This silence followed the path of evening light, spreading itself across the back ridges of the pews. It climbed up the spines, tweaked the hairs on the backs of the necks, and cast as its shadows all the words said and unsaid.

Pastor Wallace shot a puzzled look in Paster Obie's

direction. Obie had dozed off during the collection and was only now reviving himself. Pastor Wallace glanced at Warren, who was now sitting with his back straight and his chin up, seemingly the only member of the congregation who was behaving normally. Pastor Wallace was speechless. He didn't know quite where to go from there.

ACKNOWLEDGEMENTS

Bird Shadows has been many years in the making. Several kind friends have read its more primitive versions and provided insight, allowing it to develop into its present form. For this I will be forever grateful. I am particularly indebted to Esther Saulnier, who encouraged me to send it to Inanna Publications where, with the careful guidance of editor Kimberley Griffiths, it was polished up.

Jennie Morrow is a painter, a poet and, now, a novelist. She lives in Mavillette, Digby Co., Nova Scotia, not far from one of the most beautiful beaches in Canada. Much of her work is either a celebration of the effects of light or a playful consideration of the effects of religion. Growing up Catholic in a predominately Protestant village has contributed toward her agnostic sensibility. Many hours spent at her easel have provided time for rumination on the impact, both good and bad, that a strong belief in God can have on a person and on society. She chooses to use humour when sharing, through visual art and writing, the results of these reflections.

More information about Jennie Morrow and her work is available at jenniemorrow.com.